Classical Chinese Love Stor
中国古代爱情故事

The Palace of Eternal Youth
长 生 殿

Hong Sheng
洪昇（清）
Adapted by Chen Meilin
陈美林 改编

New World Press
新 世 界 出 版 社

First Edition 2000

Translated by Huang Shang and Liu Tong
Edited by Zhang Minjie
Book Design by Li Hui

ISBN 7-80005-553-1

Published by
NEW WORLD PRESS
24 Baiwanzhuang Road, Beijing 100037, China

Distributed by
NEW WORLD PRESS
24 Baiwanzhuang Road, Beijing 100037, China
Tel: 0086-10-68994118
Fax: 0086-10-68326679

Printed in the People's Republic of China

李隆基

扬玉环

高力士

安禄山

Foreword

Love is an eternal theme. Since ancient times the arts the world over have sung its praises and love stories make up a vast body of literature. Many of them are excellent, portraying spirited and worthy characters, lofty ideals, and the love shared by men and women. They allow readers to renew their souls, lift their spirits and appreciate the meaning and value of life. Readers are inspired to lead a more fulfiling life. At the same time a love story must be influenced by the author's life and environment, his economic circumstances, the existing political and social system, his philosophical and cultural background and moral concepts. Reading love stories acquaints readers with such external factors and helps them to realize their significance, thus promoting changes in society and progress. Hence reading and reviewing good love stories is most important.

Ms. Zhou Kuijie and Ms. Zhang Minjie of the New World Press have asked me to adapt the traditional love dramas *The Peony Pavilion*, *The Palace of Eternal Youth* and *The Peach Blossom Fan*, whose English-Chinese editions are to be published. In the 1980s, Ms. Zhou Kuijie, who worked for the Foreign Languages Press, caught sight of my book *The Collection of Zaju Stories of the Yuan Dynasty* (*zaju* is a poetic drama set to music, a form that flourished in the Yuan Dynasty) written under my pen name. She liked it and thought that it should be introduced to readers overseas. She contacted me through Mr. Wang Yuanhong of the Jiangsu People's Publishing House. Thanks to the efforts of Ms. Zhou Kuijie, Mr. Chen Yousheng and Ms. Yang Chunyan, the English edition of this book was published at the end of 1997, and the French edition will be published soon. After this collaboration, though I was busy, I was determined to find time to adapt the books for the New World Press.

In the 1950s when I taught ancient literature at a university I started writing ancient Chinese dramas as stories. With few teaching materials, I found it especially difficult to lecture on ancient stories and dramas. I had to briefly introduce each drama to students who knew nothing about them. The experience made me decide to rewrite the dramas as short stories or medium-length stories for my students. In the early 1980s Mr. Wang

Yuanhong thought these stories should be published. The collections, *zaju* stories of the Yuan (1279-1368), Ming (1368-1644) and Qing (1644-1911) were published in 1983, 1987 and 1988, a total of 700,000 words. In the summer of 1995, Mr. Liu Yongjian, deputy editor-in-chief of the Jiangsu People's Publishing House suggested to Mr. Wang Yuanhong that the legends that I had put aside be published. After several discussions with the publishing house, the *Collection of the Chinese Opera Stories* which included some stories based on *zaju*, *The Story of the Lute*, *The Peony Pavilion*, *The Palace of Eternal Youth*, and *The Peach Blossom Fan* was published.

When I write a story from an ancient drama I stick to the original plot and themes. The story is a different form of expression but I abide by the artistic rules and follow designated aesthetic standards. Re-writing dramas as stories is a creative process although it may appear simple.

The original versions that I adapted from the dramas *The Peony Pavilion*, *The Palace of Eternal Youth* and *The Peach Blossom Fan* range from 30,000 to 50,000 words. However, the New World Press asked that each story be about 80,000 words, and include several chapters, each with a subtitle. After careful consideration I decided to rewrite the stories from the original drama rather than extend the adapted versions. I chose this method because the extra length meant that I had to reconsider the form of the stories, re-evaluate their plots and roles. I am not sure if this new version is satisfactory and sincerely welcome comments or suggestions from readers.

Written on August 9, 1998
at the foot of the Qingliang Mountain
by the Stone City

序

爱情是文学艺术的永恒主题，在古今中外的文艺创作中歌颂爱情的作品如恒河沙数，其中为人称道的优秀之作，大都能通过对爱情的描写，肯定和赞扬人的美好心灵和高尚品德。读者在阅读这些作品时，常能经受一次灵魂的洗礼和精神的升华，认识到生命的价值和人生的真谛，从而萌发对美好生活的憧憬和追求。同时，由于作者所描写的爱情故事，离不开他们所生活的时代和生存的环境，因而必然受着一定的经济基础、政治状况、社会制度、哲学思潮、文化背景以及道德观念等等因素有形无形的制约，读者在阅读这些作品时，还可以明白造成男女爱情悲欢离合的外部因素，认识到这些外部因素的实质，从而促进社会的变革和人类的进步。因此正确地阅读、评述优秀的爱情之作，也是一项极有意义之举。

新世界出版社周奎杰、张民捷先生约我为他们改写爱情剧《牡丹亭》、《长生殿》和《桃花扇》，出版英汉对照本。早在八十年代，当时在外文出版社工作的周奎杰先生，见到笔者用笔名出版的《元杂剧故事集》一书，认为可以介绍到海外，便通过江苏人民出版社王远鸿先生与笔者联系，在周奎杰以及陈有昇、杨春燕等先生努力下，此书英文版已于1997年年底出书，法文版不日亦将出书。有此渊源，尽管手边任务甚繁，也排除万难，接受新世界出版社的约稿。

笔者尝试改写工作，起初完全是出自工作需要。五十年代在高校讲授古代文学，并无现成教材可资凭借，需要自编自讲。尤其是讲授古代小说、戏曲时，很多作品不易寻觅，学生无法知其内容，教师便无法进行评述，只能在评述之前先介绍作品的故事情节。为此，当年曾将古代戏曲的名作，效法《莎氏乐府本事》，写成一类似短篇、中篇的小说，以应付教学之需。八十年代初期，王远鸿先生认为此可发表，便先后于 1983 年、1987 年、1988 年分别出版了元、明、清三本杂剧故事集，总计七十万字。1995 年夏，王远鸿先生告知该社副总编刘勇坚先生认为当年延搁的传奇部分也可出版。几经磋商，先行将部分杂剧以及《琵琶记》、《牡丹亭》、《长生殿》、《桃花扇》四部传奇合为一集《中国戏曲故事选》先行出版。

将戏曲改写成小说，虽然题材不变，故事情节相同，但体裁不同，表现手段各异，改写者必须遵循不同体裁的艺术规则和特定的审美要求从事。尽管如此，这其实是一项看似容易却实不易为的工作，因此有识之士认为这样的改写其实也是一种“创作”。

笔者对《牡丹亭》、《长生殿》、《桃花扇》三剧原有改写本，分别为三、五万字不等。此次新世界出版社约稿，要求每本在八万字左右，同时要考虑海外读者阅读习惯，需分章立节、出小标题。为此，笔者斟酌再三，只能放弃在原改写本上增加篇幅的打算，而是按照原剧重新改写。因为篇幅的增加并不意味着简单地增加一些文字，这牵涉到全书的结构布局、故事情节的演变、人物性格的发展，甚至人物活动的场所与时序的变化等等，都需重新做全盘的考虑与安排。因此，这次改写工作不是对原改写本的简单增删，而是对原剧的重新改写。当然，改写得是否尽如人意，笔者亦不敢自信，敬希广大读者有以指正。

1998 年 8 月 9 日，时届立秋，而暑热未退，
于石头城畔清凉山麓挥汗为序

ABOUT THE ORIGINAL PLAY

The Palace of Eternal Youth

The Palace of Eternal Youth is an opera written by Hong Sheng.

Hong Sheng, a native of Qiantang in Zhejiang (Hangzhou today), was born in 1645, two years after the downfall of the Ming Dynasty. He died in 1704, the 43th year of the Kangxi period in the Qing Dynasty.

His family was well to do and he received a good education. He composed poems when he was a child and was admitted to the Imperial College in 1668. The following year he returned to Hangzhou, his native place. It is not known why he parted from his parents and lived in poverty, but in 1674 he returned to the capital and stayed there for ten years, selling articles to make a living. He went back to Hangzhou in 1691 and became poorer. He later traveled far and wide and died at Wu Town in western Zhejiang in 1704 after falling into a river.

The downfall of the Ming Dynasty and his family circumstances had great impact on his life and work as seen in the following lines, "National mourning and an unfortunate family left me sleepless the whole night." To Hong Sheng national mourning meant the occupation of his hometown by the Qing troops. The fact that two famous tutors, Mao Xianshu and Lu Fanchao, who had taught him, died rather than take official posts in the Qing Dynasty might have been a great influence on his work. The family misfortune might refer to conflict between him and his parents, the death of his daughter, or the treatment of his father who was banished to Xinjiang after a false accusation. Hong Sheng was married at the age of 20 to a woman who was born one day after him; she was from an official family. One year on the seventh night of the seventh moon the couple enjoyed the moonlight together and Hong Sheng wrote a poem for the occasion entitled *The Seventh Night of the Seventh Moon*. A year later his wife followed her father and returned to the capital. Hong Sheng wrote a poem about this called *To My Wife*. It contains the following lines: "A hundred sorrows come to me in one day, and to whom shall I tell of my hesitation?" The sorrow of this separation had an obvious bearing on his writing.

Hong Sheng was first known for his poems and he was a very productive poet. One commentator, his grandfather on the maternal side, thought his poems tended to be gloomy and sad but also noted something stately about them. Another commentator said he distinguished himself through his unrestrained and uninhibited styles. He is mainly known for his operas of which he wrote over 40. Only two, *The Palace of Eternal Youth* and *The Four Fair Women* still exist. Of the two *The Palace of Eternal Youth* is said to be the more representative of his work.

A friend of Hong Sheng wrote in a preface to his own work (*The Collection of Tianlai*), that Hong Sheng put more effort into *The Palace of Eternal Youth* than his 40 other operas. This was true; he spent a dozen years on it and re-wrote it twice. The first draft, called *The Aloes Pavilion*, was completed about 1673-1675. A second draft, *The Rainbow Garment Dance*, was written in Beijing but the opera was not finished until 1688. This was *The Palace of Eternal Youth*. It won immediate popularity and created a sensation in the literary world. In the summer of 1704, Zhang Yunyi, Provincial Commander-in-Chief, and Cao Yin, Head of Silk Manufacturing for the Imperial Palace in Southern China, each staged the opera and enjoyed it with Hong Sheng.

The story of Li Longji and Yang Yuhuan is based on an old theme. It was used by Bai Juyi in *The Everlasting Sorrow*, a poem written in the Tang Dynasty, and it appears in *Tales of the Everlasting Sorrow*, a prose poem written by Chen Hong. It is also found in more than ten literary works dating back to the Song, Yuan and Ming dynasties. *Rain on Plane Trees* was considered to be the best. Hong Sheng's two later versions reflect his impressions of the earlier works and his own treatment of the motifs. In the preface he wrote that his aim was to exalt the love between men and women. It contains such lines as, "Since ancient times, who remained true in love? As long as they were firm, they would finally unite," and "To borrow the story of Taizhen is to describe love". In the chapter on the lover's reunion he used lines from *The Rainbow Garment Dance*, "Those who are close will understand it, and love will last forever." Hong Sheng's work is about the love between Li Longji and Yang Yuhuan but there are other aspects to it. It comments indirectly on the social and political life of the time and touches on issues such as the misery caused by the excesses of those in a position to enjoy luxury and pleasure. In this respect it breaks the mold of stories based entirely on brilliant men and beautiful women and adds a deeper meaning to the opera.

The love between Li Longji and Yang Yuhuan is more than simply the love between an emperor and his imperial concubine. It comes close to a concept of love which ordinary citizens gleaned from novels written in the Song and Yuan dynasties. The desire to become husband and wife in future lives after death, with the help of the Heavenly Emperor, has parallels in the story of Du Liniang and Liu Mengmei in the opera *The Peony Pavilion*, written by Tang Xianzhu in the Yuan Dynasty.

But the story of Li Longji and Yang Yuhuan retains elements of traditional love stories of queens and kings. Excesses, luxury and over-indulgence in pleasures led to tragedy as seen in the chapters on *The Spring Festival*, *The Sending of the Lichees* and *The Disk Dance*. Privileged by his relationship with the emperor, Yang Yuhuan's brother took bribes, dominated the government, and squandered the people's money. People lived in dire poverty and to please Yang Yuhuan there was a lichee tribute which resulted in peasant's crops being trampled. These were some of the factors that led to the tragic end of their love. What the author meant is clear, but he was constrained by the conventions of the time and arranged a happy ending — a reunion in heaven because Yang Yuhuan had repented. This is not convincing and is out of keeping with the rest of the opera.

Even with such shortcomings, *The Palace of Eternal Youth* is still an artistic achievement and a literary work that shows high ideals. Since it first appeared, the opera has been played in many parts of the country. Extracts from *The Pledge*, *The Secret Vow*, *The Alarm*, *Mawei Station*, *Hearing the Bell* and *Mourning Before the Image* are part of the classical repertoire today. The complete opera has been translated into English, French, Russian and Japanese and is cherished all over the world by those who love operas. The English version, published by the Foreign Languages Press and translated by Yang Xianyi and Gladys Yang in the 1950s, is treasured by overseas readers. The book is an excellent introduction to Chinese classical opera.

原作简介

《长生殿》,洪昇作。

洪昇,浙江钱塘(今杭州市)人,出生于明亡后二年即清顺治二年(1645),卒于康熙四十三年(1704)。字昉思,号稗畦、稗村、南屏樵者。

洪昇出生于仕宦之家,家中藏书极富。他在童年时受到过良好的家庭教育,少年时便能诗。康熙七年(1668)他入京进国子监肄业,次年回到故乡杭州,不知何故,与父母关系恶化并开始分居,生活渐趋贫困。康熙十三年(1674)再次入京,过着依人卖文生涯(见陈讦《寄洪昉思都门四首》),长达十年之久。直到康熙三十年(1691)再次回到故乡,生活更加潦倒,漫游各地。康熙四十三年(1704)在浙西乌镇,酒后失足落水而死。

洪昇一生饱经"国殇"和"家难",这对他的生活、思想和创作都产生不小的影响。他曾写诗感叹道:"国殇与家难,一夜百端忧"(《稗畦集·一夜》)。所谓"国殇",对洪昇来说,他出生之际,明亡不久,清军占领他的家乡杭州。他曾师事著名学者毛先舒、陆繁弨,这两位学者在清朝一直未曾出仕,这对洪昇的影响也是可以想见的。他所创作的《长生殿》也被一些官僚"所恶"(毛奇龄《长生殿院本序》),以致贾祸。康熙二十八年(1689)八月发生所谓"演《长生殿》之祸",被革籍(国子监太学生)回乡。所谓"家难",或指其与父母不和,或指其爱女夭折,或指其父被人诬告于康熙十八年(1679)发配边疆。无论是"国殇"还是"家难",具体情况在有关记载中语焉不详,但洪昇受到外界和内里的磨难则是显然的。此外,洪昇之妻是曾任文华殿大学士、吏部尚书黄机的孙女黄兰次。洪昇于二十岁生日即康熙三年(1664)七月初一与她成婚,兰次之生日仅比他次一天。七月七日之夜,洪昇同兰次一起赏月,有《七夕》一诗,云“忆昔同衾未有期,逢秋愁说渡河时。从今闺阁长携手,翻笑双星惯别离。”婚后不久,兰次随父返京,夫妇分离,洪昇有《寄内》诗云:“一日怀百忧,踟蹰当告谁?”抒发了别离之苦。这样的生活体验,对他的文学创作同样也产生了一定影响。

洪昇最早以诗名世,创作亦丰,今存《啸月楼集》、《稗畦集》、《稗畦续集》,另有诗稿《幽忧草》和词稿《啸月词》、《昉思词》,已佚。他的外祖黄机在序《啸月楼集》中说他“于古近体靡不精究,悲凉感慨之中,有冠冕堂皇之气”;沈德潜在《国朝诗别裁》中评他的诗有“疏淡成家”之语。但他的主要成就却是戏曲创作。据有关资料记载,他一生创作戏曲四十余种,但目前有名可考者仅存《长生殿》、《回文锦》、《回龙记》、《锦绣图》、《闹高唐》、《孝节坊》、《天涯泪》、《青衫湿》、《长虹桥》等传奇九种,还有《四婵娟》杂剧一种。在这些作品中,目前可以见及的又仅剩《长生殿》和《四婵娟》二种。《长生殿》是他的代表作。

洪昇友人徐材在《天籁集》跋中说:“稗畦填词四十余种,自谓一生精力在《长生殿》。”此言不虚,《长生殿》的创作费去了洪昇十余年的精力,“三易稿而始成”。初稿大约创作于康熙十二年或十四年(1673－1675),名《沉香亭》;二稿写于北京,名《舞霓裳》;直至康熙二十七年(1688)方始写完,定名为《长生殿》。此剧一经问世,立即引起轰动,徐麟为《长生殿》所作序中云:“一时朱门绮席,酒社歌楼,非此曲不奏,缠头为之增价。”后来即使因此“贾祸”,反而流传更广。康熙四十三年(1704)春夏之交,江南提督张云翼和江宁织造曹寅还在各自驻所主持演出,并先后邀请洪昇与会共赏,一时传为盛事。

李隆基和杨玉环的故事,可谓是一个古老的题材。在唐代就有白居易的《长恨歌》和陈鸿的《长恨歌传》,历经宋、元、明三代,在很多种文艺样式中均有这类题材的作品，仅就戏曲而言，也不下十余种，以元代白朴的杂剧《梧桐雨》最为著名。这些创作，对洪昇创作《长生殿》是有影响的。《长生殿》传奇历经三稿始定，正表明作者对这一题材的认识和处理，也在逐步深化和合理。在第一出《传概》中，洪昇就表明自己创作的宗旨在于歌颂男女之情，[满江红]一曲有“今古情场，问谁个真心到底？但果有精诚不散，终成连理”，“借太真外传谱新词，情而已”；在第五十出《重圆》中，最后一支曲[尾声]中又有“旧《霓裳》，新翻弄，唱与知音心自懂，要使情留万古无穷”。可见自始至终，洪昇的创作都在表现李、杨生死不渝的爱情。但是，作者并未止于爱情，而是在他们的爱情故事中，渗透进当时的社会生活和现实政治，对“古今来逞侈心而穷人欲，祸败随之”的道理，也有所阐发，以使这一爱情题材的创作亦能“垂戒来世，意即寓焉”（《长生殿》自序）。正因为如此，此剧能突破才子佳人爱情剧的格局，具有深厚的时代内容和历史意蕴。

洪昇所写的李、杨爱情，已超越封建帝王和后妃的风流故事，从严格意义说，已和历史人物有了一定距离，而更接近于宋元以来小说、戏曲中所描写的市民阶层的爱情观念。明人传奇所反映出来的对可以生、可以死的爱情的追求，如汤显祖的《牡丹亭》等等，显然也对洪昇产生了一定影响，在《长生殿》“例言”中，作者就曾说：“棠村相国称予是剧乃一部闹热《牡丹亭》，世以为知言。”李、杨“愿世世生生，共为夫妇”的爱情，在现实生活中未能实现，死后也由玉帝降旨“命居忉利天宫，永为夫妇”，与《牡丹亭》中杜丽娘和柳梦梅的爱情故事有近似之处。

但是，李、杨的爱情故事，毕竟未能全然脱离帝王、后妃的格局。他们的“逞侈心而穷人欲”的作为，又导致他们的爱情悲剧，如《疑谶》、《进果》、《舞盘》等出所写，李隆基重用杨氏兄弟，任其招权纳贿，把持朝政，大兴土木，挥霍民脂；为取悦杨玉环，可以践踏小民赖以为生的庄稼，进献荔枝；普天之下，民不聊生，而宫廷依然豪侈无度，等等，又无一不牵连到李、杨爱情。这些做为，又导致他们现实爱情的破灭。于此，作者的寓意也就表达得极为昭显。自然，由于作者的历史局限，又安排李、杨对自己过错进行忏悔从而获得天上重圆的结局，却是缺少说服力的，自然更谈不上艺术感染力了。

尽管《长生殿》有如此不足，但它的思想和艺术的成就极高，在我国戏曲史上是不可多得的佳作。问世以来，一直在舞台上盛演不衰。《定情》、《密誓》、《惊变》、《埋玉》、《闻铃》、《哭像》等出仍然是戏曲的保留剧目。其全剧或片断还被译成英、法、俄、日等语种，成为世界人民共同喜爱的剧作之一。尤其是杨宪益、戴乃迭夫妇英译的《长生殿》全译本在本世纪五十年代由北京外文出版社出版，更为英语地区国外读者所喜爱，堪称世界了解中国古典戏曲的传世佳作。

Contents
目次

Chapter One Taking an Imperial Concubine and Making a Pledge of Love 2
第一章 纳妃定情 3
Chapter Two A Spring Outing in the River Bend 18
第二章 曲江赏春 19
Chapter Three Humiliated Because of Jealousy 34
第三章 争宠招辱 35
Chapter Four Longing and Recall 52
第四章 思妃招还 53
Chapter Five Passing on and Writing the Music 68
第五章 传曲制谱 69
Chapter Six Paying a Tribute of Lichee 86
第六章 贡荔扰民 87
Chapter Seven Shift of Affection Triggers a Grudge 102
第七章 情移生怨 103
Chapter Eight Peeping a Bath and Secret Vow 114
第八章 窥浴密誓 115
Chapter Nine Fanyang Rebellion 126
第九章 范阳叛变 127
Chapter Ten Death at Mawei Station 144
第十章 马嵬死别 145
Chapter Eleven The Spirit Followed 160

第十一章 死不泯情 161
Chapter Twelve Hearing Bells and Mourning the Image 168
第十二章 闻铃哭像 169
Chapter Thirteen The Reburial on the Way Back 176
第十三章 归途改葬 177
Chapter Fourteen Making Amends and the Lover's Reunion 194
第十四章 补恨重圆 195

Chapter One

Taking an Imperial Concubine and Making a Pledge of Love

During the Tang Dynasty, which lasted many hundred years, there were several emperors who showed determination and dedication in their task of building up the nation. After the "Enlightened Administration of Taizong Li Shimin" there was the "Enlightened Administration of Xuanzong Li Longji," both of whom have been highly commended by historians. Li Longji, third son of Li Dan, at first had the title Prince of Linzi conferred on him and later was installed as the Prince of Ping for meritorious acts. After Li Dan ascended the throne, Li Longji became the Crown Prince and in the first year of Xiantian period (712), he succeeded to the throne and changed the title of emperor's reign to Kaiyuan.

When he first came to the throne, Li Longji was cautious and attentive and followed the advice of high officials. The cabinet ministers who included Yao Chong, Song Jing, Zhang Yue, and Han Xiu were loyal and upright and helped him handle state affairs. For a time, the country was prosperous, people were rich, prices were stable and the country was at peace. Swords and spears were stored in arsenals and no one violated laws. Peace, order and prosperity reigned for almost 30 years.

The title of the emperor's reign was changed to Tianbao during the 29th year of Kaiyuan and Li Longji continued to rule for another fifteen years. During the later period, however, ranking officials who had served in the years of Kaiyuan had become old or had retired and the emperor, who had worked hard earlier on in his life to bring peace and prosperity to the country, now spent his leisure indulging in music and women. This led to the rebellion of An Lushan and Shi Siming and the loss of almost all of the Tang Dynasty's political power.

Since ancient days emperors were said to have had an enormous harem of 72 imperial concubines, but Li Longji had "three thousand beauties" in his inner court. At first he was fond of Jiang Caiping, or Lady

第一章
纳妃定情

话说唐朝开国数百年中,颇有几个励精图治的帝君。继太宗李世民的"贞观之治"后,又有玄宗李隆基的"开元之治",他们都得到史家的十分赞誉。李隆基原是睿宗李旦的第三个儿子,封为临淄郡王,后因功改封平王。李旦即位之后,李隆基就成了太子。先天元年(712年)李隆基继立为帝,改年号为开元。

李隆基即位之初,倒也兢兢业业,从谏如流,而朝中大臣如姚崇、宋璟、张说、韩休等辈,都是忠介耿直的贤相,辅助君王李隆基处理政务,一时生产发展,人民富裕,物价平稳,四海安靖,刀枪入库,刑罚不用,真是一派太平景象,这样的盛世几近三十年之久。

开元二十九年之后改元天宝,李隆基又做了近十五年的皇帝。这期间,开元年间的贤相日逐凋谢,这个皇帝老儿前半生勤于政务,眼见如今天下太平,不免追逐安逸,寄情声色,这就导致安禄山、史思明叛乱的发生,把一个大唐江山差点儿断送。

自来帝王无不有三宫六院、七十二嫔妃,这李隆基后宫更是有"三千佳丽"。起先,他钟情于梅妃江采苹,但近日来又垂涎于杨玉环。这杨玉环乃弘农人,她的父亲名杨元琰,官为蜀中司户。她本

Plum Blossom, but afterwards his eyes were on Yang Yuhuan, a native of Hongnong District; her father held a government post in Sichuan. She had been a concubine of Li Mao, son of Li Longji, so she was in fact his daughter-in-law. Although Li Longji took a fancy to her, he was unable to make her an imperial concubine straight away. He made her a Daoist priest in the court and granted her the name Taizhen before moving her to the inner court. It is said that when she was born she had a jade bracelet on her arm bearing the words Taizhen; thus she was given the name Yuhuan (Yuhuan means a jade bracelet in Chinese) and her pet name was Taizhen.

In the fourth year of Tianbao period (745), Yang Yuhuan was made an imperial concubine. Li Longji ordered that she be honored with a bath in the Huaqing Pool and sent Yongxin and Niannu, two maids, to attend to her and help her put on new clothes before bringing her to the palace. The emperor sat waiting impatiently in a side palace and ordered Gao Lishi, a eunuch, to send for her.

Gao Lishi went out the palace gate and said in a loud voice, "His Majesty orders Lady Yang to the palace." Yang Yuhuan who was anxious to receive the order was waiting at the palace gate. Though agitated she walked slowly and gracefully into the palace where she knelt before the emperor. In a sweet voice she said, "Your slave Yang Yuhuan is here. Long live the emperor."

On seeing a favorite concubine kneeling on the ground, a eunuch thought he knew what was on the mind of the emperor and said, "You may rise." How could Yang Yuhuan fail to respect the dignity of an emperor and rise in front of him at the say so young eunuch? Still kneeling, she murmured, "I come from a humble family and I am poor and plain. I was fortunate enough to be chosen as a palace maid and was given a title, but I am afraid that I can never prove myself worthy of this high honor."

When Li Longji saw that she was so humble, he could not restrain himself and praised her, "You come from an illustrious family, and you are as beautiful as you are virtuous. I am happy to have you as an imperial concubine."

"Long live the emperor! Long, long live the emperor!" That was all Yang Yuhuan could utter at the time to show her gratitude.

Gao Lishi used the opportunity to say, "You may rise." Yang Yuhuan rose slowly only on his order because she knew that unlike the other eunuchs he was the emperor's confidant and had been appointed General of the Imperial Cavalry; he enjoyed greater power than any minister.

是李隆基的儿子李瑁的妃子，也就是李隆基的儿媳妇。被老公公看中后，一时不能纳为自己的妃子，就先让她入宫做了女道士，号为太真，然后再迎进宫中。据说她出生之际，左臂套有玉环，上面隐隐有“太真“二字，因此名叫“玉环”，小名叫“太真”。

天宝四年(745年)杨玉环入宫被册封为贵妃。李隆基传旨，宣她入宫之前，先行在华清池中沐浴一番，又命宫女永新、念奴二人服侍她洗漱，里里外外又换了新衣。皇帝老儿急不可待地坐在便殿中专候，命太监高力士传见。

高力士走出殿门，高声呼道：“万岁爷有旨，宣贵妃杨娘娘上殿！”候在殿外的杨玉环巴不得有此旨意。不过她虽然内心急切，但行步却平缓，姗姗行入殿来，跪下拜倒，娇滴滴地说道：“臣妾杨玉环见驾，愿吾皇万岁！”

小太监对皇上的心思极其明白，见这样一个正在得宠的妃子跪倒在地，就传旨说道：“平身。”杨玉环何许人？她能不知道皇帝的尊严？又岂能听从一个小太监的传话就此起身，仍然稳稳地跪着不动，口中喃喃地说道：“臣妾出自寒门，姿质丑陋，今被选入宫廷，又受宠加封，不胜惶恐之至。”

李隆基见她如此谦恭，不禁褒美道：“妃子出自世家大族，德容兼备，选为贵妃，朕心甚喜。”

“万岁！万万岁！“杨玉环此际只有以此来表示自己的感激之情、知遇之恩了。

高力士则趁机传旨：“平身。”杨玉环知道高力士的身份与一般小太监不同，乃是皇上心腹大太监，官拜骠骑将军，六宫太监的头儿，权势在百官之上。听他这般说，方才慢慢立了起来。

Li Longji gave an order, "Let the feast begin." A group of eunuchs passed the order on and in no time a feast was ready, accompanied by music. The emperor and Yang Yuhuan advanced to the table, the emperor to the host's seat with Yang beside him. Yang Yuhuan offered the emperor wine and Li Longji asked the palace maids to give her wine on his behalf. After few cups they were relaxed and chatting to each other.

Li Longji said, "I gave orders for a nationwide search for lovely girls but failed to find the loveliest. Today I have a truly matchless beauty. You were given to me by the gods in heaven and should be the leader of the three thousand beauties in the inner palace. Therefore, I confer on you the title Guifei (Imperial Concubine)."

Yang Yuhuan was clever and used the moment to express her devotion, saying, "I am overwhelmed by your praise, for I do not deserve such an honor. I am plain and clumsy and am afraid that I could never properly serve at your side. Your sudden favor has raised me to the skies. I can only learn from outstanding imperial concubines of the past, such as Feng Si and Ban Ji, while waiting faithfully on my lord."

Feng Si was an imperial concubine of Emperor Yuan of the Han Dynasty. One day, when a bear suddenly broke out its enclosure, Feng Si immediately shielded the emperor with her own body to stop its attack. The other imperial concubine, Ban Ji, was a female official at the time of Emperor Cheng of the Han Dynasty. The emperor once wanted to ride in same cart as her, but she refused, saying that an emperor should be with his ministers instead of favoring an individual woman. Li Longji knew these stories by heart, but he was glad to hear what the newly appointed imperial concubine said. They flirted and drank together. The palace maids who liked to join in the fun said that from now on Lady Yang would be most happy. She would be like Lady Swallow who won the love of Emperor Cheng of the Han Dynasty. They wished the emperor and Lady Yang a long life and eternal love. The palace attendants did not wish to be left out and followed the maids' example by wishing that the love between His Majesty and Lady Yang would endure as long as the earth. Li Longji and Yang Yuhuan were happy to hear these sweet words and honeyed phrases and they continued to drink cup after cup together. Their spirits were high.

Gao Lishi said to them, "The moon has risen. Would Your Majesty like to have the table removed and take a rest?"

Li Longji did not wish to rest and said, "The moonlight is bright. I

李隆基吩咐道:“摆宴。”自有大小太监奔走传呼,不消一会儿,酒席摆好,奏乐之声也细细传来。李隆基与杨玉环入席,皇上自然坐了主位,杨玉环侍坐一旁,并且先行向皇上献酒,李隆基也命宫女代他送酒给杨玉环。几杯酒后,彼此心情舒畅,未免喁喁细谈。

李隆基先行开口道:“朕曾下令,在全国范围内遍求窈窕淑女,但没有一个可以领袖群芳的人。今日得到你,真是上天赐给的绝世无双佳人,后宫三千,都该让你居先,所以朕褒封你为贵妃。”

杨玉环是个十分乖巧的女子,便趁机表白忠悃,说道:“蒙君王过份夸奖,实不敢当。臣妾只怕平庸的姿貌、粗笨的躯体,不堪陪侍皇上。如今一朝受宠,顿时从人间拔至天上。臣妾当努力效法冯嫄、班姬那些贵妃,永远效忠皇上。”

杨玉环说的冯嫄,是汉元帝的皇妃,当大熊突然从兽圈中跑出时,她挡在元帝身前,以免元帝受伤。班姬是汉成帝的女官,成帝曾经要和她同乘一辆车,她说皇帝应该和大臣在一起,不该宠幸女色,推辞了。这些后妃故事,李隆基何尝不知晓?如今听得新册封的贵妃这样表白,更是龙心大悦。宫女们更是善于凑趣,一会儿说自今以后,贵妃当是宫中第一,犹如赵飞燕受到汉成帝的宠爱一般;一会儿祝皇上、贵妃千秋万岁,恩情美满。内侍们也不落后,紧跟着宫女们祝愿万岁与娘娘合殿春香、地久天长。李隆基与杨玉环听了这些甜言蜜语,十分受用,便你一杯我一盏,不断对饮,兴致越发浓烈起来。

高力士在一旁却提醒道:“月亮上来了,时辰已不早,万岁爷还是撤宴歇息吧!”

李隆基仍不想就此安歇,说道:“月色正好,朕与妃子在阶前

shall watch the moon from the courtyard with Lady Yang." A young eunuch quietly repeated this to musicians and after a while soft and lovely music was heard from afar.

Li Longji went down a few marble steps and led Yang Yuhuan by the hand to the courtyard. He turned her slightly to gaze at her under the moon and saw a ravishing beauty, more delightful than all the flowers in the garden. Stepping back half a pace, he looked at her figure which appeared perfect under the close fitting garment; he was very pleased. No longer able to wait he said, "Light the lanterns and lead us to the west palace."

Surrounded by eunuchs and maids, the procession immediately went towards the west palace where Gao Lishi reported, "May it please Your Majesty, we have reached the west palace." Li Longji told the eunuchs to withdraw and just the maids were left wait on them while they changed their clothes. After a while, the maids withdrew and the two of them were left in the sleeping palace.

Touching her shoulders, Li Longji said, "Our love begins this evening. Let us love each other as long as we live." He withdrew from his sleeve a double golden hairpin with two carved phoenixes and a jewel box wrapped in a piece of silk with a love knot on it. To pledge their love the emperor gave them to Lady Yang. Li Longji wished that they would like the phoenixes on the pin, always flying together, and like the love-knot on the box, two hearts as one. Lady Yang said gratefully, "Thank my lord for your gifts. May our love be as close and as firm as this hairpin and the jewel box, may the phoenixes never be parted, and may the box never be divided." Hand in hand, they went to bed. From that day on, Li Longji indulged in pleasure day and night, and neglected state affairs all the more.

After Yang Yuhuan won favor with the emperor, all her relatives received high honors. Her cousin Yang Guozhong, through repeated promotion, became the prime minister with powers second only to the emperor. Afterwards he accepted bribes, took private property by force, lived luxuriously and indulged himself in pleasures.

At that time, there was a military officer, An Lushan, who was a native of Liucheng, Yingzhou. His mother's second husband was a Tartar tribal chieftain called An Yanyan, so An became his surname. An Lushan had joined the army when he was young. Afterwards he was enlisted under the Youzhou Military Governor Zhang Shougui, who was struck by his uncommon appearance, adopted him and appointed him a frontier

闲步赏月。”小太监悄悄告知乐工,一时不远处便飘来柔和动听的乐声。

李隆基一手搀住杨玉环,下了台阶,走至庭院,一手将杨玉环身躯微微挪动,对着月色,细看玉环容颜,觉得确实美丽非凡,胜过庭院中奇花异卉多多;又退后半步,细观玉环身躯,只见合身的衣服衬托出她的丰满绰约姿态,更是欢喜无限。此际,他也按捺不住了,吩咐道:“掌灯往西宫去。”

立刻,太监、宫女前呼后拥,一行人向西宫行来。不一会儿,高力士报道:“启奏万岁爷,到西宫了。”李隆基随即吩咐太监回避,只留宫女侍候更衣。其后,宫女也自行退出,一时寝宫中只剩他们二人。

李隆基抚摸着杨玉环的双肩,说道:“从今夜开始,朕与妃子永结白头偕老之盟。”说着,从袖中取出金钗、钿盒,作为定情之物,送与贵妃,表示今后要比翼齐飞,牢扣同心。杨玉环先行谢恩,又感激地说:“谢皇上赏赐,但愿臣妾与皇上情似金坚,钗不单分。”说罢,二人携手进入帐内寻欢。从此,李隆基更是日夜耽于欢乐,愈发不理朝政了。

杨玉环一人得宠,全家升天。她的兄长杨国忠不断受到擢升,直至作到相当于中书令的右相,权势仅次于皇上。从此更是招权纳贿,穷搜恶刮,过着挥霍奢侈、寻欢作乐的生活。

此时,有个武将安禄山,原是营州柳城人,他的母亲阿史德曾改嫁给突厥族酋长安延偃,方始更姓为“安”。他早年投军,在幽州节度使张守珪帐下奔走。张节度见他生有一副不同寻常的异相,收为义子,不时提拔,直作到平卢讨击使、左骁卫将军。张节度派

lieutenant. He was sent to fight the Khitan tribesmen who defeated him and forced him flee. An Lushan had lost because he was a braggart who boasted of his courage and had made a reckless advance. His failure warranted execution but Military Governor Zhang did not carry this out; instead he sent him to the capital to be court-martialed. This gave An Lushan a chance to find means of approaching powerful officials and offering bribes.

An Lushan was experienced in bribery and knew how to win the support of people who worked for high officials. These skills were exactly what he wanted today. He had a sworn brother named Zhang Qian who was a steward in the Prime Minister Yang Guozhong's house and had done good service there. Yang now had power and could do whatever he wanted; the way for An Lushan to seek his help was through Zhang Qian.

As the saying goes, "A servant of a prime minister equals to an official of 7th rank." Zhang Qian was also devious and been entrusted by An Lushan to give a large sum of money to the guards asking them to be lenient on him. He sent gold, silver and treasures to the house of the prime minister. Yang Guozhong accepted the gifts with a smile and said that he would see An Lushan in his mansion.

An Lushan was elated as the reply indicated that there was a chance he would live and he went there at once. On the way he thought about what had happened to him in the last few years. Fate and other people were to blame; a dignified man like him had been tripped up by trifles. He was like a dragon that was able to ruffle the sea but he had fallen into a ditch and had been treated like a turtle. However, he was fortunate to have bought off the prime minister with such a large sum, otherwise he would have died for no reason. While he was thinking about these things he reached his destination. Zhang Qian greeted him at the door, "So you have come, Brother An. His Grace has accepted all the gifts which is a good omen. He is now waiting to see you in the hall."

"Many thanks for your great help."

"Don't stand on ceremony. We are sworn brothers. Would you please wait in my office?"

Yang Guozhong was sitting in the hall. He had accepted the handsome gifts from An and wanted to do something to exempt him from a death sentence. It was an easy thing for a prime minister to do as there was always an element of luck in war and to be defeated occasionally was excusable. Also he could say that he saved An because he wanted to save

他去攻打奚契丹部落，他却恃勇轻敌，吃了败仗逃回。按他的败绩，论罪当死，他的义父张守珪，为了使他有求生机会，没有在帐前就地执法，却命人将他押解赴京，听凭圣上发落。这就让安禄山有了寻找关系、打通关节的机会。

幸亏安禄山这厮平时就会收买人心，笼络大官，今日正好用得着。他有个结义兄弟唤作张千，曾在丞相府中做过干办，为杨国忠效过力。如今杨国忠势焰熏天，力可回天，托他去求丞相出力相救，当是一条捷径。

俗话说“宰相家人七品官”。这张千也颇有手段，如今受了安禄山重托，拿出许多银两重重地酬谢押解官儿，求他们宽松宽松；又将安禄山为他准备的一份厚礼送进府中。杨丞相自然笑纳，并传出话来让安禄山今日前去杨府听回话。

安禄山得此回话，求生有望，自然欣喜，即刻前往。一路上想到近年来的遭遇，不免怨天尤人：自己是一条堂堂好汉，未想到居然在阴沟里翻了船；就像翻河决海的莽龙，反成了瓮中的龟鳖。又想到：幸亏这一大笔金银珠宝买通了丞相，否则不是死得太冤枉？边想边行，已走到丞相府。一到门口，张千迎了出来，悄悄说道：“安大哥来了。丞相爷已将礼物全都收下了，这是个好兆头。现在等你进府相见。”

“多谢兄弟大力周旋。”

“自家兄弟不必客气，请安大哥先到班房少待。”

杨国忠已坐在大客厅上，收了安禄山这份厚礼，要将他免死发落，对丞相来说，这事也不难。胜败乃兵家常事，临阵偶然失利，也属情有可原。他想，还可说免他死罪，是为朝廷爱惜人材。如此

a useful officer for the state. This thought put him at ease as it made his acceptance of the bribe and his disregard of official policy.

He had made up his mind when Zhang Qian appeared again and reported, "An Lushan is waiting outside."

"Bring him in."

"I will, Your Grace." Zhang Qian went out and beckoned to An from the door of his office. An Lushan had been sitting sullenly on a bench and stood up at once to follow Zhang to the hall.

From the hall's doorway An Lushan saw the prime minister sitting on the host's chair. He was in trouble and his behavior was exemplary. He at once knelt down and advanced on his knees to face Yang Guozhong. He kowtowed and said, "The wretched An Lushan salutes Your Grace."

"Rise," said Yang.

"I dare not, since I deserve to be sentenced to death."

Assuming the airs of a prime minister, Yang Guozhong said, "Zhang Qian has told me why you are here. Give me your own account of the offense."

Still kneeling, An Lushan replied, "I beg to inform Your Grace that I, the wretched, was ordered to attack the Khitan tribesmen...." Yang Guozhong was sitting up and could not clearly hear what was said. He said, "Rise and speak." Only then did An Lushan stand up. His head hung down and he pressed his hands against his body. He continued, "Relying on strength and boldness, I, the wretched, charged with my men, but the tribesmen made a sudden attack at night and surrounded our camp. Although we resisted as best we could, we ran out of arrows."

"How did you escape?"

"I rode a horse and fought my way out with a sword. I hoped to be pardoned for my past service and did not expect to face a court martial." An went down on his knees again and kowtowed, saying, "Your Grace, please be generous and have mercy on me."

Although Yang Guozhong had accepted the presents and was prepared to help, he would not let An off lightly. He said haughtily, "To lose an army and bring humiliation to the country is a serious matter and you should be punished according to law. Though I handle state affairs, I cannot make a decision without authorization. I fear I can do nothing for you."

一想，明明是收受贿赂，因私废公之举，倒可心安理得、堂而皇之地实行了。

正当他拿定了这一主意，张千又上来禀报："安禄山在外伺候。"

"叫他进来。"

"领钧旨。"张千应答着退出，来到班房门口，坐在长条凳上垂头丧气的安禄山，立即站起身来，跟在他后面朝客厅走去。

走到客厅门口，瞧见杨丞相正安坐在主位上，安禄山落难之际也不能不乖巧些，赶紧跪下，双膝着地前行到丞相面前跪拜，说："犯官安禄山，叩见丞相爷。"

"起来。"

"犯官是应死囚徒，理当跪禀。"

杨国忠摆出丞相气派，开口说道："你的来意，张千已讲过了。且把犯罪情况，仔细说来。"

安禄山仍然跪在地上答话："丞相爷听禀：犯官遵奉军令，去征讨奚契丹……"高高坐在上面的杨国忠听不清楚，又吩咐道："起来讲嘛！"安禄山这才站起来，低头垂手，继续说："犯官恃勇出战，未曾料到番兵夜里偷袭，一时被团团围住，犯官仍然拼命抵抗，无奈箭却射完了。"

"你又怎能脱围？"

"那时犯官杀条血路，单刀匹马奔出重围。原指望凭过去的一点儿功劳抵挡这番失利的罪责。哪里想到要受刑罚。"说罢，又跪倒在地，连连叩头："望丞相高抬贵手，可怜可怜犯官。"

杨国忠虽说受了礼，有心援之以手，但却不能如此便宜这个武夫，就故作姿态地说："据你丧师辱国的罪行来看，该受刑罚，事情太

This frightened An Lushan and he cried out, "I can live a second life only with the help of Your Grace." Winning gratitude by granting a favor was exercising power and it pleased Yang Guozhong to see him panic. He gave a strange laugh and said, "I have a little power, the emperor will follow what I say. There are certain formalities which are hard to explain and which I cannot tell you about."

An Lushan was astute and understood the meaning implied in the words; he saw a chance of life. He continued kowtowing and said, "My life is in your hands."

"Very well. Tomorrow when I go to court, I shall see what can I do. If it is possible, I shall save your live."

An did not stop kowtowing and said gratefully, "I own Your Grace such gratitude that I can only repay you by serving as your dog or horse. As you are busy, most humbly I take my leave." Yang Guozhong asked Zhang Qian to show him out.

When one receives presents from others one should do something in return. Sitting alone in the hall Yang Guozhong thought, "This An Lushan is a junior officer who was at the frontier and has never distinguished himself. He should now be sentenced to death for his offences. If I try to save him, the emperor will suspect that something is wrong." He stretched his hand and took down the memorial to the throne sent by Governor Zhang and read it carefully. As he read it a plan formed in his mind and he said, "Ah, I have it! The memorial to the throne mentioned that An's knowledge of six barbarian languages and his military skill qualified him for the post of a frontier general." He could make something out of this. He decided not to be involved himself, but to drop a hint to the Ministry of War to propose to the emperor that An be summoned to court to be tested by His Majesty himself. If this worked, An's life could be saved. After he had made this decision he returned to the inner hall.

Naturally, the Minister of War acted on the Prime Minister's suggestion; he knew what Yang Guozhong wanted and did not need a detailed explanation. He presented a memorial to the throne. As was expected, Li Longji gave his assent and what is more asked Yang Guozhong to give the test on his behalf. In the meanwhile the emperor whiled away the time with Lady Yang in the inner court.

大,有关刑典,我虽然总揽朝政,也不便擅自做主,怕也无力回天。”

安禄山听得此言，不禁惊恐万端，放声大哭：“丞相爷假若肯救助,犯官就得生了。”杨国忠见他这副惶恐的神情,不无得意,故作神秘地笑了一笑，卖弄地说：“我还有些小权，皇上对我也还能言听计从。这其中的关节,说不清,也不对你说了。”

安禄山何等乖巧,听话听音,眼见求生有望,又连连叩首:“全仗丞相爷作主。”

“好罢,等我明日上朝,见机而行,如有一线希望,当保全你一条性命。”

安禄山又连连叩首，感激不尽地说：“蒙丞相爷大恩，犯官将来变狗变马也一定要报答。丞相事繁,就不打扰了。”杨国忠吩咐张千领他出去。

受了人家重礼,就不能不为人消灾。杨国忠独自坐在客厅上细想计谋:这安禄山乃守边的一个小武官,从未建有功劳,如今犯了死罪,我若直截了当地救他,必然会引起皇上疑心,得想个法儿。想到此际,又随手将张节度使守珪的奏章拿起来细看,不禁十分得意,自言自语地说道:“这不是有办法了?奏章中说他通晓六番言语,又精熟各种武艺,可充当守边之将。在这番言语中就可以做文章了。他决定不必自己出面,准备暗示兵部以此为理由,召他御前面试,果真如此,便可救他一命了。想好主意,他也回后厅去了。

兵部主官自然也看丞相颜色行事，不待杨国忠细说，便已心领神会,上奏玄宗李隆基。李隆基果然允其所请,又居然派杨国忠代他主持面试,自己却呆在后宫里与贵妃戏耍无厌。

Chapter Two

A Spring Outing in the River Bend

After Li Longji made Yang Yuhuan an imperial concubine, he lavished all his love on her. They feasted and spent day and night together. Yang Yuhuan on her part did all she could to please the emperor and keep his love. However, she became physically tired after a while and when the emperor attended to state affairs she rested. One drowsy day in mid-spring Yang Yuhuan fell into a deep sleep. The palace was still, the smoke of incense curled up; outside Chinese crabapples blossomed and orioles sang. Yongxin and Niannu, two maids, stood outside the gate, talking quietly from fear of waking up Lady Yang.

The sound of music and singing in the neighboring courtyard suddenly woke Yang Yuhuan, who asked, "Where does the music and singing come from?"

Yongxin and Niannu hurried in and kowtowed, saying, "There was a gathering in the neighboring courtyard, and the noise unexpectedly woke Your Ladyship. It is now about noon. Would Your Ladyship like to get up? All is ready for Your Ladyship's make-up."

Yang Yuhuan stood up listlessly and walked slowly to the mirror; Yongxin and Niannu helped her sit down. Looking in the mirror she combed her black hair. Yongxin handed her a hairpin saying, "Your Ladyship please use the hairpin." She presented the rouge and said, "And here is the rouge, my lady." Then she asked Her Ladyship to pencil her eyebrows.

After Yang Yuhuan had made up she was still a little tired and stood up slowly moving her waist as if to shake off fatigue. Niannu suddenly cried out, "Ah! You have forgotten the flowers, my lady." She picked up two cherry blossoms which had just been sent from the palace and pinned them lightly on the hair to either side of Yang Yuhuan's head. The maids stepped back half a pace and looked at Lady Yang. They were moved by her beauty and said, "Your countenance looks so delicate that one fears a

第二章
曲江赏春

话说李隆基自从得到杨玉环后，对她百般宠爱，终日宴饮，彻夜嬉乐。杨玉环侍候皇上，求其欢心，不敢懈怠，天长日久，也未免云娇雨怯，体力不支。每当李隆基坐朝理政之际，她便抽暇睡卧休憩。如今正值春深，更是人懒身倦，不觉沉沉睡去。宫中一片寂静，沉香袅袅，窗外海棠盛开，流莺声啼。宫女永新、念奴静静守在门外，悄声细语，怕惊起宿醉未醒的贵妃娘娘。忽地笙歌齐鸣，原来是邻院中嫔妃欢会，杨玉环蓦然醒来，问道："何处笙歌？"

永新、念奴赶紧进来跪下叩头："隔院笙歌聚会，不想惊动娘娘——时近晌午，娘娘也该起身，镜奁已备齐了，请娘娘上妆。"

杨玉环懒慵慵地抬起身来，缓缓走近镜台，永新、念奴两人扶她坐了下来。她对着镜台，轻轻撩起细丝般的乌发，永新递上花钿："请娘娘贴上花钿。"又送上胭脂："请娘娘点胭脂。"接着，永新又请娘娘画眉。

梳妆已毕，杨玉环不免有些倦意，慢慢立了起来，将柳腰宽摆，似乎要抖掉一身的疲惫。念奴忽而惊道："呀，娘娘忘了戴花了。"说着，便在镜台上拿起宫女刚刚送进来的两朵樱桃花，轻轻

breeze outside the window may harm it." The two praised her beauty and helped her take off her sleeping gown, then dressed her in an apricot colored silk dress, a Hunan embroidered skirt and embroidered slippers. Her form was matchless and she had thousand charms. When she looked in the mirror, she could not help loving herself.

After Yang Yuhuan had spent much time dressing up and admiring herself, she had nothing to do; she yawned sleepily and stretched herself. Yongxin and Niannu had nothing to do either and said, "My lady, since you're so tired, why not sleep some more?"

"Yes, I will. I am still tired and think I'll rest a little longer. You two draw the bed curtains for me." She went to bed, lay on her side and was soon fast asleep.

The two maids left the room and sat outside the gate, chatting. Yongxin said, "Has the emperor not come because he has gone to see Lady Plum Blossom?"

"Sister, don't you know? Lady Plum Blossom has been forced to move to the Shangyang Pavilion."

"Surely not!"

"Sister Yongxin, recently the emperor has been so devoted to Lady Yang that he often comes here and doesn't even bring his attendants. We must take care and wait on them."

Let us ignore the chattering of the two maids. After Li Longji had made Yang Yuhuan his concubine, he took such delight in his new mistress that he wanted to be with her day and night. That day, after attending the morning imperial court session, he hurried on his own to the west palace. The two maids were at the gate. He walked over quietly. As he approached, the maids greeted him saying in a low voice, "Long live the emperor! Our Lady has just gone to sleep."

Li Longji, the romantic emperor whose heart was ruled by the fair sex, waved his hand and hushed them saying, "Don't wake her." He walked lightly to the bed and quietly parted the curtains; Lady Yang's body gave off a warm aroma. He looked at her and was overjoyed; she was like a piece of warm jade lying beneath the light silken bedcover. He stood there lost in thought.

Yongxin and Niannu were dumfounded by this and said, "With such gallantry it is no wonder that he has become the king of lovers!"

Maybe the gaze of Li Longji made Yang Yuhuan react and roused her from her deep sleep. She woke suddenly but still looked drowsy and

插在娘娘双鬓。两个宫女忍不住倾倒在娘娘的花容月貌前,赞叹道:"看了娘娘这般娇嫩的容颜,只怕被窗外的阵阵风儿吹破哩。"两个宫女你一句我一句不断称赞,同时又帮着娘娘将睡衣更换,穿上件杏色罗衫,一条湘绣裙,头上插着行走时自会摇动的首饰步摇,脚上一双紧贴脚跟的半弯绣花鞋,真是百种娇态、千种风流。

杨玉环上妆半晌,无所事事,顿觉疲乏,呵欠不断,伸腰不停,永新、念奴便劝道:"娘娘,既然这般困倦,何妨再去床上躺躺。"

"也好。身子确实疲乏,略睡片刻也好,你们两个替我放下帐子。"吩咐已毕,侧卧床榻,不一会儿便沉沉睡去。

两个宫女见娘娘睡去,便去门外坐下闲谈。永新自言自语地说:"万岁爷怎么到此时还不来,是不是到梅娘娘那边去了?"

"姐姐,你还不知道,梅娘娘已被迁到上阳楼去了!"

"哦,有这样的事!""永新姐姐,近来万岁爷只爱杨娘娘,时不时地来到此处连贴身侍从也不带。我与你须随时小心伺候才好。"

李隆基自从纳了杨玉环为贵妃以后,心满意足,浑身舒畅,恨不得从早到晚相守在一起。今日下了早朝,便独自一人急急来到西宫,两个宫女看见,赶紧上前迎驾,"万岁爷!娘娘刚才睡去。"

李隆基这个风流皇帝倒也会怜香惜玉,悄悄说道:"不要惊醒她。"悄无声息地走到床前,轻轻撩起绞绡纱帐,一阵龙脑清香扑鼻而来,原来这香气发自贵妃身体。李隆基顿时感到欢畅无比,瞧着贵妃压着一床锦缎薄被睡得正香,便一言不发地看出了神。

永新、念奴在旁看呆了,两人不禁低低说道:"你看皇上这般温存,怎不夺得天下的风流!"

也许是心灵感应,李隆基热灼灼的目光,唤醒了沉睡中的杨

asked in a frightened voice, "Who is it that dares to part the curtains?"

Still taken by her beauty, Li Longji murmured, "Even though she has just woken up and half her powder has been rubbed off, her lipstick gone and her hair in disorder, she is still a celestial beauty!"

Yongxin and Niannu saw that Her Ladyship was awake and went to help her get up. Yang Yuhuan opened her eyes, gave the emperor a listless look then closed them again. She got up, but was too weary to stand and sat down.

Full of sympathy, Li Longji saw that the two maids wanted to help her get up. He went forward to help them, saying in a low voice, "You're so sleepy you'd better have a rest." Aware that it was the emperor Yang Yuhuan leaned over his shoulder and murmured, "Long live and long, long live...."

"On this sunny spring morning it would be pleasant to stroll outside. Why do you sleep at noon?" Li Longji asked.

Yang Yuhuan blushed at this and whispered, "Last night I was favored by Your Majesty. You honored me so much that today I am weary and when I tried to dress I fell asleep again. That is why I failed to welcome Your Majesty just now."

Hearing this Li Longji laughed and said, "So this is my fault!" Yang Yuhuan blushed and remained silent. Li Longji said softly, "My love, you still look drowsy. Let us go to the front palace to pass a pleasant hour." Yang Yuhuan nodded. Li Longji took her hand and the two left the west palace for the front palace.

It goes without saying that a group of eunuchs and attendants in the front palace waited on the emperor and Lady Yang, who had tea and snacks in a hall.

While they were talking to each other Yang Guozhong sought an audience. Eunuch Gao Lishi entered the hall and said, "Long live the emperor! In accordance with Your Majesty's orders the prime minister has given An Lushan a test. He is now waiting outside the palace to make his report."

"Let him in."

Yang Guozhong entered the hall and kowtowed to the emperor, saying, "Long live the emperor! Long live Lady Yang!" After being ordered to stand up he said, "I have tested An Lushan and beg to report that I find him a worthy fellow, skilled in six tribal languages as well as archery and horsemanship."

玉环。她突然惊醒，惺眼尚自朦胧地问道："谁人？怎敢撩咱绡帐！"

李隆基仍在欣赏贵妃娇美的容颜，自言自语地赞叹道："尽管一觉醒来，粉容浅淡，朱唇褪色，发形零乱，但仍是掩不住你的国色天香啊！"

永新、念奴见贵妃娘娘已经醒转过来，便上前扶她起身。杨玉环方才睁开惺眼，懒懒地看了看皇上，沉重的眼皮又垂了下来。李隆基看在眼里，怜在心里，便趋步向前，一把托起杨玉环腰肢，轻轻说道："你睡得这般朦朦腾腾，先休息休息。"杨玉环知是圣上，索性歪倒在李隆基臂膀上，口中呢呢喃喃地："万岁，万岁……"

"春昼晴和，正好及时游赏行乐，为何日头当午还兀自沉睡不起？"李隆基悄悄问道。

杨玉环闻言不觉胀红了半边脸，在李隆基耳边低声细语说道："夜来承宠，雨露恩浓，不觉花枝力弱，经受不起，因此失迎圣驾。"

李隆基方知昨夜欢乐过度，不禁笑道："这样说来，倒是寡人唐突贵妃了！"杨玉环满脸发红，娇羞万般，一言不发。李隆基又软语劝说："妃子，看你神思困倦，且同到前殿去消遣消遣。"杨玉环点头称是。李隆基便牵着她的手，双双离开西宫，向前殿行去。

前殿自有一般内监侍候皇上与娘娘，摆上茶点酒肴，两人随意取用，悄悄谈心。正当李隆基与杨玉环深情蜜意、你恩我爱之际，杨国忠来回奏了，高力士入殿通报："启禀万岁爷：国舅杨丞相，遵旨面试安禄山，现在宫门外等待回奏。""传他进来面奏。"

杨国忠闻召进后宫面圣："臣杨国忠见驾。愿吾皇万岁，娘娘千岁。"拜罢，口称："臣启陛下：承蒙皇上委托面试安禄山，此人果然是个人才，身高力大，弓马娴熟。特此复旨。"

Li Longji was glad to hear it and said, "Yesterday I read General Zhang's memorial which said that this An Lushan knew six tribal tongues and all the arts of war so he had been made a frontier general. But he has been defeated in war and should be executed. That is why I sent you to test him. Since General Zhang's statement is true, you can tell An that his mistakes are pardoned and order him to appear in court tomorrow morning. I shall appoint him to a post in the capital and see how he conducts himself."

"It shall be done, sire." Yang Guozhong was, of course, happy with the result and he could now give a satisfactory reply to An. But he did not anticipate that An's presence in the capital would cause him trouble in the future.

After Yang Guozhong had gone, Gao Lishi said, "Sire, the peonies at the Aloes Pavilion are in full bloom. Would Your Majesty and Her Ladyship care to see them?"

Li Longji was glad to hear this and said, "With such a lady and rare flowers, you must send Hanlin academician, Li Bai, to the pavilion to compose a new poem for me."

Gao Lishi left to summon Li Bai. Li Longji rose from his seat and helped Yang Yuhuan to her feet, saying, "My love, let us go to see the flowers."

It was no mere accident that Gao Lishi, a personal attendant, held a post of first rank. Scheming and guessing the emperor's moods from his words and looks he catered to his whims and had ingratiated himself. He enjoyed the emperor's confidence and had won repeated promotions to achieve prominence in officialdom.

Gao Lishi was well aware that the emperor was infatuated with Lady Yang and did his best to please him. He thought that the emperor and Lady Yang were just having a good time and would surely tire of each other in the long run. People in the capital went on an outing during the Spring Festival which fell on the third day of the third lunar month and he might persuade the emperor and Lady Yang to go as well. There were many scenic spots such as the River Bend Pond, Yichun Garden, Ziyun Tower, Furong Garden, Apricot Garden, and Ci'en Temple in the southeastern part of the city; the emperor and Lady Yang would surely like them. Later they would remember how he had contributed. He made up his mind and found a chance to tell the emperor about it.

李隆基听罢，也还高兴，说："朕昨日见张守珪奏章，说他通晓六番言语，精熟各种武艺，可以充当守边之将。今失败当斩，所以委你面试。既然张守珪所奏不虚，你可传旨安禄山，赦他前罪，明日早朝引见，授他一京官，以观后效。"

"领旨。"有这般结果，杨国忠自然高兴，对安禄山有个交代了。可是却不知道，安禄山留任京官，对他来说却是埋下了无穷祸根。

杨国忠退下后，高力士又趋前报告："启奏万岁爷，沉香亭牡丹盛开，请万岁爷同娘娘前去赏玩。"

李隆基圣心大悦，说道："今日对妃子，赏名花，岂可无新词？你可告诉翰林李白，让他立刻写几篇新词来。"

高力士奉命前去宣召李白，李隆基便走下座位来，扶起杨玉环，说："妃子，和你赏花去。"

近侍高力士，官至从一品，并非偶然。此人很有心机，极善于察颜观色，揣摸圣情，投其所好，曲意小心，因而得到李隆基宠信，从一个内侍步步高升，乃有今日之显赫权势。

高力士深知近来皇上日夜迷恋贵妃杨玉环，因而就变着法儿迎合凑趣。他想：近日来帝、妃二人只是呆在宫中戏嬉作乐，日久必感乏味，趁此三月三日上巳节，倾城士女去郊外踏青，正可劝说圣上与娘娘也去郊游。何况京城东南有曲江池、宜春苑、紫云楼、芙蓉苑、杏园、慈恩寺等许许多多风景名胜，皇上与娘娘必定会玩得欢畅，自然也就会想到咱家也有一份功劳。主意一定，便伺机奏知皇上。

Li Longji happily accepted his suggestion. It would please Lady Yang but Li Longji had other reasons for accepting. After Yang Yuhuan became the favorite concubine, her cousin Yang Guozhong, now brother-in-law of the emperor, had been repeatedly promoted until he held the post of prime minister, with only the emperor over him and millions answerable to him. Yang Yuhuan's three sisters had been made Duchess Qin, Duchess Han, and Duchess Guo respectively. As an emperor, Li Longji could not simply call on them when he liked and the suggestion of a spring outing gave him a chance to meet the three ladies. He ordered Gao Lishi to go to the prime minister's house at once to tell him and the three duchesses to accompany them on the outing.

Gao Lishi rode out at once heading for the house of the prime minister and then to the houses of the three duchesses. His galloping horse aroused the interest of the people in the city who guessed that the emperor and Lady Yang would be going on an outing accompanied by the prime minister and the three duchesses. Yang Yuhuan was a beauty and government officials and ordinary people knew it. Her three sisters were also renowned for their comeliness. But one was in the court and the others lived in mansions. Who could see them? The speculation that they were going on an outing and visiting River Bend created a sensation in the capital. All the people, in groups of three to five, men and women, old and young, ugly and beautiful, turned out to watch the matchless beauties.

It was acceptable to make a show for the people but the act would allow one scoundrel to sow the seeds of trouble. The scoundrel was none other than An Lushan. He had lost his army and should have been put to death, but his life had been saved because he offered a large bribe to the prime minister Yang Guozhong. Afterwards, he had been given a post in the capital. He was not a generous person, in fact he was malicious and his intentions were evil. He lived in the capital and saw that Yang Guozhong had used his position as brother- in-law to the emperor to behave arrogantly to the people. Although government officials of all ranks said nothing they thought it was unsatisfactory; even the emperor sometimes disliked him, but he curbed his anger because he doted on Lady Yang. An understood the subtle relationship between the two. He also thought of how he had been humiliated the other day when he sought Yang's help; he wanted revenge. Because of this An tried hard to please the emperor in the hope that he could bring about the downfall of Yang Guozhong and avenge himself.

李隆基欣然接受他的建议，除了讨好贵妃杨玉环之外，还另有心思哩。自从杨玉环得宠后，她的兄长杨国忠贵为国舅，自然升迁不断，官至丞相，真可谓一人之下、万人之上了。杨玉环的三个姊妹也分别被封为秦国夫人、韩国夫人和虢国夫人。李隆基虽贵为圣上，但也不能随时和三位国夫人相聚。高力士建议上巳节春游，倒为他提供了一个亲近三位夫人的极好机会。他便命高力士速速前往丞相府，召唤杨丞相和三位国夫人一同去曲江游春。

高力士奉了圣旨，飞骑直奔丞相府，又去三位国夫人府，路上风风火火，早惊动了满城士女，一传十、十传百，都知道皇上与娘娘游春，并传召丞相与三位国夫人随驾同游。杨玉环的国色天香，早已盛传朝野，她的三个姊妹也是秀色可餐，啧有名声。然而一位深藏宫中，三位深居府中，平素哪能一睹芳容？如今同出踏青，游幸曲江，哪能不轰动京城！倾城士女，不论老的、少的、娇的、丑的，无不三五成群，结伴而行，一睹绝色。

惊动别人犹可，就中惊动了一个歹徒，便栽下了祸根。此人非他，乃是安禄山。他曾军前失利、罪当处死，只因用重金贿赂杨国忠方得以赦免，之后又留在京城任职。安禄山原非善良之辈，实在是一个包藏祸心的野心家。留京以后，他看出丞相杨国忠自恃国舅身份，待人接物，处处傲慢无礼，朝臣上下虽口中不言而心实不满，甚至连皇上对他也有些厌恶，只因宠爱着杨玉环，才容忍未发。安禄山窥测到这种君臣关系，又想到当年求救于杨国忠时所受到的屈辱，自然寻机思图报复解恨，便竭力巴结皇上，求得欢心，以便斗败杨国忠，一洗前次受到的羞辱。

When Li Longji was with them, Yang Guozhong became more arrogant and An Lushan more cautious. In time Li Longji thought that An was loyal and intended giving him more important assignments and promoting him. This upset Yang Guozhong who was jealous, but An Lushan naturally disregarded his feelings.

An Lushan was born with a big belly. One day, when he was with Li Longji in a side hall, the emperor pointed to his belly and asked playfully, "What is inside? Why is it so big?"

Shrewdly, An Lushan replied, "Your Majesty, there is nothing inside except my loyal heart." His answer pleased Li Longji who favored him more and intended making him prince. An learned that on that day the emperor would be taking Lady Yang and the three duchesses for an outing. He longed to have a glimpse and changed into civilian clothes, mounted a horse and galloped along the banks of the River Bend in search of them.

After a while a procession of carriages and horses approached. There was a smell of sweet perfume and the three duchesses appeared. Duchess Han wore an embroidered dress which contrasted with the white one worn by Duchess Guo and the red one of Duchess Qin. They were surrounded by a group of attendants and maids. Men and women thronged the road, vying with each other to catch a glimpse. An Lushan also saw the procession. He held the reins tightly and suddenly charged the carriages. The servants of the Yang family immediately stopped the horse shouting, "Halt there! The prime minister is here! Who are you? How dare you charge past?"

An made no reply, but gazed around trying to spot the beautiful duchesses in the assembly of carriages and horses. He saw that they were matchless beauties and stared at them. While admiring them, he felt envious of the emperor and murmured, "Ah, emperor of Tang, emperor of Tang! You have not only Lady Yang, but her sisters too! You are the most fortunate of men! You have all the beauties in the country and only by this means can you become the Son of Heaven!" As it was a rare opportunity to see the duchesses, An disregarded the shouts of the servants and spurred his horse on to take a second look. The Yang family servants blocked his way and shouted at him. Prime Minister Yang was putting on airs as he rode slowly at the back of the procession. Hearing the commotion he whipped his horse to a gallop and met An Lushan face to face. Instead of greeting the prime minister, An turned his horse and left swiftly by a side way.

在李隆基面前，杨国忠越是恃宠傲慢，安禄山便越是谨慎谦恭,两人形成强烈对照。自此,安禄山便渐渐得到李隆基宠信。这更加招致杨丞相的嫉恨,安禄山自然不会考虑杨丞相的意愿。

安禄山生就一个大肚皮，一日在便殿上与李隆基相对，李隆基指着他的大肚皮,戏问道:“你这肚皮中有啥东西？为啥这么大？”

安禄山机伶地回奏道：“皇上，这大肚皮中并无他物，只有一片忠心。”李隆基大喜,更加宠眷,有心要封他为王。安禄山早就怀有觊觎之心，今日他听说皇上不但携了贵妃而且还带了三位国夫人同游,便换了便服,故意纵马奔驰,穿梭般地在曲江周围往来寻觅。

不一会儿，一队车马驶来，随着一阵香风拂过，原来是三位国夫人前来了。只见韩国夫人穿着一身绣花衣服，虢国夫人是一身洁白素衣，而秦国夫人却又穿着一袭红色缎服，三位夫人身边各有一众随从、丫环，前呼后拥地踏青而来。自然，这队车马也逃不过安禄山四面观察的贼眼,他勒起缰绳,突地向车队飞闯过去。杨府家人赶紧上前迎着马头拦住,大声呵责:“咄！丞相爷在此！你是什么人？怎敢在此乱撞！”

安禄山也不答话，只是把一双贼眼在如云的车马中寻找如花的夫人。果然被他瞧个仔细,真是个个天姿国色！赞赏之余,不禁流露出强烈的既羡又妒的感情，自言自语地说道：“唉，唐天子呀唐天子！你有了一个如花似玉的贵妃，又添上这几个国色天姿的阿姨,真的占尽了天下风流！”杨府家人自然又是拦阻又是疾呼。杨丞相原先摆着官谱儿不疾不忙地行在车队后面，听得前方喧嚷不断,乃策马向前,正好与突奔而来的安禄山迎面相撞,安禄山也不打招呼,勒回马头从斜刺里疾奔而去。

The family servants were very angry and said to Yang Guozhong, "We do not know the fellow who has just fled. He just rode towards us on a horse and no one could stop him!"

"Ah, it was An Lushan. Why did he run away when he saw me?" Yang Guozhong had not yet given much thought to An's insolence but the full force of it came home to him and he said to the servants, "Where are the three duchesses carriages?"

"In the front."

Yang Guozhong was suddenly enraged and said, "Aya, that fellow An Lushan is rude! How dare he look down upon the imperial relatives. He charged at them openly and rudely. The scoundrel." He spoke sharply to his family servants. "Go at once and protect the carriages of the three duchesses. Use your gilded whips to lash anyone who comes near. No idlers or people not connected with them are allowed to approach the carriages."

This order was too late to stop An Lushan having a peep, but the men and women pressing forward were whipped. Instead of seeing the duchesses, they were now trying to hide and had to hold their breath until the carriages and horses of the Yang family had passed. They ended up behind the carriages and horses calling out to each other as they walked in small groups on the grass.

Someone suddenly cried, "Ah, there is a hairpin!" A young woman picked up the ornament dropped from a carriage and held it happily in her hand. Several young women surrounded her and wanted to see the hairpin. "Ah, there is a ruby on it." Just then someone else called out. "Let's keep on searching, there might be something good!" The girls dispersed, searching in the grass. Someone found a slipper, someone else an inlaid box and another girl, a silk hanky. Each searcher found something and they said to each other how rich and extravagant the imperial relatives were.

The carriage procession with the three duchesses went fast and drew away from the crowds that had surrounded it. Family servants went ahead and bowed before their carriages to say that they had arrived at River Bend."

Duchess Han asked, "Where is His Grace, the prime minister?"

"His Grace has gone to Wangchun Palace, where His Majesty is now."

The three duchesses alighted at the same time and before them was

杨府家人气忿忿地向丞相禀报："刚才逃走的那个人，也不知是什么人，骑马乱撞过来，向前拦阻也阻挡不住！"

"啊，那厮是安禄山，怎么见了咱就远远避异了？"此刻，杨国忠还未想到安禄山的无礼。继而醒悟过来，便问家人："三位夫人的车儿在哪里？""就在前面。"

杨国忠陡然大怒："啊呀呀，安禄山这家伙怎敢如此无礼！他居然敢藐视皇亲国戚。公然无礼冲撞，令人好恨！"继而又吩咐家人道："你们赶紧护着三位夫人的车儿行走，对围上来的人，不论是何人，甩起金鞭，将他们赶得远远的，不许任何闲杂人等近傍夫人车儿！"

此命一下，并未禁得住安禄山的窥视目光，吃苦的倒是争先恐后的男男女女，被鞭儿抽得七倒八歪，忙着东躲西藏，好不容易等杨府车马驶过，方才喘过气儿来，整整零乱的衣衫，依旧跟在车马后面，寻机一睹芳容。

忽地一声惊呼："呀，这是一枝簪子！"一个少女拾起车队遗下的首饰，喜不自禁地攒在手中。听到她的叫声，立刻拥上来几个女子，争着观看："呀，上面还嵌有一块红宝石。"赞叹之余，又传来一声："我们再去找找，兴许还能找到好东西！"围观的女子一时散去，在草地上四处寻寻觅觅，有的寻到绣鞋，有的寻到钿盒，有的拾到鲛绡手帕，各有所获，互相讲说丞相、夫人的富有，叹息皇亲、国戚的奢侈。

且说三位国夫人的车队在周围喧闹的人群中疾驶而过，渐行渐远。不一会儿，家人趋前打恭："禀报夫人，到曲江了。"

韩国夫人先开口问道："丞相爷在哪里？"

"万岁爷在望春宫，丞相爷到那儿去了。"

a beautiful scene. Water wound between banks covered in red flowers and green grass. There were slender willow tendrils and young cattails; it was spring everywhere.

A young eunuch approached and said, "By His Majesty's orders, Duchess of Han and Duchess of Qin will feast in the second pavilion, while Duchess of Guo is to ride to Wangchun Palace to feast with Lady Yang." The duchesses knelt down and said, "Long live the emperor!" They rose.

The eunuch urged Duchess Guo to go at once which made her uneasy and she said, "Why should I hurry! How can I leave my sisters here."

Tactfully, duchesses Han and Qin said, "You are summoned to the palace thanks to your natural charm. You can appear before the emperor with your face unpainted. Go ahead, don't keep the emperor waiting."

说话之间，三位国夫人一齐出了车，眼睛顿时觉得明亮起来，只见环岸曲水，红花绿草，细柳新蒲，春意盎然，心神为之一畅。

一个小太监迎了出来，朝着三位国夫人说："皇上口敕：韩国夫人、秦国夫人，在别殿赐宴；虢国夫人立即乘马入宫，陪杨娘娘饮宴。"三位国夫人闻旨，齐齐跪下，口称"万岁"，随后立起身来。

小内监不断催促虢国夫人快行，她倒有些不好意思起来："何必催得太紧！怎能让俺一人偏背了姐姐妹妹。"

韩国、秦国两位夫人自然识趣，劝说道："宣你进宫，正是不辜负你这副娥眉淡扫的容颜。快快去吧，别让皇上等急了。"

Chapter Three

Humiliated Because of Jealousy

No one would have anticipated that the pleasure tour arranged by Li Longji would have ended in discord. They had been in high spirits the day that he and Yang Yuhuan had gone to River Bend. But after just one night Yang Yuhuan came back alone while the emperor returned the second day.

Although Gao Lishi was a confidant of the emperor, he did not know much about the harems of the inner palace. He saw that the emperor was very angry and he spoke to the palace maid, Yongxin, "Can you tell me why the emperor has stopped going to Lady Yang's chamber?"

"Ah, Your Grace, don't you know? The two have quarreled and neither will give way."

"What did they quarrel about?"

"It was over an extra flower on the two-headed lotus flower." Yongxin did not explain further. Gao Lishi understood that there was a third person, but he did not know who it was. Yongxin refused to name the person and said with a smile, "Your Grace, you're so clever; if you guess, you will certainly solve the puzzle."

"How should I know! Sister Yongxin, please tell me."

Gao Lishi repeatedly pressed her for an answer and Yongxin told him the whole story. She said, "Well, it was Lady Yang who started the trouble."

Bewildered, Gao Lishi said, "How?"

"Her Ladyship often tells the emperor that Duchess Guo is a great beauty with good figure. This made the emperor summon her to the feast in Wangchun Palace. After a few cups, the two shared erotic feelings and they made love in secret. That was how it happened."

When he heard this, Gao Lishi clasped his hands and laughed, saying, "Aya. I suspected as much. But why then should Lady Yang be angry?"

Yongxin, a woman, knew more about love than Gao Lishi, a eunuch,

第三章
争宠招辱

哪里知道李隆基安排的这场宴游却落得个不欢而散，去时大家欢天喜地，不过一宵，杨玉环却先行回宫，皇上今日才返驾。高力士虽为皇上亲信，但对皇上的宫帏之情却不能十分了解。见圣上不悦，未免向宫女永新询问："万岁爷为何不到杨娘娘宫中去？"

"唉呀，公公，你还不知道么？他们两个闹了点儿别扭，都在装腔作态呢。""为什么事儿闹别扭？"

"还不是为了并头莲之外又开了一枝花。"永新仍不说明，但高力士已知道是有第三者了，只不知道第三者为谁人。永新还是不点出人来，只是笑着回答："公公，你是聪明人，自己去参悟，肯定能解开这个谜。""咱哪里能得知！永新姐，你还是说给我听吧。"

禁不住高力士一再恳求，宫女永新只得娓娓道来："只为娘娘经常在皇上面前说虢国夫人美貌动人，天生一副好身段。这才惹动万岁爷，召她在望春宫侍宴。三杯酒后，彼此情浓，暗中结下连理。"

高力士听得此言，拍手笑道："啊呀呀，咱也猜测到这上头——只是娘娘又为何烦恼呢？"

宫女永新到底是女流，对男女之情要比太监高力士有更多的

and explained, "Lady Yang was afraid that someone might take her place in the emperor's affections. That is why she was angry and spoke rudely. But Duchess Guo is clever and left, saying nothing. The emperor was very angry because Lady Yang did not press Duchess Guo to stay and he has not come to the west palace today. Lady Yang is there, crying."

"I think Lady Yang carries matters too far. She is too self-willed and intolerant. The other day she insisted that Lady Plum Blossom move to the east wing of the Shangyang Pavilion and now she cannot even tolerate Duchess Guo, her own sister. She lacks sisterly feelings."

Yongxin was aware that they should not discuss the matter further and said, "Your Grace, let's drop the subject. There is one thing though. Usually the emperor never leaves Lady Yang's side and now he is staying away from her. What can we do?"

"What can we do? We can only wait and see...." At that moment someone from the inner court announced, "His Majesty sends for His Grace Gao." Gao at once went into the inner court.

Duchess Guo was also upset after she returned from the tour of River Bend; she stayed alone at home, reflecting. She had married into the Pei family, but her husband had died and left her a young widow. Nevertheless, she was careful and seldom went out for pleasure. Her sister had become the favorite of the emperor and she was now a duchess; she had to go on the outing because the emperor required her presence. Simply dressed and with no powder on her face, she went. She had not anticipated that, discreet as she was, she would not be able to escape the lascivious attentions of Li Longji. He had singled her out to force his attentions onto her in the Wangchun Pavilion.

During the feast, after a few cups Li Longji had become captivated by Duchess Guo's beauty and took her to bed; she had resisted but he took no notice. They spent the night together, but Li Longji was not satisfied and wanted her to stay at the palace. Duchess Guo thought that her sister was his favorite so she repeatedly declined his importuning and returned home. Her sister Yuhuan was angry and certainly did not ask her to stay; as for Li Longji, he failed to find a pretext to keep her from going. She went home. The affair had enraged her sister, aroused gossips and afterwards she had been most unhappy pitying herself over her sad lot. But her sister, Duchess Han, knew nothing of this and had only heard that she had fallen ill after returning from Wangchun Pavilion, so she visited her accompanied by maids.

理解："娘娘还不是担心日后被夺了宠爱！因此嫌弃这桩事儿。言语就不善，虢国夫人乖觉，便悄悄出宫去了。万岁爷怪杨娘娘不留住虢国夫人，所以今日就偏偏不进西宫去，丢下娘娘一人在那里哭哩。"

"这就要怪杨娘娘了。她也太恃娇任性，厉害得让人受不了。前些时候，把个梅妃逼得迁到东楼。如今这个虢国夫人是自家亲姊妹，也容她不得。真也没有一点儿姊妹情谊了。"

永新知道这个话题是不能说下去的，连忙止住："公公，这话不说吧。只是万岁爷和杨娘娘行坐不离，如今两下不见面，如何是好？"

"咱们又有什么办法？且等着瞧机会吧。"高力士话音刚落地，内里已传出："有旨宣高公公。"他连忙答应着进内宫去了。

且说虢国夫人自那天侍游曲江归来之后，心情也极不平静，闭门不出，独自沉思。她原先嫁给裴家，哪知夫婿早年命丧，青春年华就已寡居。不过，她也不是放荡的人，轻易不肯出游。只因亲妹妹杨玉环得宠，自家沾光，被封为虢国夫人。圣上召陪游赏，才不得不出门。穿着一身素衣，更不搽粉涂脂，就去面见圣上。哪知即令如此谨慎，也逃不出性喜女色的李隆基的手心。

在宴席上，李隆基几杯酒下肚，面对裴氏绝色，春意盎然，径自将她搀入帐中，彼此春风一度，还要邀她一同回宫去。她自忖，妹子玉环正得宠，此事如何行得，便再三再四地辞归。玉环妹子已经嗔怒了，自然不会挽留，李隆基一时也找不出借口留住她。这样，方才得以脱身归来。但即令如此，不但引起了亲妹妹玉环的不满，也招来人言藉藉。因此近日来心情不佳，颇为自己的身世际遇而伤心不已。但是，她的亲姐姐韩国夫人却不知道这些，只知道那一天她从望春宫回来后生了病，便带了院子、丫环前去虢府探视。

"Duchess Han has arrived," an attendant of the Guo Mansion announced.

"Show her in at once," replied Duchess Guo.

Duchess Han entered the inner room slowly. The two sisters greeted each other, sat down and tea was served. Duchess Han said, "Sister, congratulations!"

"Why should I be congratulated?"

"The other day only you were honored. This beautiful flower has blossomed at the side of the emperor."

Duchess Guo blushed. "Sister, do not say so. I was summoned to Wangchun Pavilion just to attend the emperor during the feast. His Majesty holds us in equal favor, there is no difference."

"Aya, although you say so, a feast outside and a feast inside the palace are quite different. Sister, do not pretend, among the thousands of flowers, you were picked by the emperor!" Duchess Guo felt unable to defend herself and she lowered her head without saying anything. Duchess Han noticed this and at once changed the subject. "How was Sister Yuhuan when you saw her at the palace?"

"Recently, Sister Yuhuan has been in high favor and the emperor cannot leave her for a moment."

"How much does the emperor love her?"

"I just know that they are together all day, but outsiders should not know how much they love each other."

Duchess Han pressed her. "Didn't you get any idea?"

Duchess Guo had to reply. "The only thing that is certain is that Sister Yuhuan has become even more quick tempered than she was before. She found fault in others and insisted on having her way."

"That has always been the case. Sister, you should give her some advice."

"No one can and no one wants to," Duchess Guo unwittingly complained.

"She was proud of her gifts and accomplishments and has had a bad temper ever since she was a child. As sisters, we should not gossip behind her back. Now that she is a favorite in court, she will certainly have her own way all the more. No one can compare with her."

These remarks of Duchess Han unintentionally touched a nerve and Duchess Guo said loudly, "Who has competed with her to be favorite? There is nothing I can say about the temper she was born with, but I can

“韩国夫人到！”虢府院子进来禀报。

“快去请进。”虢国夫人答道。

韩国夫人缓步进入内室，姐妹彼此见过，坐下，上了茶。韩国夫人试探地说道：“妹妹，大喜。”

“有何喜事？”虢国夫人惊讶地问道。

“那一天，独独你得到特别的宠幸。你这朵美丽的花儿已开到皇帝身边了。”

闻得此言，虢国夫人羞怯万状，边解释边诉说：“姐姐，你说到哪儿去了！我被召进望春宫，也不过陪陪酒而已。圣上对我的恩幸与对姐姐的恩幸都是一般的，哪有差别！”

“啊呀呀，话虽然如此说，但外边赐宴怎比得上内宫赐宴。”这一番话，说得虢国夫人也难以辩白，只得低头不语。韩国夫人见状，立即换了个话题，问道：“你在宫中，看见玉环妹子的情况怎样？”

“那玉环妹妹，近来更是有身份了。皇上一时也离不开她。”

“不知皇上怎样与她恩爱？”

“只知他们终日不离，究竟如何恩爱，外人怎能得知。”

韩国夫人仍不放过，追问道：“你难道一点儿情况也未发觉？”

虢国夫人不得不说了：“只见玉环妹子的脾气越发大了，不免倚宠使骄，对他人更是挑剔，太任性了。”

“她从小就如此。妹子，你也该劝劝她。”

“哪个能劝得她。”虢国夫人不觉流露了几分怨气。

“她从小就依仗自己长得好模样，性子骄，脾气坏，我们是姊妹，也不必说她了。如今在宫内得宠，自然更是恃宠放纵，有谁能与她争高低。”

say that the emperor is unpredictable!"

Duchess Guo's answer was revealing and Duchess Han stood up and murmured, "Ai, there must be some reasons behind what this sister from the Pei family says. She hides something while revealing something else and does not give a straight answer. I only hope that nothing will happen."

Just then an attendant rushed in and said, "I have something to report, Madame, an unfortunate thing has happened!"

"What is it? What's there to be alarmed about? Say it slowly." Duchess Han was alarmed while Duchess Guo, although not surprised, stood up.

"Her Ladyship has offended the emperor. The emperor was in a rage and ordered His Grace Gao to take her back to the prime minister's house."

Duchess Han was frightened and said, "Ya! Can it be true?"

"I said her temper would get her into trouble. Now it has happened."

"Even so, we are sisters, and this relates to our honor or humiliation. I think we should go to see her."

"You are right," Duchess Guo was unable to sit down. The two sisters rode to the prime minister's house in a carriage. On the way Duchess Han panicked as she spoke about it and Duchess Guo said, "Sister, won't Lady Plume Blossom find Sister Yuhuan's situation amusing?"

Without realizing what she was saying Duchess Han replied, "It is worse than Lady Plum Blossom, for though she has been cold-shouldered, she remains in the court."

Duchess Guo fully agreed and said, "Yes, our sister's situation is really worse than that of Lady Plum Blossom."

As the saying goes, "In nature sudden storms spring up and men's fortunes may change overnight." After his cousin had been made an imperial concubine, Yang Guozhong had been promoted many times and now he enjoyed great power as brother-in-law of the emperor and prime minister. But who could have told him when he got up that morning that he would learn that Her Ladyship had offended the emperor had been dismissed from the palace. He trembled at the news and did not know what to do. This shows the truth of the saying that "when you sit at home, a disaster descends from heaven".

Now we will set aside Yang Guozhong's fright and the coming visit

韩国夫人这番无心的话，倒触动了虢国夫人的心病，声音也高了几分，说道:“谁与她争！只是她生性如此，别的倒没啥，只怕君心不测！”

虢国夫人这样的回答，倒让韩国夫人窥得一些内情，不觉立起，自言自语地悄悄叹息:哎，这番言语，说得藏头露尾，必有原因。

正当她担忧之际，院子一头闯了进来，叫道:“禀夫人，不好了。”

“哇，什么事？为何大惊小怪！”

“贵妃娘娘忤旨，圣上大怒，命高公公送归丞相府去了。”

韩国夫人听到如此禀报，惊恐万端:“呀！有这样事。”

“我说她这般心性，总要惹下事来。果不其然。”

“虽说如此，但你、我与她都是姊妹，而且事关大家荣辱，我们还是去看看她才是。”

“正是。”虢国夫人也不能坐视了。说罢，两姊妹一同乘车前往兄弟杨国忠丞相府中去。路上，韩国夫人还心有余悸地谈说此事，虢国夫人则话中有话地说道:“姐姐，玉环妹妹这般下场，可不被梅妃看笑话？”

韩国夫人有口无心地说道:“真还不如梅妃，虽然遭到冷遇，还留在宫中哩。”

虢国夫人极表同意地说:“是呀，妹妹的下场真不如梅妃。”

真是“天有不测风云，人有旦夕祸福”，杨国忠自从妹子杨玉环被册封贵妃后，不断升官，既是国舅身份，又是丞相大人，权势滔天，不可一世。岂料今日早晨起来，就传说贵妃得罪圣上，被谪出宫。顿时惶惶不知所措，真是“人在家中坐，祸从天上来”。

of the two duchesses and turn to how Gao Lishi brought Lady Yang home.

As personal attendant of the emperor Gao Lishi was able to gauge his thoughts extremely well. Although the emperor had sent Her Ladyship home in a fit of anger, like other emperors, he would long for his former lover later on when he had had enough of other women. Thus, as he advised Her Ladyship not to cry on the way, he was planning how to make the emperor change his mind. They arrived very soon at the prime minister's house. Yang Guozhong was already standing outside the gate with a group of men and women attendants and servants waiting to welcome them.

Gao Lishi got down from the carriage and Yang Guozhong who dared not neglect Gao when things were going well was especially attentive today. He bowed deeply; Gao Lishi waved his hand. Yang Guozhong turned and knelt before the carriage of the imperial concubine, saying, "Your subject Yang Guozhong welcomes Your Ladyship." Without waiting for orders, maids and servants pushed forward to help Yang Yuhuan out of the carriage.

Yang Guozhong turned to speak to Gao Lishi, but Gao did not consider himself to be an outsider and neglected the formality. He said, "Prime minister, show Her Ladyship in and I would like to have a word with you."

Yang Guozhong immediately ordered attendants and maids to take Her Ladyship to the house for a rest. Again he bowed deeply to Gao Lishi and said politely, "Please be seated. I wonder how this happened?"

"Generally speaking, Her Ladyship has been the most favored since she entered the palace. No one knew what happened yesterday. Her Ladyship offended His Majesty and suddenly they were estranged. Don't be offended if I speak bluntly. Her Ladyship is inclined to be arrogant because she is a favorite and she cannot tolerate the other ladies."

Yang Guozhong knew all about his cousin's temper and accepted the truth of what Eunuch Gao said. But the most important thing now was to reverse the situation and he asked Gao directly, "Your Grace Gao, what can be done now that she is dismissed?"

"Prime minister, you'd better go to the palace to apologize for her, see how things are, and watch for an opportunity."

"Your Grace, I shall depend on you to put in a good word for me to the emperor."

Gao Lishi replied with confidence, "Sure. Something should be done to help Her Ladyship return to the palace." Then he left and Yang

且不说杨国忠胆颤心惊，也不说两位国夫人车乘急驶而来。只说高力士奉召遣送杨玉环回府。

这高力士身为李隆基近侍，当然深知他的心思。他知道，圣上虽然不满贵妃忤旨，一时怒起，将她遣出宫来，但哪个君王不是喜怒无常！隔段时日，采够了野花，吃饱了禁果，又会回转心思，眷恋故人的。因此，高力士一路上一边劝说、安慰哭哭泣泣的贵妃娘娘，一边也在思谋如何再使圣上回心转意。不一会儿，已到了丞相府，杨国忠早已率领一般男妇大小，在府门外迎接。

高力士先下了车，杨国忠平素也不敢轻视内侍高力士，更何况此刻！赶紧上前长揖到底，高力士挥手作答，杨国忠转身上前，跪在娘娘车门边，口称："臣杨国忠迎接娘娘。"不待吩咐，身后丫环、婢女个个趋前搀扶杨玉环下车。

杨国忠又转身与高力士搭话，高力士也不见外，并不理会这些繁文缛节，说道："丞相，快请娘娘进府，咱和你还有话说。"

杨国忠即刻吩咐院子，叫丫环搀扶娘娘先去休憩。再向高力士长长一揖，恭谨地招呼："老公公请厅上坐，不知此事因何而起？"

"按说起来，自娘娘进宫以来，皇上对她最为宠爱。昨天不知何故，不讨皇上欢喜，顿时间有了隔阂 —— 丞相，不要怪咱家多嘴，说起娘娘啊，一向恃宠放骄，容忍不得他人。"

杨国忠何尝不知自家妹子的脾性，高力士所说又何尝有不实之处，但事到如今，还是赶紧扭转局面为要，便直截了当地问道："高公公，如今被遣送出来，怎么办呢？"

"丞相不妨先去朝门请罪，看看动静，趁机而行。"

"高公公，全仗你在圣上面前美言了。"

Guozhong went with him to the palace to apologize.

Yang Yuhuan's banishment from the palace had filled her with alarm and she was sad. When Meixiang, a maid, took her to the back hall, she just sat silently at a table, grief stricken, her face covered in tears. She thought that at the palace she had been the emperor's favorite; she could trust him and their happy union would last for a hundred years. Who would have thought that she would have been sent home when the emperor was angry? Once she had left the palace, she felt that she was as far from it as earth is from the ninth heaven. She recalled the moon in the palace; it would not see her shadow there any more. Now that she was outside the palace she was like a flower that had dropped off a branch, she could not return. Her future looked bleak and she wept in self pity.

Meixiang did her best to soothe her and Lady Yang gradually calmed down. She took out the clothes that she had brought back, but the sweet smell of imperial scent made her sad. The emperor had given in to her every whim and had been with her day and night. How he had loved her! Now they were separated because he wished to be with her sister as well. Could she return to the palace? She wished that the emperor would change his mind and said to Meixiang, "Girl, where can I see the palace from here?"

"Look northwest from the Yushu Pavilion at the front, my lady, and you can see the palace wall."

"Come with me to the pavilion." Yang Yuhuan stood up at once and Meixiang led the way. In pavilion the maid pointed northwest and said, "Your Ladyship, can you see the yellow glazed tiles over there? That is the inner court of the palace."

When she looked to where the maid pointed, Yang Yuhuan saw the court, felt sad again and murmured, "Oh, heaven, I gaze at the palace from the pavilion, it is so near and yet the mist separates me from it. I was there yesterday. Now though I am still young, the emperor loves me no more. How can I make the emperor remember our former love and recall me?"

As if in response to her longing, Meixiang spotted something and said, "There in the distance I can see a eunuch on horseback. He may be coming to call you back, my lady."

Yang Yuhuan also saw the eunuch and hoped that instead of bad news he would bring good luck. As there was no time for her to ponder over it, she hurriedly descended the steps.

高力士极为自信地说："这个自然。总得让娘娘重进宫来。"说罢，便要回宫。杨国忠也跟着前往请罪。

杨娘娘被送出宫来，自然又惊又悲。丫环梅香送入后堂后，她也不洗漱，不饮食，默默坐在案前，泪痛满面，愁思万端，仔细思量：自入宫闱，受宠过甚，只认为君心可托，百年和合。谁想命运不济，逢上君皇之怒，被遣出宫，放归私第。宫门一出，如隔九天。想起宫中明月，再无照影之日；宫外飞花，已无上枝之望。前程何在，不免自伤自悼，独自落泪不已。

梅香在旁不断劝慰，杨娘娘心情渐渐平服，便把宫中带回的衣着取出，阵阵香气扑鼻而来，又触发她的愁思：这全是御香熏过的呀！又想起皇帝对自己的百依百顺，从晨至暮，相亲相伴，何等恩宠！只为这一"横枝"插入，陡然把两人分开，难道真的不能再回宫去？一念及此，她又渴望皇上回心转意，便向梅香问道："丫环，这里何处可看见宫中？"

"前面御书楼上，朝西北望去，便是宫墙了。"

杨玉环即刻立起身来，梅香引路前行，上楼，指着西北方向说道："娘娘，你看那一片黄黄的琉璃瓦，不就是皇宫内殿嘛！"

杨玉环随着丫环手指所向朝前望去，果然是皇宫，不禁又伤心起来：天呀，天呀，凭高远眺，咫尺云天。昨日还是宫内人，今朝却已是头未白而君恩尽了。怎能使得皇上重恋旧情，复召回宫呢？

好似与她的思虑相感应，丫环梅香眼尖，连忙招呼娘娘："娘娘，你看，一个公公远远骑马而来，说不定是召娘娘入宫哩。"

杨玉环此刻也看到了，只是希望别是又传来什么不好的讯息，但愿带来的是好的命运。也来不及多考虑了，她便匆匆下楼而来。

Gao Lishi had arrived when she entered the front hall and he knelt before her, saying, "Gao Lishi kowtows to Your Ladyship."

"Gao Lishi, what brings you back here?" Yang Yuhuan asked anxiously.

"Just now when I reported your return to His Majesty, he asked me to tell him what had happened here in detail as if he regretted what had taken place. Now he is sitting alone in the palace, sighing. He must be longing for you, so I came to report this to Your Ladyship."

"Oh no, how could he be thinking of me?"

Gao Lishi assured her it was so and said, "I am stupid. Forgive me if I advise you, madame. Do not be too stubborn. The emperor is actually thinking of you. Have you anything that you could give me to take to His Majesty when I get the opportunity? You never know, it might soften his heart."

Yang Yuhuan thought this was reasonable. She had been obstinate and said anxiously, "Gao Lishi, what can I send to the emperor?"

Gao Lishi could think of nothing at the moment and made no reply. Yang Yuhuan thought, "What would soften his heart?" Besides herself, all that she had was gifts from the emperor. How could she string together on a golden thread her tears, which dropped like pearls? Ah, yes! She could send a lock of the glossy hair which once lay near his head on the pillow. That might move his heart.

"Girl, bring me the mirror and the scissors." Lady Yang let down her hair but could not help shedding tears, crying out, "Hair, hair, you have been with me all my youth. How can I cut you off? To show that my heart is faithful I have to give you up!" She wept and cut her hair with a trembling hand then held up the lock and said, "His Majesty, your servant has only this lock of hair and she hopes it will reunite us."

She stood up and gave the lock of hair to Gao Lishi, saying, "Gao Lishi, take it and give it to the emperor. Tell him that I deserve ten thousand deaths as I shall never see his face again in this life. I present him with this lock of hair as a token of my love."

Gao Lishi took the lock of hair with both hands and placed it on his shoulder. He said, "My lady, please don't worry. Your servant will leave you now. By this lock of silken hair, your servant will do his utmost to make the emperor change his mind so that you will be reunited with him until your hair turns gray."

After Gao Lishi left, Yang Yuhuan felt tired and sat down. She did

等到娘娘走下楼来，高力士已是急冲冲地进了内堂，跪下：“高力士叩见娘娘。”

“高力士,你又来此为何？”杨玉环急不可待地回答。

“奴才刚才去复旨，万岁爷细问娘娘回府情况，好像有些懊悔。现今独坐宫中,长吁短叹,因此奴才特地赶来告知。”

“唉,哪里还想着我？”

高力士颇不以为然，说道：“奴才愚笨，不该向贤德娘娘进言。不过,娘娘也不可太固执了,皇上真的思念娘娘，娘娘倘有什么亲近的东西,奴才乘机进呈皇上,或许能感动圣心,也未可知。”

杨玉环觉得有理,便急切地问道:“高力士,献什么东西好？”

高力士一时想不出来,也就未答话。杨玉环想:什么东西可以感动君心呢？想我一身之外，全是皇上所赐，如今惟有愁泪千行，但哪能有穿连泪珠的金线把它贯穿,用金盘呈献？哦,有了！这一头青丝长发,曾与君王并头共枕,以此进呈,或能感动皇上。

“丫环,把镜子和剪刀取来。”说罢,她松开一头美发,叹道:“头发,头发,你曾经伴我青春年华,我怎忍心剪去?只为表我衷肠,不得不舍弃你！”她抖抖索索地一剪下去,一束青丝刹时在手,不禁放声痛哭:“我的圣上呀！但愿这长长青丝能重将咱们系在一起。”

哭罢，立起身来，将一束头发递与高力士，说道：“高力士，你拿去转献皇上,说妾罪该万死,谨献此发,以表依恋。”

高力士双手接过,将它搭在肩上,说道:“娘娘请不要愁烦,凭这缕缕青丝,奴才尽力使皇上回心转意,与娘娘重结白首之缘。”

杨玉环见高力士去了,全身像是散了架,有气无力地坐了下来,不知此后命运如何,忐忑不安,泪珠儿就似断了线,默默地流淌。

not know what fate held in store for her and she shed tears in silence.

While she was weeping, Duchess Han and Duchess Guo arrived at the prime minister's house. On the way there the two sisters had been very worried. They feared that, after Her Ladyship was dismissed from the palace, their cousin Yang Guozhong would lose power. It would be a big blow to the Yang family. They knew that they were powerless, and their only hope was that the emperor would recall Yuhuan. Attendants greeted them when they arrived and they asked, "Where is Her Ladyship?"

Meixiang reported their arrival immediately, "My lady, duchesses Han and Guo are here." Yang Yuhuan wept and did not reply; the duchesses walked in by themselves.

Duchess Han consoled her sister, "Your Ladyship, don't be distressed." She shed tears in sympathy but Duchess Guo took pleasure in Yang Yuhuan's misfortune and said, "That day in the Wangchun Pavilion, the emperor was very fond of you. How could this have happened?" Yang Yuhuan lowered her head and said nothing and she continued, "I thought that the love between the emperor and you would last a thousand years and however badly you behaved he would never take offence."

Duchess Han detected a hidden meaning in her words and at once stopped her. "Sister of the Pei family, you're too talkative. Her Ladyship, why is the emperor offended? What is the reason?" Yang Yuhuan said nothing. Duchess Han did not mind her silence, but Duchess Guo could not stand it and said, "Your Ladyship, excuse me for speaking frankly, but being too much in favor can only lead to trouble. You must know that the emperor's love is like autumn leaves...." Duchess Han immediately cut her short and said to Yang Yuhuan, "We have come to show our concern. Why do you pretend not to hear us?"

Yang Yuhuan had to reply, "It is my fate to be discarded by the emperor and I am grateful that my sisters show such concern. You can shower me with thousands of words but I shall try to keep my sorrows to myself." After she said this, she paid them no more attention and went into the other room.

"Sister! See how she treats us!"

Duchess Han was angry too and said, "Yes, indeed. We came specially to see her, but she goes to the other room. Next time you go to the Wangchun Pavilion make sure you don't behave like that." Duchess Guo blushed at this and said, "Pah, pah."

正当杨玉环伤心万分之际，韩国夫人和虢国夫人已迤逦而来。杨玉环这两位姊妹心事重重，一路上不免对此事的后果担忧，生怕娘娘被放出宫来，自家兄弟杨国忠就要失去权势，这对杨氏家门也会带来极大的冲击。她们只望皇上重召玉环入宫。来到府第门前，自有丞相家人迎接出来，两位夫人边走边问："贵妃娘娘在哪里？"

丫环梅香赶紧向内室禀报："娘娘，韩、虢两位夫人到了。"杨玉环闻言并不答话，犹自垂泪不已，听任两位国夫人自行入内。

韩国夫人开口便劝慰道："贵妃娘娘，千万不可终日愁烦。"虢国夫人却流露出幸灾乐祸的情绪，问道："前日在望春宫，皇上十分欢喜你，为何有此突变？我原以为你与圣上千秋万代恩结连理，即使有些过失，也不会和你计较！"

韩国夫人已听出她的话外之音，连忙止住她说："不要说这些闲言碎语，贵妃，皇上为何事生你气？"杨玉环并不答理，韩国夫人倒不介意，虢国夫人又忍不住要说几句："贵妃，你莫怪我说，从来宠多就要生嫌，君恩如同秋叶……"韩国夫人赶紧打断她的话，又面向贵妃说："姊妹们关心情切，特地来问候，为什么你总像未听见似的？"

杨玉环再不好不开口："我被圣上嫌弃是我自家的命，谢谢姊妹来慰问。不过，纵有千言万语，我也只能在自家心中忖思。"说罢这些话，她也不再搭理姊妹二人，竟然走入另一间内室去了。

"姊姊，你看她这个样子，如何使得？"

韩国夫人也有几分不快："是呀，我们特地来看她，她却竟然进房去了。妹子，你如再次被召进望春宫，可不能学她那个脾气。"这句话倒把虢国夫人说了个大红脸，连声"啐，啐"。

Chapter Four

Longing and Recall

Naturally Yang Yuhuan was sad about her dismissal but Li Longji was not happy either. He sat alone in the court, miserable. He thought, "Lady Yang is handsome and jealous. I love her but I sent her away in a fit of anger. I did not realize how hard it is to find such beauty. Moreover, we love each other and since she left all that I see disgusts me. Everything reminds me of the pain of our separation. There is no one that I can bare my heart to and that is very distressing. When her cousin Yang Guozhong came to apologize, I was embarrassed and did not see him. The more I think about it the less I know what to do. It would shame me to give the order to recall her. If she is not recalled, I will never know happiness again. This is a hard decision. I have behaved rashly with no regard for her sensitive feelings and should have understood that her jealousy affirms her deep love for me...."

"May it please Your Majesty, dinner is served." While he had been lost in thought a eunuch carrying food entered and broke his train of thought by urging him to eat. Li Longji was angry and said, "Who told you to come?"

"Your Majesty has eaten nothing since early morning and the ladies of the inner court told us to prepare a meal."

The mention of the inner court and the interruption made Li Longji angry and he called out, "What inner court? Attendants!" At once two attendants entered the hall and Li Longji said to them, "Give this fellow a hundred lashes and put him in prison." The attendants held the eunuch's arms and took him away. Still angry, Li Longji thought, "I was thinking of Lady Yang and was disturbed by this fool. Ah, how I long for her. Even if I had wine made in heaven and precious imported food, I would find them tasteless. Only the presence of Lady Yang will make me happy!"

Another eunuch came in and knelt before him. "Would it please Your Majesty to feast at Aloes Pavilion and hear the new music composed

第四章
思妃召还

杨玉环被放出宫，自然悲戚万端，但李隆基也并不愉快，独自在宫中悲思万分。心想：贵妃既娇且妒，心中不忿，一时失计，将她遣送回家。哪里知道，佳人难得，且彼此情深。自她去后，看什么事物都不顺眼，看什么景色都感到离恨。这无端烦恼又不好对人说起，真正愁煞人呀！贵妃的兄长杨国忠入朝谢罪，自家也觉无趣，未曾召见。越想越难受，越想越无主意。

"请万岁爷进餐！"正当他出神之际，一个内监捧了一盘膳食进呈，打断他的思绪，李隆基不禁恼怒起来："哇，谁叫你进来？"

"万岁爷自清晨以来不曾用餐，后宫传话，备膳伺候。"

听见"后宫"二字，李隆基不由更气恼："哇，什么后宫！叫内侍。"立即有内侍二人前来，李隆基吩咐道："将这家伙拽去打一百杖，关押起来。"两个内侍捉了这个内监左右两只臂膀下去。他还气恼不平，"哎，朕在此想念贵妃，却被这个家伙来扰乱，真扫兴。唉，想起贵妃来，纵有天上琼浆，海外珍味，知它什么滋味！除非中人意的贵妃娘娘立在眼前，才能解咱家的饥渴！"

"请万岁爷沉香亭上赴宴，听赏梨园新乐！"又一内监跪请。

by the imperial musicians?"

Aloes Pavilion was where Li Longji and Lady Yang had viewed flowers. To be reminded of it made him unhappy. "What Aloes Pavilion? I shall have you beaten! Take this fellow and give him a hundred lashes, then send him to be a keeper of charcoal." Unhappy at being disturbed by the two eunuchs Li Longji bid two attendants to stand at the door and allow no one to enter. If they disobeyed, he would have them thrashed within an inch of their lives. Standing by himself he murmured, "Ah, how could I drink and enjoy new music!"

Gao Lishi entered with Lady Yang's hair on his shoulder. He saw the two attendants standing at the door and asked, "Where is His Majesty?"

"His Majesty is sitting alone."

Gao Lishi moved to enter, but the attendants stopped him. "His Majesty is very angry. He has had two eunuchs punished, and has forbidden us to admit any one."

"Very well, I shall wait outside." Gao was clever.

After ruminating for such a long time, Li Longji was despondent. He took a stroll and saw the green grass growing by the marble steps. But there was no silken skirt and the pearl-decked shoes of Lady Yang were absent. He felt sad again. Gao Lishi saw him and knew that he must not act rashly. He hid by the door and waited for a chance.

A few steps beyond the palace gate Li Longji lowered his head and murmured, "I long for her here. I wonder whether she is thinking of me. Gao Lishi told me this morning that she was weeping when she left the palace. It breaks my heart to hear of it. That was several hours ago and there has been no more news. That scoundrel Gao Lishi has been keeping out of my way."

Gao Lishi heard him and knew that his chance had come; he advanced to kneel before the emperor, saying, "Your slave is here."

"Gao Lishi, what have you there on your shoulder?"

"Her Ladyship's hair."

Thinking that Gao Lishi was making fun of him, Li Longji smiled and said, "What hair?"

Gao Lishi said, "Lady Yang said that she was sorry that she had offended Your Majesty and that she deserved ten thousand deaths. She will never be able to look upon your face again. She has cut off this lock of hair which she asked your slave to present to Your Majesty as a token of her love." He presented the hair with both hands.

听得“沉香亭”三字，李隆基心头一阵牵痛，这可是他与贵妃赏花所在：“唗，说什么‘沉香亭’，这家伙该打！拽这家伙下去，打一百杖，罚他管柴炭去。”先后两个内监来打扰，李隆基十分不悦，随即吩咐两个内侍看守宫门，不许人擅自进入，违者重打。他又一人独立几前，自言自语地说道：“唉，朕此刻还有什么心情去听歌饮酒！”

正当此际，高力士肩上搭着贵妃的青丝长发，兴冲冲地向宫中走来，见到门口站着两个内侍，开口问道：“万岁爷在哪里？”

“一个人坐在宫中哩。”

高力士想跨门而入，两个内侍即刻拦阻：“万岁爷此刻十分气恼，刚刚处罚过两个内监，特派我们守着宫门，不许人擅自进入。”

“呀，原来如此，咱家且在此候着。”高力士自然乖巧。

李隆基在宫中沉思过久，也着实觉得无聊，便步出宫外闲走。只见沿阶碧草成片，却不见贵妃珠履印痕，不禁又伤心起来。

李隆基走出宫门不远，又俯首低语：“寡人在此思念妃子，不知妃子又怎样思念寡人哩！早晨问高力士，他说妃子出宫时，双眼泪水不干，真叫朕寸心如割。这大半天，也无从再知消息。高力士这家伙也真可恶，大半天也不到朕跟前来。”

高力士闻言，知道时机已到，乃上前叩见：“奴才在这里伺候。”

“高力士，你这肩上搭的是什么东西？”“是杨娘娘的头发。”

李隆基莞尔一笑，以为高力士在逗他：“什么头发？”

高力士却一脸正经地回答道：“娘娘说，只怕自己愚昧无知，惹圣上生气，罪该万死。今生今世，再也不能够看见圣上了，特剪下这一绺青丝，叫奴才献给万岁爷，以表依恋之意。”说罢，双手将头发献上。

Li Longji took the hair and wept bitterly, "Ah, my darling! I smelt the perfume of your hair on my pillow two nights ago, but today it is shorn for me. Your glossy hair is obviously a token of your sorrow. It breaks my heart. This lock of hair is like the love between us which has been cut as if by a pair of scissors."

"Your Majesty, do not grieve. Lady Yang is your favorite so why begrudge her a small space in the palace and make her stay outside? This flower-like imperial lady would return to the palace anytime you wish." Gao Lishi was tactful.

Li Longji thought for a while and said, "But I have already dismissed her. How could I recall her?"

"It is nothing. To dismiss her because of her mistakes and then recall her because she has repented that would show the divine mercy of the Son of Heaven." Li Longji nodded and thought that what he said made sense. Seeing that the emperor was about to agree Gao Lishi continued, "Besides, it was barely dawn when she left in a single carriage so no one knew. Now it is dusk. If we open the gate in Anqing Quarter we can let her in from the Taihua Residence and no one will know. Your slave begs that she be pardoned and recalled. Your slave will bring Her Ladyship back at once. Her return will surely alleviate Your Majesty's grief."

Li Longji gave his consent for he found reason in what Gao said and the arrangement was right. He said, "Gao Lishi, I order you to bring Her Ladyship back."

"As Your Majesty commands!" excited, Gao kowtowed and withdrew.

Alone in the palace, Li Longji pondered. "How shall I meet her when she returns? She always tends to be angry. What shall I say to her? Well! Well! Well! I am to blame, let her have her own way."

Gao Lishi returned swiftly and entered the inner court, followed by a fragrant carriage with Her Ladyship in it. He reported, "Her Ladyship is here."

"Let her in at once."

"It shall be done. Lady Yang calls on His Majesty," announced Gao. Yang Yuhuan entered immediately and said, "Your slave Yang pays her respects to Your Majesty. She is under a sentence of death." She knelt and prostrated herself on the ground.

Li Longji felt pity for her and told her to rise. Gao Lishi sensibly withdrew leaving them alone. Yang Yuhuan said, "As your slave I acted

李隆基接过头发,大恸,“哎哟,我那妃子呵。记得前天枕边还闻着你发上的香气,今朝却剪下来给我。这缕缕青丝,分明夹杂着你的愁思。看着这齐根剪断的头发,怎不叫寡人伤心断肠!就好像寡人与妃子的恩情,被这无情的剪刀一下两断。”

“万岁爷,请别伤心。奴才想,杨娘娘既然得到皇上恩幸,万岁爷又何惜宫中一席之地,让她沦落在外?只要皇上回心转意,名花一样的贵妃便能立刻回到宫中来。”高力士委婉地进言。

李隆基说道:“只是寡人已经放出宫去,怎好又重新召还?”

“这又有什么!有罪放出,悔过召回,正是圣上的大度。”李隆基听得高力士这样说法,颇觉有理,点头称是。高力士见皇上有允准之意,继续说道:“何况今晨一辆小车送出,黎明时分,没有人见到;此刻已是傍晚,开了安庆坊,从太华宅入宫,外人又怎能得知。”继而又进一步恳求:“望皇上原谅娘娘一次,赐她回宫。”

李隆基觉得高力士话也说得有理,事儿也安排得妥当,便允其所请:“高力士,就派你迎贵妃入宫。”

“领旨。”高力士兴冲冲地叩了一叩,退出宫来。

宫中只剩下李隆基一人,他想:妃子来时,怎么与她相见呢?罢,罢,罢,这原是自家不是,只有讨好她了。

李隆基主意刚定,高力士已急速而回,一辆香车拉回了杨娘娘,进入大内,禀报道:“杨娘娘到了。”“快宣她进来。”

“领旨,杨娘娘进见。”高力士返身宣旨。杨玉环立刻进见:“臣妾杨氏见驾,死罪,死罪。”说罢,跪下,俯身在地。

李隆基更加怜惜地说:“平身,平身。”高力士识趣,及时悄悄退出,内宫只剩下他们两个。杨玉环又说:“臣妾不是,以致获遣。

wrongly and was sent away. Now that I behold Your Serene Countenance, I shall die content." While she spoke tears coursed down her cheeks. Li Longji also sobbed and said, "Do not say that, my love."

"My guilt weighs down on me as heavily as a mountain, yet Your Majesty is as merciful as Heaven. Now I should repent. In future I shall keep my proper place and never ever show my jealousy."

Li Longji saw that she had repented and stepped forward to help her up. He said, "I was unreasonable for a moment. Let us not speak of it again."

"Long live Your Majesty!" was all that Lady Yang could say. Li Longji took her hand and wiped away her tears. He said lovingly, "A taste of parting has increased our love tenfold."

Realizing that the emperor and Her Ladyship were on good terms again, the maids waiting outside came in. "A feast is ready in the west palace, Your Majesty, Your Ladyship." Li Longji took Yang Yuhuan's hand and they walked slowly. Ever since that moment they have been deeply in love.

Li Longji favored Yang Yuhuan even more after she returned to the palace; the pair cherished lost love and became more intimate. The emperor stayed with her all day neglecting state affairs and leaving everything, big or small, to Yang Guozhong. The three duchesses received higher honors and many gifts from the emperor and the Yang family's authority became higher than the throne. This made men with lofty ideals discontent.

Guo Ziyi, a native of Zhengxian County, Huazhou, had been a successful candidate in the provincial examination of military officers. Since childhood he had held lofty ideals. He was well versed in both polite letters and the martial arts and he dreamt of becoming a mighty hero who helped to bring peace and stability to the country. After passing the examination, he went to the capital to wait for an appointment.

There were hardships on the trip but Guo Ziyi arrived in the capital and stayed in a hotel where he waited for instructions. People like him meant nothing in the capital but he did not realize it. It was boring sitting all day in the hotel so he sometimes took a stroll in the street or went to tea houses and restaurants. In this way he learned many things about affairs of state and became much more knowledgeable. What worried him was power had fallen into the hands of the Yang family, An Lushan had become a favorite and the government was going to rack and ruin. By himself he

今日得以重见圣上,死亦瞑目。"说着,泪水沿颊而下。李隆基也抽泣道:"妃子为何说这般话?"

"臣妾罪重如山,荷蒙皇恩包容,也当自我反省。自今而后,愿意依次而进,再也不敢嫉妒了。"

李隆基见她已认错,上前扶起她来,说:"寡人一时处置失措,从前的话,也不要再提了。"

"万岁!"杨玉环只有谢恩而已。李隆基一手携着她,一手替她擦泪,恩恩爱爱地对她说:"经过这番分离之愁,恩情更添十倍。"

侍在门外的宫女,知道皇上已与娘娘和好,进来禀报:"西宫宴席已备好,请万岁爷、娘娘去上宴。"李隆基便携着杨玉环之手,缓缓前行。从此,两人的恩情也的确更加亲密无间了。

自从杨玉环重新入宫以后,更加得到李隆基的宠信,彼此都是失而复得,倍觉珍重,也格外亲密。终日在宫中寻欢作乐,全然不问朝政,事无巨细,全由丞相杨国忠掌管。杨氏家族权倾当朝,天下有识之士,无不为之侧目。

华州郑县有一武举人姓郭名子仪,自幼就有远大抱负,长成之后更是学得文韬武略,满腹经纶,一心要做个顶天立地的男儿,干一番安国定邦的事业。既然中了武举,就赴京城等待选用。

他不辞辛劳地来到京城,找了一个住处,一心等待朝廷任命。他哪里知道像他这样的武举,在京城是排不上号的,终日枯坐寓中,也是百无聊赖,不免去大街小巷、茶楼酒馆闲散闲散,倒也了解了不少朝政状况。他眼见杨氏家族擅权,安禄山又十分得宠,朝纲弄得不成模样,而自己又无从出力,更是忧心如焚。

could do nothing about this.

One day when he had nothing to do he went to Chang'an Market for a drink. As he walked there the jostling crowds reminded him of drunkards and he thought it would be hard to find a sober man like Qu Yuan, a great patriot of the State of Chu in ancient times. He wanted to find someone who shared his ambitions and aspirations so that they could accomplish great tasks together. It was sad that people like Lu Shang, who helped the emperor to establish Western Zhou, Li Guang, a famous general in Western Han and Fan Kuai, a renowned general in the Han Dynasty, were nowhere to be found.

As he was pondering over this, he reached a place between the east and the west markets, a prosperous area in Chang'an. He looked up and saw a signboard — Xinfeng Restaurant. He entered and called out, "Do you serve wine?"

"Please go upstairs, sir." His manner had impressed the waiter who led him to a room upstairs. "Are you drinking alone, sir, or are you waiting for other guests?"

"I will have a few cups by myself. Bring the best you have."

"We have the best wine. And you'll like it." The waiter went to bring the wine.

Guo Ziyi got up to look outside where large crowds hustled and bustled. A procession of people suddenly came from somewhere nearby. A eunuch led a group of richly dressed officials; attendants, carrying gold, silk, sheep and wine followed. He thought it strange.

"Sir. Your wine is heated." Guo Ziyi turned and said, "Waiter, tell me where are those officials outside going?"

"Sir, I'll tell you while you drink. The emperor has ordered new mansions in Xuanyang Quarter for his brother-in-law Yang Guozhong and the three duchesses. The four mansions are next to each other and each is like an imperial palace. Nowadays every family wants to outshine every other one. When one family sees that their neighbor's houses are better than his, he pulls his houses down and rebuilds until they have one exactly the same. In this way a single hall may cost millions. The new buildings were finished today so all the government officials are going there to offer their congratulations and give presents of sheep and wine. They all pass this way."

"Ah, is it possible?" Guo Ziyi sighed. If the favorite concubine's relatives were indulging in such a display, what would it lead to! They

这日闲来无事，又到长安市上去买醉。沿街行来，只见来往人众，一片闹昏昏，全像是一批醉汉酒徒，很难找到一个像楚国大夫屈原那样清醒的人。他很想找个志同道合的人，好建功立业，只是像西周开国功臣吕尚、西汉名将李广、功臣樊哙那样的有为之士却无处寻找了，不免怅然神伤。郭子仪虽然思虑万千，脚下却没有停步，不觉已来到东、西两市之间，他抬头一看，“新丰馆大酒楼”的招牌赫然入目，便信步而入，口呼：“酒家有么？”

“客官，请楼上坐。”店小二见来人气度不凡，便引入楼上雅座。“客官是自饮，还是待客？”

“独饮三杯，有好酒呵，取来。”

“有好酒，保客官满意。”店小二连声应答着取酒去了。

郭子仪走至楼前伏在栏杆上眺望，只见人头攒动，熙来攘往。忽又见不远处来了一队人，打头的分明是一个内监，身后几名官员，都穿着一身吉服，随从又捧着金币彩缎，牵羊担酒迤逦而来，不免诧异。

“客官，热酒在此。”店小二一声招呼，郭子仪回转身来，且不取酒，却开口问道：“酒保，我问你，那些官员，是往何处去？”

“客官，你一面吃酒，我一面告诉你，国舅杨丞相，还有韩国、秦国、虢国三位夫人，当今皇上各赐造府第一座，就在这宣阳里中。四家门府相连，完全按照宫廷模式建造。这一家造了，就要胜过那一家；那一家造了，就要赛过这一家。若看见别家造得华丽，这家便拆了重造，一定要与那家一样方才住手。一座厅堂，造价就费了千万贯钱钞。今日总算完工，因此朝中大小官员，都备了羊酒礼物，前去各家庆贺，从楼下经过的就是这些去祝贺的人。”

vied with each other in ostentation; their displays of luxury came from hard-won wealth of the people. And none of the courtiers, hangers-on, ministers or men of influence dared tell the emperor that these vermilion roofs and brilliant tiles were stained with the people's blood. The more he thought about it, the angrier he became. The wine had gone to his head and he had to rest for a while in the restaurant. He stood up and slowly paced the room. On the wall a few lines of poetry were written and one poem caught his eye.

When the people desert Yan city,
And no horses return from the Han Pass.
He comes to the ghost beneath the hill,
And there hangs a silken dress on a ring.

It surprised him and he said, "What a strange poem!" He read it carefully again. He thought the poem seemed rather sinister and looked for the name of the author, "Written by Li Xiazhou." His brows were knit in thought. The name sounded familiar. "Ah, yes," he finally got it. Li Xiazhou was a renowned fortune-teller who could tell the future. The poem must have a hidden meaning, but who could explain the riddle? A noise downstairs interrupted his thoughts and without thinking he said, "Where is the waiter?"

"Yes, sir?"

"What is the meaning of that hubbub downstairs?"

"Well, sir, just take a look out of the window." He looked in the direction indicated by the waiter and saw a lord riding past preceded by retainers. "Who is that?"

"Sir, just look at the big belly! That is the famous An Lushan, a great favorite with the emperor. His Majesty even allowed An Lushan to sit beside him. Today he was made Prince of Dongping and he is on his way back from the court to his new palace outside Donghua Gate."

"Ah, so that is An Lushan, and what has he done to be made a prince? He has the face of a rebel; he will certainly bring ruin to the empire!" He wondered how the court had come to admit such a jackal. What was the difference between this fellow and the Yangs? It was hard to tell what would happen, but the poem of Li Xiazhou contained a bad omen. He was angry. "Why do you look so gloomy, sir?" asked the waiter.

“哦,有这样的事!”郭子仪万分意外地叹息,心想外戚得宠到了这一步,如何结局呵!他们竞相比豪奢,全都是搜刮的民脂民膏。朝中那般大小官儿又争相趋附,有谁人敢向皇帝进言?越想越气,不觉酒涌上来,有些醉意,一时不便步行回寓所,索性在酒楼上稍作憩息,绕着四壁漫步,闲看壁上题诗,忽然见到这样一首诗:

燕市人皆去,函关马不归。

若逢山下鬼,环上系罗衣。

顿时惊讶万端,不自觉地发出声来:“呀,这诗好怪异!”又从头仔细读过,细细思索,觉得此诗大不吉祥。看是何人所作,“李遐周题”,不免皱紧眉头,这名字好生熟悉!“哦,是了!”他终于想起来了。这李遐周原来是名享遐迩的术士——也就是预言家。他这首诗中必定藏有哑谜,令人费解!楼下又传来喧闹之声,打乱了他的思索,脱口而出:“酒保哪里?”

“客官,有何吩咐?”

“楼下为何又闹起来?”

“客官,你来窗前,往下看去。”随着酒保的指点,郭子仪向窗外楼下看去,只见一个王爷骑在马上,前面一队仪仗队导路,缓缓行了过来:“那是什么人?”

“客官,你看他那个大肚皮!这个大肚皮就是有名的安禄山。万岁爷十分宠爱他,招呼他坐在御座旁边哩。今朝封他为东平郡王,方才谢恩回朝,又赐给他东华门外新造的王府一座,正从这儿经过哩。”

“呀,这、这家伙就是安禄山么?有什么功劳,居然就封王?唉,我看这家伙一副反相,乱天下者,必是此人!”说罢,又暗自思虑:

"I am so angry that my hair stands on end and I am beside myself with rage. My sword on my waist has also been disturbed!"

The waiter did not understand what he meant and said, "Don't look so depressed, sir. Let me get you another pot of wine."

"A thousand cups and a hundred pots of wine could never wash away my gloom. Here is your money." He walked down the stairs.

The waiter was perplexed and murmured, "After three cups other men are at peace with the whole word, but this gentleman has a thousand sorrows. It is none of my business; I just take the money to the counter."

After leaving the restaurant Guo Ziyi returned to the hotel; he had nowhere else to go. When he arrived his attendant who had come with him to the capital reported, "Master, the bulletin has come." He passed it to him with both hands. The bulletin read, "The Ministry of War announces that by Imperial Decree Guo Ziyi is now appointed military commissioner for Tiande."

"So the decree has come. We should pack our things and go to my post at once." The attendant went to prepare.

Guo Ziyi's mood changed from excitement to sadness. He was excited because he was able to serve the state, but he worried about the throne which appeared to be tottering and in danger. He thought, then decided. "Since I have been appointed by the emperor, I must not fear wolves ahead or tigers behind, even dark forces. I must dispel jackals and wolves and restore the great Tang."

朝廷怎引来这样一个野狼？他与杨氏贵戚又有何两样？天下事难说了，难怪李遐周题诗不吉祥哩。越想越气恼，并且已形之于色，店小二不禁问了一句："客官，为什么事生气啊？"

"不由人不怒发冲冠，不由人不气破胸肠。你看，俺这腰间的宝剑也有反响！"

这没头没脑的话，店小二怎能理解？只是劝说道："客官，请息怒，再吃一壶吧。"

"就是吃上百壶千盅，也消不了我的愁 —— 不吃了，收了这酒钱去。"说罢下楼而去。

店小二莫名其妙，自言自语地说："别的客官来'三杯和万事'，这个客官可真怪，是'一气惹千愁'。咱也不管他，收了酒钱交账去。"

郭子仪出了酒店，别无他处可去，只得气忿忿地回到寓所。随他来京城的家将见主人回寓，立刻禀报："爷，朝报已到。"双手送上朝报，郭子仪见上面写着："兵部一本：有选授官员事。奉圣旨，郭子仪授为天德军使。钦此。"

"哦，原来旨意已下，咱们干脆早早收拾行李，即日上任去。"家将应声而出，做赴任准备。

郭子仪颇为兴奋，继而又十分忧虑。兴奋的是：俺郭子仪从此可以报效朝廷了；忧虑的是：朝政日非，处境险恶。沉吟良久，下定决心：既然受了朝廷委派，就不能前怕狼后怕虎，纵有奸邪当道，也要力除豺狼，把大唐江山重整。

Chapter Five

Passing on and Writing the Music

Li Longji and Yang Yuhuan feasted and played day and night and the discontent of people outside the court reached fever pitch; upright officials were worried. But the emperor and Lady Yang knew nothing about that nor did they wish to know. All that interested them was carnal pleasure and sensory enjoyment.

Since Yang Yuhuan had returned to the palace, Li Longji showed her greater favor than before. The situation was like the poem: "His love for all his three thousand palace ladies seems to center on one, / And none of the others in the six palaces can compare with her." Naturally Yang Yuhuan did her best to please Li Longji to consolidate her position.

One morning, when Yang Yuhuan got up, she ordered Yongxin and Niannu to clean the Lotus Pavilion because she wanted to compose music there. Niannu helped her dress and Yongxin set up the brushes, ink slabs, paper and ink stones. When all was ready, Yongxin smelt musk and heard the tinkle of jade pendants and said to herself in a low voice, "Ah, Her Ladyship is early this morning."

Since Lady Yang had come back to the palace the emperor stayed with her in the morning and absented himself from his audience. Why should she come to the Lotus Pavilion so early this morning? It turned out that Lady Plum Blossom was good at singing and dancing and the emperor often praised the Frightened Swan Dance which she had written. Could Yang Yuhuan concede defeat? She planned to compose a music that would be better than that of Lady Plum Blossom. This would win the exclusive love of the emperor.

It is said that Yang Yuhuan in her previous life was a fairy on Penglai Mountain; she had lived in the moon and was very clever. Now she thought day and night about the melody and this moved Chang'e, the goddess of the moon. There was a melody called the Dance of the Rainbow and Feathery Garments that had stayed on the moon and

第五章
传曲制谱

李隆基与杨玉环朝朝夜夜耽于欢乐，宫廷外的民怨沸腾、正直官员的忧思，他们哪里知道，又哪愿知道？只是想着法子、变着法子享受声色之乐。

杨玉环自从重新入宫以后，李隆基更是恩幸有加，正如诗人所写“三千宠爱在一身，六宫粉黛无颜色”。自然，杨玉环也自出心裁，想方设法取媚李隆基，以固其宠幸。

今朝起床，她就吩咐永新、念奴两个宫女去收拾荷花亭，她要去制作曲谱。念奴服侍她梳洗打扮，永新去打扫荷花亭，将文房四宝——笔、墨、纸、砚一一铺设整齐。诸事刚刚安排好，一阵兰麝之香飘入亭中，忽而环佩之声也传入耳中，永新不禁低低呼道：“呀，娘娘今晨到得好早呀。”

杨玉环入宫来一直与李隆基过着“从此君王不早朝”的生活，何以今朝一大早起床急急地来到荷花亭呢？原来梅妃极擅歌舞，皇上时常夸奖她的《惊鸿》舞，自家怎能认输？一直想制作新曲以超过她，从而获得皇上的宠爱。

传说杨玉环前身是蓬莱仙女，曾经在月宫中生活，聪明绝顶。如今日思夜想，一心要自谱新曲，终于感动月中嫦娥。月宫中

was unknown to men. She thought, "Now the Tang emperor on the earth below is fond of music and Yang Yuhuan is his concubine. I will summon her spirit to hear the tune again. When she awakes she can transcribe it and bring the music of heaven to mortals on earth. This will be a praiseworthy deed!" She called her fairy maid, "Hanhuang, come here."

"What do you want, my lady?"

"Go to the Tang palace on the earth and bring the spirit of Yang Yuhuan to hear our music. When the dance has been played, you may send her back."

Hanhuang left the moon palace, crossed the Milky Way, passed the starry sky, and arrived at the Tang palace. She flew over the palace wall, reached the inner palace and stopped right beneath the window of Yang Yuhuan's palace. But the gate was locked and the curtains drawn. Yang Yuhuan looked like a cherry blossom and was fast asleep, cuddling a pillow. Hanhuang called gently, "Get up, Lady Yang. Get up, Lady Yang."

Yang Yuhuan was sound asleep, her hair to one side and her face covered with powder and rouge. She opened her sleepy eyes a little and then closed them again at the repeated calling of Hanhuang.

Seeing this, Hanhuang raised her voice, "Please get up, lady."

"Who is that calling from the palace gate?"

Yang Yuhuan got up unwillingly and yawned. She went to the window, looked out and said, "Oh, it is a palace maid."

"I am not a palace maid who sweeps and waits on others."

"Not a palace maid? Are you a beauty from one of the other courtyards?"

"I am not a concubine either."

"Who are you?"

Hanhuang said proudly, "I am a fairy maid of the moon, and my name is Hanhuang."

Yang Yuhuan was startled and said, "Oh, so you are a fairy from the moon! How did you get here?"

"Chang'e, the goddess of the moon, ordered me to invite you to come with me and enjoy our cassia blossoms."

"Can it be true?" Yang Yuhuan asked.

"Don't hesitate, my lady; let me lead the way. Come with me." So saying, Hanhuang waved her hand, and Yang Yuhuan flew towards the

向来就有一部《霓裳羽衣》仙乐，从未传到过人间。嫦娥公主自忖：如今下界人间唐朝皇帝知音好乐，杨玉环既为他的贵妃，何不将杨玉环魂魄召回月宫，让她重听此曲，醒来后凭着记忆谱写出来，被之管弦。这不就将天上仙音传入人世，不也是为后人留一段佳话么！主意一定，立即吩咐仙女：“寒簧，你过来。”

“娘娘，有何事吩咐？”“你可去下界唐宫之内，引杨玉环魂魄来此听曲；曲终之后，仍将她送回人间。”

寒簧奉嫦娥公主之命，出了月宫，渡银河，穿星空，刹时已飘至大唐宫庭，越过宫墙，深入后宫，直到杨玉环寝宫窗下。只见宫门紧锁，鲛帐下垂，那杨玉环拥枕而卧，好似一朵鲜艳海棠，惹人怜爱。寒簧乃轻轻呼道：“贵妃起来，贵妃起来。”

杨玉环正睡得香酣，一头乌云斜堕，满脸残花腻粉，在寒簧反复呼叫中惺眼微微睁开，随即又双眼紧闭。

寒簧见状，不得不稍稍抬高声调：“贵妃，请起。”

“呀，深宫之内，是谁人在窗外呼唤？”杨玉环满不情愿地起床，呵欠连天，懒洋洋地走近窗前，朝外一看：“呀，原来是个宫女！”

“俺不是专司洒扫、侍奉他人的宫女！”

“不是宫女，大概是别院的美人？”“俺也不是。”

“那么，你究竟是何人？”

寒簧不无自豪地说：“俺乃月宫中仙女，名唤寒簧。”

杨玉环闻言倒有些吃惊：“呀，原来是月中仙女！为何到此？”

“奉嫦娥娘娘之命，请贵妃到月宫中花下消暑。”

“哦，有这样的事！”

“贵妃不必迟疑。俺在前引导，就请同行。”说罢，用手一招，杨

sky with her. Clouds floated beneath their feet and the wind whispered softly into their ears; they gazed at the stars so near they could reach out a hand to pluck them. Before their eyes was a glorious palace. Cool breezes dispelled the summer heat.

Yang Yuhuan said, "Ah, this is mid-summer. Why do I feel so cold?"

"This is known to men as the Palace of Boundless Cold. You may enter now."

When she went in, she thought that she may have seen the decorations, the yard, the flowers and other things there some time before. But she had no time to recall it in detail and she smelt the fragrance of cassia. A group of fairies in white tunics and red skirts played music under the cassia tree. The music was sweet and Hanhuang told her that this was the Dance of the Rainbow and Feathery Garments. They both listened to it beneath the cassia tree. The melody was moving and lovely and the fairies played earnestly. The music, though, could not remind Yang Yuhuan of her previous life or wake her from the nightmare of riches and power on earth; nor could the music help her free herself from the infatuations and greed of the mortal world. She could only go her own way, rising and falling with the world.

Yang Yuhuan did not know the intentions of Goddess Chang'e but she was carried away by the fairy music and exclaimed, "Marvelous, it is so clear and melodious; it moves me. It certainly is not a tune from earth!" She asked Hanhuang whether she could meet Goddess Chang'e but the time was not right for her to return to the moon and Hanhuang declined saying, "The time for that has not yet come. It is nearly dawn, and Your Ladyship should return to the Tang palace." Hanhuang waved her hand and Yang Yuhuan woke from her dream. The fairy music and rhythms still rang in her ears and she got up early to order Yongxin to clean the Lotus Pavilion. She wanted to compose music in serene surroundings.

When Yongxin saw Lady Yang approaching, she went to greet her. "I beg to report to Your Ladyship that the brushes, ink slabs, paper and ink stones are ready."

"You and Niannu may stay here." Yongxin waved a fan and Niannu burned incense to inspire her.

Water surrounded the Lotus Pavilion; the scent of lotus came through the gauze-screened window and mixed with the smell of musk. Sitting at the table Yang Yuhuan straightened the paper and took up a brush to transcribe the music of the moon. She was inspired and expressed her

玉环也就不由自主地跟着寒簧冉冉升空，不一会儿足下生云，耳际起风；又一会儿，点点星辰似可随手而摘，幢幢殿影突兀呈现眼前，阵阵凉气逼人而来，顿时暑热消除。

杨玉环紧跟一步，问道："呀，目今正是仲夏季节，为何这般寒冷？""这就是人间所传的广寒宫——就请进去。"

进得宫来，那陈设，那庭院，那花卉，那景物，杨玉环都似曾相识。不待她细想，一阵浓香扑鼻，原来是月中桂子。又看到一群素衣红裳的仙女，在桂树下奏乐，十分动听。寒簧不失时宜地告诉她："这就是《霓裳羽衣》之曲。"这几位仙女认真吹弹演奏，音韵优美，十分动听。不过，似曾听闻的仙曲依然唤不醒杨玉环对前生的记忆，惊不醒贪富恋贵的人间梦魇。自然，也不能引导杨玉环摆脱人世间的痴恋贪欲，只得任她自行其是、浮沉人世了。

杨玉环此刻哪里明白嫦娥公主用心？只是耽于动听的仙乐，惊呼道："妙啊，这仙乐清高宛转，动人心魄，真非人间所有！"继而她向寒簧提出要见嫦娥娘娘，寒簧见她痴梦未醒，还不是回归月宫的时机，便推辞道："要见嫦娥娘娘为时还早，如今天色渐明，贵妃还是回大唐后宫去吧。"说罢，举手一挥，杨玉环便从梦中醒来。梦中所听仙曲，音节宛然在耳。因此今日清晨起来就吩咐永新打扫荷花亭，借那清幽之处，细细配合宫商，谱制新曲。永新见贵妃走进，迎出亭外，口称："启禀娘娘：笔、墨、纸、砚已安排齐备。"

"你与念奴一同在此伺候。"于是永新打扇取凉，念奴洗手焚香，以助神思。

荷花亭四周全是水面，微风过处，阵阵荷香透过纱窗，渗入亭内，与兰麝之香混为一体，沁人心脾。杨玉环坐在案前，把笺纸摊

thoughts carefully, considered all the details, made every word fit and wrote the stanzas in their proper sequence. An oriole sang on a willow branch. Yang Yuhuan put down her brush and was moved. She said, "Wonderful, wonderful," and altered the score. She wrote the music at her first attempt and it was soon finished.

Li Longji sat for an audience and thought about the inner palace. He hastily appointed a group of officials for various posts, concluded the audience, sent the officials away and went to the Lotus Pavilion when he learned that Lady Yang was there.

Niannu spotted the emperor in the distance and went to meet him, "Long live Your Majesty!"

"Niannu, where has Her Ladyship gone? What are these? Brush and ink stone?"

"Her Ladyship has been composing music and has just gone to change her dress."

Li Longji nodded and said, "My darling! My darling! You have all the accomplishments that could grace a lovely woman. What music have you been composing? Let me have a look." He sat down and read the score on the table. The words were written meticulously; they were excellent and there was not the slightest dissonance in the score. He hummed the tune and wondered. The melody had an unearthly quality, as if it came from heaven. It was rare music indeed. He could not help saying, "My darling, my darling not only is your beauty unsurpassed, but this music shows the talent of a genius. In intelligence alone you outshine the three thousand beauties in the inner palace."

The silk evening dress that Lady Yang had changed into made her look more delicate. She walked with light steps to the Lotus Pavilion accompanied by Yongxin. When she saw Li Longji sitting there reading the score, she knelt down and said, "Long live the emperor!"

Li Longji helped her to rise and said, "Take a seat, darling." Yang Yuhuan was not as restrained as she was the first time she came to palace and sat down as ordered.

Li Longji had not seen her for half a day and ran his eyes over her from head to foot. He said, "My darling, the silk dress makes you look more charming than ever. You are like a lotus glimmering in the lake and with the orchid in your hair, your face is doubly enchanting...."

Lady Yang was delighted to hear what he said, but tried to be modest and said, "Why has Your Majesty returned from court so late today?"

开，手握犀管毛笔，回忆月宫之曲，调合自家心思，将曲调的转移过渡、细微曲折之处，细细审处，一字安插，也要合拍，一段曲调，也得入化。忽然亭外柳树枝上，一阵莺啼，杨玉环暂停手中之笔，凝神细听，颇有感悟，连声称赞“妙呀，妙”，将原先谱的一节抹去，融入自家心灵感受，重新谱写。一气直贯而下，顷刻谱完。

再说李隆基身在坐朝，心系后宫，匆匆任命一批官员后，立即遣散众官，罢了早朝，听说娘娘在荷花亭上，就一路寻来。念奴眼尖，远远看见皇上急步赶来，立即走出亭子迎接：“万岁爷到了。”

“念奴，怎不见娘娘？怎么，这里还有笔、砚？”

“娘娘在这儿制作曲谱，方才更衣去了。”

李隆基点头称赞：“不知娘娘作的什么曲谱，待寡人看看。”说罢，坐了下来，将案上的曲谱从头仔细看到尾。只见蝇头小楷，笔笔银钩，字字如划；又见宫商谨守，没有半点儿差池，未免仔细哼了一遍，好不奇怪，咱家可谓懂曲的了，这谱连寡人也不知晓。细按音节，不是人间所有，似是天上仙乐，真是曲高和寡。仅凭你这一点儿灵性，又有谁人及得上？怕不压倒后宫三千佳丽！”

杨玉环换了一身生绡晚妆，更添了几分潇洒，在永新陪侍下，来到荷花亭，见李隆基兀自坐在那儿读谱，便上前相见：“臣妾见驾。”

李隆基闻声，上前扶起：“妃子坐了。”

半日未见，李隆基已觉耐受不住，如今见了，便从头到脚重新打量一番：“妃子，看你穿了一身轻装，更添几分妩媚，云鬓处斜插一朵兰花，更衬托出你脸儿的风流俊俏……”

杨玉环听见这样赞美，心中自然高兴，但又不能不表示一点儿谦虚，故意岔开话题，“陛下今日因什么事一直拖至此刻才退朝？”

“Because I had to appoint a new governor for Lingwu Province, an important post. I discussed the matter with my ministers the whole morning but we could not find a suitable man. Finally Guo Ziyi was promoted to the post. That is what delayed me.”

“I had nothing to do while I was waiting for Your Majesty in the Lotus Pavilion and tried to learn a new tune. It falls far short of the Frightened Swan Dance which won much acclaim after it was performed.” Lady Yang was jealous.

“I have just seen and hummed it; it is quite unique. How can that Frightened Swan Dance compare with this?”

“I wrote it hastily, without much thought; I hope Your Majesty will correct its mistakes.”

“I shall go through it carefully with you.” As Lady Yang sat beside the emperor, Yongxin and Niannu crept out of the Lotus Pavilion.

Li Longji became passionate and sat close to Yang Yuhuan; each pointed to the score with one hand. Li Longji said, “You are a rare beauty and the music you wrote is flawless. Tell me, what do you call it?”

“Last night I dreamt that I was on the moon and saw a group of fairy musicians dressed in rainbow colored feathery garments. I want to call it the Dance of the Rainbow and Feathery Garments.”

“Good. The Dance of the Rainbow and Feathery Garments is a good title. It is certainly a music of the moon.”

Li Longji looked at her again and said, “Your unearthly beauty makes me think that you must once have been a fairy on the moon. We must give this tune to the conservatory. But I am afraid ordinary musicians will not fully appreciate its excellence. I would like Yongxin and Niannu to copy the script and learn it from you. After that they can teach Li Guinian and he will pass it on to his musicians. We should do it that way.”

“Yes, Your Majesty.”

Li Longji stood up and looked around. He held Lady Yang’s hand and said, “It’s getting dark; let us return to the palace.”

After Yang Yuhuan returned to the palace, Li Longji constantly indulged himself in pleasure. He paid little attention to state affairs; it was peaceful and nothing irregular was happening in the country. He did not know that in his absence royal relatives and civil and military officials in the court contested for privileges and wealth; they formed cliques to further their own interests.

“只为灵武太守一职缺员，此地为紧要之地，需要选一干员去任，朕就破格任用郭子仪去补此缺，因此退朝迟了。”

“臣妾候陛下多时，独坐荷花亭，学着谱了一曲新声，怕不如《惊鸿》之舞那样，演完之后满座喝彩。”杨玉环不无酸意地说道。

“寡人刚刚见到此谱，细细哼了一遍，真是千古奇音，《惊鸿》何能与它相比。”

“妾只凭一己之见，草草写成，其中错误，还望陛下更定。”

“还是与妃子一同点勘。”

李隆基与杨玉环并肩而坐，各自用一只手翻着曲谱，李隆基说：“这谱何名？”

“妾于昨夜梦入月宫，见一群仙女都穿着霓裳羽衣，在那儿奏乐。妾拟取这‘霓裳羽衣’四个字命名。”

“好，好，好个《霓裳羽衣曲》！

李隆基说罢，又将贵妃端详一番，赞不绝口地说：“看你的仙姿，上一辈子一定是月宫中的女娃。—— 此谱当即宣付梨园，但那些伶工俗手，怕不能尽其曲妙。不如先叫永新、念奴抄好图谱，妃子亲自教授她们，然后再由她们二人传授给李龟年，去教习梨园子弟。这样才妥。”“领旨。”

李隆基立起身来，看看四周景色，牵着杨玉环的手说：“天色渐晚，咱们回宫去吧。”

李隆基自从有了杨玉环以后终日沉浸在你恩我爱之中，不认真处理朝政。他哪里知道，满朝皇亲国戚、文臣武将正利用他深居后宫的机会，相互争权夺利，各自培植私党。

An Lushan had been favored by the emperor and received several promotions. He was a changed man; his wild ambitions became apparent; he was arrogant and overbearing. Other officials allowed him to have his way, but he and Yang Guozhong were antipathetic, like fire and water. Yang Guozhong looked on An as an ingrate who had forgotten that he had saved his life. Moreover, An often opposed him and this made him unsatisfied. Earlier Yang Guozhong had warned His Majesty that An was an ambitious fellow with treason written on his face. He would be trouble in the future, but the emperor had not listened. He was determined to warn the emperor again and was bent on having An Lushan dismissed by the emperor.

One day when he was approaching the palace gate he told his attendants to withdraw and went in alone. There was a sudden uproar and he wondered who dared make such a noise inside the palace. When the procession came near, he sneered, "Oh, it's An Lushan!"

"Old Yang, did you call me?" An Lushan answered back sarcastically, because Yang Guozhong had called him by name.

Yang Guozhong made no reply to this but reproached him. "This is the palace. How can you make such a noise here?"

Rejecting the reproach An Lushan pointed to his clothes and said, "Old Yang, see here. The robes I wear were given to me by the emperor; the horse I ride is from the imperial stable. I have been summoned to confidential discussions on important matters and leave the palace after all the others have left. What can you do with me? Since I am a prince there can be no objections when my attendants call out to clear the way for me. Can you, a prime minister, compare with me? Can you tell your attendants to call out to clear the way for you?" He looked triumphant.

"What? An Lushan, when have you become so high and mighty?" Yang Guozhong laughed coldly.

"I have always been like this."

"An Lushan, think back a little."

"To what?"

"To the time when you first came to see me. Were you like this then?"

An Lushan did not mind Yang Guozhong laying bare the past. He was brazen and said, "Old Yang, that was different. There is no comparison. Why harp on the past?"

"Well, An Lushan, you lost an army and should have been beheaded

且说安禄山自从得到李隆基的赏识后，不断受到提拔，大大不同于往昔，狼子野心逐渐暴露出来，骄横跋扈，不可一世。朝中百官见了他都让他三分，惟独自恃为当今国舅的丞相杨国忠，却与他不相水火。尤其是安禄山，全然忘了当年求救于杨国忠的恩情，经常出言顶撞，遇事毫不相让。引起杨国忠极大的不满。日前他已在皇上面前进言，说安禄山野心极大，面有反相，说不定日后要闯祸。但是皇上却未听从他的进谏。他决心上朝去再次禀奏。

当他走近朝门时，忽然听到那边一群人前呼后拥、高声喝道而来，未免一惊。“什么人敢大胆在宫内喧哗？”说着，那队人已来到跟前，他放眼一看，不禁讥笑道：“哦，原来是安禄山！”

“老杨，你叫我什么？”安禄山见他居然直呼其名，便也毫不相让地反唇相问。杨国忠却不正面回答，而是斥责他：“这是皇宫内地，你怎敢在此大声呼叫？”

安禄山不以为然，指手划脚地道：“老杨，你看，咱身上穿的是皇上自家穿的御衣，皇上还赐我入宫乘马，我常奉密旨进朝商议机密大事，有时要很迟很迟才出宫，你管得了吗？我做郡王的，便喝道一声，也不妨。像你这个右相，怎能比我？又怎敢喝道？”一副得意非凡的气势。

“好，好个‘不妨’！安禄山，我问你，你这般大模大样，是几时摆起的威风？”杨国忠冷笑地问道。“咱从来如此。”

“安禄山，你也还应该回去仔细想一想。”“想什么？”

“你只想当年来见我的时候，可是这副目中无人的模样？”

安禄山脸皮厚，不在乎杨国忠揭疮疤：“这是彼一时、此一时。”

“唉，安禄山，你当年军事失利，论罪当斩，本是刀下之鬼。那

for your crime. You knelt at my feet to plead and I covered up your offences in the memorial to the emperor and thus saved your life. How could you forget all that?" Yang Guozhong was uneasy.

An Lushan did not take this into account in his rebuttal. "His Majesty in his mercy pardoned me and restored me to my post. What did you have to do with it?"

"Well said, indeed! You sin against your conscience! You are ungrateful." Yang Guozhong had not convinced him so he scolded him.

This made An Lushan angry, so he touched a sore spot. "Yang Guozhong, things are changeable; fame and disgrace depend upon chance. Do not think that because you have power and influence you can bully colleagues in the court. You mentioned my failure but do you remember your attack on Nanzhao? Did you not hide the truth from the emperor and cover up for Xianyu Zhongtong, the defeated general?"

"Who would dare deceive our sovereign? This is slander." Yang Guozhong was touched to the raw and gave a weak defence.

"Have you never deceived him? How many posts and official ranks have you sold?"

Yang Guozhong could not withdraw and had to fight head on. "Hold your tongue. You talk about the sale of official posts. How did you get your wealth if not through such means?" He laughed cynically.

"That is not all by any means. How many tricks have you played while relying on your cousin's influence? You are guilty of thousands of crimes against the state." An Lushan's attack avoided the matter of selling positions.

Yang Guozhong shouted himself hoarse. "These are baseless slanders!" He seized An Lushan and said, "Come with me to see the emperor!"

"Who is afraid of you? Let us go! Let us go!" An Lushan also seized Yang Guozhong and gripping each other they went before the emperor.

Yang Guozhong spoke first. "Your Majesty, An Lushan is disloyal and hides a dagger in his heart. He poses as a simple man but is at heart more treacherous than Shi Le." To convince the emperor, he added, "Once An Lushan did not bow when he saw the crown prince; he is cocky and impolite. Such insolence is not to be endured and evil must be struck down. I beg Your Majesty to mete out justice immediately while there is time!"

Not bowing to the crown prince just showed that An Lushan was

时，你长跪阶前向咱苦苦哀求，我在奏章中为你多方掩饰，才救了你一条命，你怎么全忘了。”杨国忠气急败坏地呵责道。

安禄山仍不领情，反驳道：“赦罪复官，出自皇上之恩，与你有什么关涉？”“好啊！你倒说得干干净净，只是太没良心了。做人全不讲恩义！”杨国忠说不过他，只得痛骂了。

安禄山被骂得火起，不禁也揭起杨国忠的疮疤来：“唉，杨国忠，常言说道：三十年河东，三十年河西。你可晓得，世上的荣枯都在变动，偶然机遇也太多。你不要自以为权势大，欺压朝中群僚。你说军事失利之罪，你恐怕也忘了你自家的南诏之事了吧？你不是也包庇了败将鲜于仲通，欺骗了皇上？”“圣明在上，谁敢欺骗？你这不是诽谤皇上？”戳着痛处，杨国忠无力地辩解着。

“还说不欺骗！你卖官鬻爵得到多少财利？”杨国忠被逼得无退处，也只能迎面反击：“住口，你说什么卖官鬻爵，只问你的富贵是从哪里得到的？你不是也靠钱财买来的？”说罢，不断冷笑。

“你的罪也不仅仅这一桩！论起你依仗皇戚，耍了多少鬼花样？论起你的误国大罪，又何止千条！”安禄山避开了买卖官爵一事，从其它方面继续攻击。杨国忠声嘶力竭地说：“你这全是污蔑之辞！”伸手扯着安禄山说：“我与你同去面圣！”

“谁怕谁呀？一道去，一道去！”安禄山也反过手来扯住杨国忠，两人撕拉着上了金殿。

杨国忠抢先奏道：“皇上，臣看安禄山胸怀异志，腹里藏刀，假作痴愚之态，奸诈不让大奸石勒。”为了说动皇上，他又把安禄山不认太子只认当今的事儿揭了出来，说：“他不拜太子，桀傲不驯，如此无礼，实难容他在朝中有立脚之地。望皇上立即罢斥，早除祸苗！”

loyal only to the emperor and Li Longji knew this.

An Lushan refuted him. "The royal favor shown to me has made Yang Guozhong jealous. I am simple, unable to protect myself and sooner or later I shall be his victim." He seemed to be in a state of fear and his story and his tears contrasted with the haughtiness shown by Yang Guozhong in his capacity as brother-in-law of the emperor. This impressed Li Longji favorably.

An Lushan saw that the emperor did not intend punishing him and said, "Only the emperor knows my loyalty. I beg permission to leave the capital to serve Your Majesty at the frontier."

The pair had often accused each other and Li Longji was unable to reconcile them. A military general and prime minister who are at odds cannot work together in the court. As An Lushan wanted to work at the frontier, wouldn't this be a good way of solving the conflict? So he appointed An Lushan Military Governor of Fanyang, and ordered him to proceed at once to his post. After kneeling to receive the imperial edict, Yang Guozhong and An Lushan said together, "Long live the emperor!" but their minds were on other matters.

When they left the palace An Lushan bowed merrily to Yang Guozhong and said sarcastically, "Veteran prime minister, I am going now. You will be troubled no more by my insolence. In future, you can bare fangs and brandish claws and run amuck in the court, while I build my principality in Fanyang and do as I please." Yang Guozhong did not know what to say and just gave a sarcastic laugh.

An Lushan started leave and turned back to mock Yang Guozhong, "One last word, prime minister. I suppose my new appointment comes through your help." He saluted by bringing both hands together and said, "Well, when I arrive at Fanyang, I will bide my time to see the end of you." He left without saying goodbye. Yang Guozhong was stupefied.

It was only after An Lushan had gone that Yang Guozhong realized what had happened. He reflected, "Ah, what a bad business! How can I rid myself of the hatred I feel in my chest? I wanted to overthrow him, but added to his accomplishments. Will I become a laughing stock? I honestly hope that An Lushan will make trouble this time; then the emperor will see that I was right in warning him. Your Majesty, Your Majesty, when that happens you will regret the decision you made today."

其实，安禄山不拜太子，只不过在李隆基面前表示自己效忠他一人而已，李隆基完全知悉这桩事儿，杨国忠的攻讦并不能对他产生任何影响。安禄山反驳道："微臣因受到皇上恩宠，致使杨丞相生嫌。小臣生性愚笨，恐难自保，迟早会落进他的圈套。"他一副诚惶诚恐的模样，声泪俱下的诉说，与杨国忠依仗国舅身份、气势汹汹的指责，形成鲜明的对比，李隆基对他倒也有几分好感。

安禄山见皇上并无罪责之意，进而奏道："微臣一片忠心，只有皇上知道。不如放臣出朝，去为皇上镇守地方。"

李隆基见这文武二臣老是闹矛盾，自家也调和不来，将相不和，确实难以共理朝政。听到安禄山自愿去地方任职，这又何尝不是解决矛盾的一个办法？就任命他为范阳节度使，并命他早早赴任。两人见圣旨已下，各自抱着不同想法口称"谢恩"而退。

走出宫门，安禄山喜气洋洋地向杨国忠拱手为礼，不无讥讽地说："老丞相，下官今日去了，你再也不要看不惯我这般大模大样。今后朝廷内，随你如何张牙舞爪，胡作非为了。我去范阳，独挡一面，建立自家府署，倒也逍遥自在哩。"杨国忠无言以对，只能冷笑而已。

安禄山正待离开，复又转过身来，再次讽刺杨国忠，说："还有一句话儿说给丞相听。今日下官得此任命，大约也是仰仗你的回天之力相提携的。"说罢，又举起手来："请了，我去范阳后，总会看到你的下场。"说完，也不告辞，把个杨国忠气得目瞪口呆，丢在一旁。

安禄山走后，杨国忠才回过神儿来，自言自语地说道："唉，居然有这样的事！我胸中积恨怎消？原想抹倒他的威风，哪曾想反替他添了荣耀。但愿安禄山这次出去，闹出些事儿来，方才信我今日这番话儿是忠告。皇上，皇上，到那时你也会后悔今日这样的处置哩。"

Chapter Six

Paying a Tribute of Lichee

After Li Longji sent An Lushan away, no one in the court dared provoke Prime Minister Yang. He thought the country was at peace and stayed all the time with Yang Yuhuan in the inner palace trying to please her and satisfying her desire for good food. Yang Yuhuan was fond of fresh lichee, a delicate fruit that grows in Hainan and Fuzhou thousand miles from the capital. How could he bring lichee to the capital to please his imperial concubine? Was this a problem for an emperor? Certainly not. He just ordered the two places to pay a tribute of lichee each year.

Some things are easier said than done. Fuzhou was in Sichuan Province, far away from the capital, while the distance to Hainan was further. Fresh lichee usually loses its flavor seven days after it is picked so it would have to be sent to the capital before the first day of the sixth moon, Lady Yang's birthday. Only a feudal emperor who did not care about the misery of his people would make such an order.

Each year in the second half of the fifth moon special envoys from Fuzhou and Hainan galloped towards the capital carrying a basket of lichees suspended from a pole. It was especially hard for envoys from Hainan, which is further from the capital; they had to offer the tribute the same day.

Usually, the envoys took shortcuts off the road, sometimes across wheat and rice fields. They had a hard time but the ordinary people along the road suffered more.

An old peasant of East Village, in Jincheng County, not far from the capital, and his family of eight lived on a few *mu* (one *mu* equals to 1/15 of an acre) of infertile land. He heard that envoys would pass that morning and was afraid that his crops would be trampled; he got up early and kept watch on the field. He waited and saw no envoy but a man with a bamboo stick and a woman with a stringed instrument walked slowly towards him.

第六章
贡荔扰民

李隆基打发走安禄山，朝中再也无人敢招惹杨丞相了。他就自以为政事太平，终日在后宫与杨玉环厮混。为了讨好杨玉环，千方百计地满足她的口腹之欲。杨玉环特别喜欢吃新鲜荔枝，但这种鲜果十分娇嫩，又非京城附近所有，产地远在千里之外的海南和涪州。贵为天子，这又有什么为难？诏命这两处年年进贡就是了。

话虽说得轻易，事儿却不容易做来。涪州属四川，离京城千里之遥；那海南更远过涪州。而荔枝这种鲜果离枝七日味道便变，又要在六月初一杨贵妃生日之前送到，于是每年五月下旬，涪州的使臣、海南的使臣，都选派干员，骑着骏马，手持竹竿，挑着盛满荔枝的竹篮，向京城飞驰。尤其是海南的使臣，任务更为艰巨，因为他们离京城更远，而进呈时日却是与涪州一般。

照例，进呈荔枝的使臣，只拣近路走，不问有路无路，不问麦地稻田，向京城冲刺而去。进呈荔枝的使臣固然备尝辛苦，而沿途的老百姓却加倍遭殃。

且说京城附近金城县东乡的一个种地的庄户，全家八口人只靠几亩薄田过活。老汉听说今早进呈荔枝的使臣要路过这一带，生怕自己的庄稼被毁，就起了一个大早，来到田头守望。老汉等了一会

When they came near, he saw that they were a couple of blind fortune-tellers, and heard what they said.

"We have traveled a long way today, husband, and my feet are aching. I can't go any further."

"There is someone there, wife. Let me ask him where we are." He took a few steps and called out, "Pray, sir, what district is this?"

The peasant replied, "This is East Village, Jincheng County, next to the West Village, Weicheng County." The blind man bowed and thanked him.

While they were talking horse bells were heard. The peasant at once looked up and saw a group of people on galloping horses. Leaving the blind man and woman he ran towards them shouting at the top of his voice:

"Commander, keep to the highway, and don't trample on the grain!" But who listens to a peasant? The commander just took them through the green field, as that was the shortest way.

The blind couple continued walking along a path, talking. The man said, "It is not far to the capital, wife. Let me go ahead and I may be able to hire a donkey for you." There was a beat of hooves and a group of envoys from Fuzhou rushed past. The blind man at once stepped aside, but before he had stopped moving another group of horses with envoys from Hainan rode up. Unable to avoid them, the blind man was trampled to death and lay on the ground.

No thought was given to the living, still less to the crops. The peasant staggered after the horses crying out, "Heaven! My crops have been trampled and destroyed by these people. There is nothing left for us to eat. What can I use to pay tax? The peasant's lot is hard!" He sat down and beat the ground with his fists.

The blind woman's husband was silent and she crawled on the ground feeling with her hand. Finally she touched her husband's body but it did not stir and she exclaimed, "Alas, something is wrong. Someone has been trampled to death! It is my husband. Save his life please. Let the local authorities know."

Only then did the peasant stop howling. He looked round and said, "Oh, the fortune-teller has been killed." When the blind woman heard this, she cried, "Please sir, call the local authorities and asked those on horseback to pay for my man's death."

"You have no sense of propriety. You'd better not do that! Do you

儿,尚未见到使臣,却见不远处走来一男一女两个瞎子,男的手持竹竿探路,女的弹着弦子哼唱,原来是一对闯荡江湖的算命瞎子。

女瞎子说:"老公,我们走了很多路,脚疼的要命,真走不动了。"

"妈妈,那边有人,待我去问他。"男瞎子说道。只见他走上几步,叫道:"请问客官,这里是什么地方?"

老汉答道:"这是金城东乡,与渭城西乡交界。"

谈话之间,忽然一阵铃响,老汉赶紧抬头望去,只见一队骑马的奔驰而来。他丢下这两个瞎子,迎着马队奔去,口中大呼:"马上长官,往大路上走,不要践踏了田苗!"使臣哪里听他这个庄稼汉?仍然率一队人马朝田中禾苗密处驰去,因为那块田地有条直径。

两个瞎子也正坐在那条小路边上低低谈话哩。男的说:"妈妈,此处离京城不远了,我们再走几步,到大路上也许能雇到一头毛驴子,与你骑着。"话音才落地,只听马蹄声急,一队涪州使臣人马冲了过来,他赶紧闪身让过,脚跟尚未站稳,哪知海南使臣的马队又奔过来,躲让不及,顿时被一队飞马践踏而死,倒在地上。

活人都不管,还管什么庄稼?老汉跌跌爬爬地一路追一路哭:"天啊,你看一片庄稼,都被踏得稀烂了,眼见全部被毁了。不要说一家食用全靠它,如今官租催得那样紧急,拿什么交官啊!"

那边女瞎子听不见自家男人的声息,一面爬一面摸,终于摸到男瞎子的躯体,却不见动弹,不禁大叫起来:"哎呀,不好了,踩死人了!我那老公,地保救命呀!"

老汉这才停止了哭叫,转过身来一看:"呀,算命先生被踏死了。"女瞎子听见有人答话,叫道:"请客官去叫地保,让那跑马的人来偿命!"

know who those people on horseback are? They are sending fresh lichee as tribute for Lady Yang. No one knows how many people they have trampled to death on the road, but who dares to ask for compensation? What chance would a blind woman have?" The peasant was resigned to his lot and advised the blind woman.

"What's to be done, then?" The woman cried and said, "Oh, my husband, how am I going to bury your corpse?" The peasant had a generous nature and said, "I will help you to bury him nearby."

Ordinary people were not the only sufferers. Low ranking officials in feudal bureaucratic offices could not escape the mayhem. One example of this was the posting station in Weicheng near the capital, a place where officials changed horses and had a rest. The station had spent its budget on envoys sending tributes of lichee each year and only had a skinny horse left. It was time for the lichee tribute again and the station master cleared off leaving a groom in charge. He had difficulty managing the station and did not know what to do with the envoys.

One afternoon an envoy from Fuzhou galloped up and called out, "Station master, give me a new horse quickly." The groom left the room to hold the reins while the envoy carefully lowered his fruit basket and dusted his clothes. Another envoy from Hainan arrived at a gallop and cried out, "Station master, a change of horse for me." He carefully put down his fruit basket and after greeting the envoy from Fuzhou said, "Groom, where is our meal?"

"It is not ready."

The envoy from Fuzhou wanted to make up time and was not worried about the food. "Never mind, we won't eat now. Just bring out the horses quickly."

"I am sorry, gentlemen, but there is only one horse left at the station. You yourselves can decide who will have it."

The envoy from Hainan had come a long way and his horse was not fit. The groom's reply enraged him and he shouted loudly, "What! Such a big station and only one horse? Call your rogue of a station master out and I'll ask him what he's done with the horses."

The groom spread his hands out helplessly and said, "The station had many horses. In the last few years they have been ridden to death by envoys with the fruit tribute. The station master was at his wit's end. That's why he made off."

The envoy from Hainan pressured him, "If the station master is not

“你真不识相了！我说你呀，还是省了这份心吧！你知道那跑马的是什么人？他们是进贡鲜荔枝给杨娘娘的。一路上，不知踏死多少人，谁敢要他们偿命？何况你这瞎子？”老汉自认吃亏，又劝说她。

“如此怎了？”说着，女瞎子又哭了起来：“我那老公呀，你这个尸首，怎么断送？”老汉倒仗义：“我来帮你埋在附近吧。”

其实，遭殃受害的又何止是普通平民？就连封建官僚机构的下级吏卒，也逃不出这一灾难。只说天子脚下渭城驿吧，原是供应来往官员换马、休息的机构，只因连年支应进贡荔枝使臣所需浩大，弄得驿站没有钱粮，无力招待来往官员，只养了一匹瘦马。眼看又到了进贡之期，主管官儿干脆一走了之，只剩下一个驿子在这里看门。这个驿子也是过一天是一天，并无办法应付使臣需要。

这日晌午时分，涪州进贡使臣先到，远远就呼叫：“驿子，快换马来。”驿子闻声而出，接下马来。使臣轻轻将果篮放下，抖抖衣上灰尘，还未住手，又一匹马闯来，马上人大呼：“驿子，快换马来。”原来是海南使臣接踵而来，驿子上前接下马来，使臣也轻轻放下果篮，与涪州使臣相见为礼。接着，转身向驿子：“驿子，酒饭在那里？”

“未曾准备。”涪州使臣要赶路，也顾不得吃饭了：“未准备就算了，我们不吃饭了，快带马来。”

“两位老爷听禀：本驿只剩一匹马，任凭哪位老爷骑去。”

海南使臣赶了远路，马匹已不堪再骑，闻言大为恼怒，喝道：“哇，这么大的一个渭城驿，怎么只有一匹马？快唤你的狗官来，问问他驿马弄到哪里去了。”

驿子无可奈何地摊开双手回答说：“说起驿马，本驿原先倒有不少匹，都被连年进呈荔枝的老爷们骑死了。驿官没法，如今也走了。”

here, we can demand horses from you."

Although the groom was angry, he dared not talk back. Pointing to the stable he said, "Is there a horse in the stable?"

The envoy from Fuzhou was clever and he knew that as long as they argued there would not be another horse. He wanted to have the one that was there and said, "I got here first; let me have it."

"I come from Hainan which is farther away; you should let me have it."

The Fuzhou envoy went to change his horse; he did not want to quarrel with the envoy from Hainan. Angered, the Hainan envoy pulled him back. Immediately the envoy from Fuzhou picked up his basket of lichee to defend himself and said, "Don't you dare touch my lichee basket!" The envoy from Hainan also picked up his fruit basket and moving towards the envoy from Fuzhou saying, "Don't you dare touch my basket!" They were locked in a stalemate.

"Please keep your temper, gentlemen," the groom said. "Why don't both of you ride the horse?"

The envoys reacted to his suggestion by venting their anger on him. The Hainan envoy roared, "Nonsense! I'm going to beat you, you rascal!"

"I'm going to beat you too, you trickster!" The Fuzhou envoy was not one to lag behind.

The groom protected his head with his hands and knelt down, begging for mercy. The envoys said in unison, "If you want us to let you off, bring the horse quickly."

"There is only one horse."

"We need another."

"I can't get you another."

The two beat him again. The groom could not escape and took off his clothes saying, "Please don't beat me, gentlemen. Even if you beat me there is still only one horse. Please take my jacket to buy wine." The envoy from Fuzhou wanted the horse and not the coat. The envoy from Hainan examined the jacket, put it on and said, "All right, I must hurry. I shall change my horse at the next station." The envoy from Fuzhou mounted the skinny horse and rode off.

The horse had gone and so had the groom's jacket. He was very sad and sighed, "Oh, Lady Yang, Lady Yang! This happens just because you want to eat lichees!"

“驿官走了,只问你要！”海南使臣无理地要挟道。

驿子虽然恼怒, 却不敢顶撞, 指着棚子中说: “这棚内不是有一匹马么？”

涪州使臣乖巧, 知道再与驿子纠缠也不能变出马来, 便赶先抢了这匹马再说:“驿子,我先来,就让我先骑了去。”

“我从海南来,路途更远,还是让我先骑去。”

涪州使臣只是换马,不与海南使臣斗口。海南使臣急了,前来拉扯。涪州使臣赶紧用果篮挡住:“你敢把我这些荔枝乱丢?”海南使臣见状, 也如法炮制, 举起果篮向涪州使臣面前顶去: “你敢把我这竹篮打碎? ”一时之间,两人相持不下。

驿子劝说道:“请二位不要发脾气,不如你二位同骑这匹马走。”

哪知驿子好言相劝, 两个使臣顿时迁怒于他, 先是海南使臣吼道:“哇,胡说！我只打你这个坏蛋！”

“我也打你这个刁贼！”涪州使臣也不甘落后。

驿子被打得抱头跪在地上求饶, 两个使臣都说: “若要饶你, 快换马来。”“马只有一匹。”“再添一匹来。”“一匹也没有。”

两个使臣又痛打,驿子没法,脱下身上衣服,说:“请二位爷不要打,再打也无马。我这身衣服,与你们当酒钱吧。”涪州使臣只要马, 不要衣服; 海南使臣仔细看了驿子的衣服, 也还能穿, 就随手披在身上, 说: “算了, 赶路要紧。 我还骑了自家的马, 到前站换去。”涪州使臣只得换了驿中那匹瘦马上路。

驿子见马也被骑走了,还贴了自家一身衣服,不禁悲苦万分,叹息道:“咳,杨娘娘,杨娘娘,这一切都是为了你要吃荔枝啊！”

The lichees arrived at Chang'an, the capital, on time, but Li Longji had taken Lady Yang to Mount Lishan to spend summer there.

The emperor ordered a feast to be held in the Palace of Eternal Youth on Lady Yang's birthday, the first day of the sixth lunar moon. He sent Gao Lishi to summon the musician, Li Guinian, and his orchestra to play the Dance of the Rainbow and Feathery Garments which had been composed by Lady Yang. They would enjoy themselves from morning to night.

Ever since she had returned to the palace, Yang Yuhuan had done her best to keep Li Longji's favor and strengthen his love. The Dance of the Rainbow and Feathery Garments had been composed for this purpose.

When the score was finished, Yang Yuhuan had followed the emperor's instructions and had taught it to Yongxin and Niannu, who learned it quickly.

The two palace maids passed what they had learned on to Li Guinian, the orchestra leader, each night at the Chaoyuan Pavilion. One night when they had taken the score to the pavilion and were waiting for Li Guinian, Yongxin pushed open the window and said to Niannu, "Look, the moonlight lights up the outside as if it were under water and there is a cool breeze. This is a perfect night to learn music."

Niannu said, "We have finished the prelude and will begin the main parts." Li Guinian soon arrived.

He was an outstanding figure and had been appointed head of the orchestra by the emperor. There were excellent musicians, such as Lei Haiqing a famous lute player, in his group. After Li arrived the three started.

The Dance of the Rainbow and Feathery Garments was music from heaven and not only officials but ordinary people in the capital all knew about it and longed to be the first to hear it. A certain young man by the name of Li Mo from South China heard of it during his visit to the capital. He was young and talented. As a child he had studied music and was known for his fine flute playing. He did his utmost to find a way to hear the music.

His efforts paid off. Someone told him that Chaoyuan Pavilion had been built by the palace wall and that music played in the palace could be heard from the outside. Taking his flute he went that particular moonlit night to Lishan where he walked around the red palace wall and leant against a spot near the pavilion. He looked up to see the dancing light from the red lanterns and moving shadows. Patiently he waited.

荔枝终于如期送至京城长安。不过，唐玄宗李隆基已携着贵妃娘娘杨玉环同去骊山避暑了。六月初一是杨玉环生日，李隆基特地吩咐在长生殿中设宴庆贺，并令高力士召来乐工李龟年等梨园弟子演奏娘娘新制的《霓裳羽衣曲》,以便与贵妃作竟日之欢。

杨玉环自从重新被召入宫之后，千方百计讨好李隆基，求其欢心,以固其宠,制作《霓裳羽衣曲》,也是为了献媚。曲谱写定之后,她奉皇上之命,亲自口耳相传,教会永新、念奴两个宫女。

从此,这两个宫女每晚就在朝元阁上,传授给乐师李龟年。今夜也不例外,两人携了曲谱先上了朝元阁。李龟年此时尚未来到，永新对念奴说:“你看今夜月明如水,凉风习习,正好演习哩。”

念奴说:“序曲已传授了，今日说演习曲谱正段拍序了。”说着,李龟年也上了朝元阁。

这李龟年也非等闲之辈，是万岁爷亲自点名为梨园班首的，在他戏班中颇有一些技艺高超的艺人，如雷海青的铁拨琵琶就赫赫有名。如今他奉命前来向两个宫女习学新谱，以便及早传授给梨园弟子们。两个宫女见李龟年已到,招呼几句,便开始传授了。

岂知他们习学的《霓裳羽衣曲》，原非人间所有，而是天上仙曲。他们三人在此习学,仙曲之名早已传出宫外,无论朝野,人人争欲先闻。此曲也惊动了一个江南少年,这少年名李暮,自小就精通音律,以能吹奏铁笛闻名遐迩。为人又生性风流,颇多逸兴。如今来游京城,闻知宫中新制一曲,便想方设法要得到这一曲谱。

工夫不负有心人，他终于打听到传曲之所为朝元阁，便趁此月明之夜，携了铁笛，赶来骊山，绕着红墙，走到宫门西首朝元阁下,倚墙而立,翘首而望,只见红灯灿灿,人影幢幢,便耐心等待。

After a while the mixed sound of pipe, flute, gong, woodenfish drum and other musical instruments was heard. It was very pleasant to the ears, like the sound of scattered pearls falling on jade plates. After listening for a while, Li Mo grasped the essence. He took out his flute and lightly played the tune accompanied by music from the pavilion which sounded like the clatter of autumn bamboo and the crackle of spring ice. He listened to the music, played his flute then left happily when the lights and people in the pavilion had gone and the moon had moved to the west.

No one knew that Li Mo had stolen the music while Yang Yuhuan was preparing to dedicate the piece to the emperor on her birthday.

Now that the emperor was sitting in the center of the Palace of Eternal Youth giving orders to others to request Lady Yang to come. Helped by Yongxin and Niannu, Lady Yang had been gorgeously attired and now she walked slowly to the Palace of Eternal Youth. She curtseyed to the emperor and said, "Your slave Lady Yang is here. Long live the emperor! May Your Majesty live ten thousand years."

"Long live to you, my love." Li Longji said happily and added, "This is your birthday. I have prepared a feast to celebrate it. Let us spend the day in pleasure."

"I am overwhelmed by your royal favor, and would like to drink to your eternal life." Eunuch Gao Lishi at once handed Lady Yang a cup of wine and she presented it to Li Longji with both hands. Li Longji drank it and ordered a cup of wine for her. Lady Yang drank kneeling to show her thanks and kowtowed, saying, "Long live the emperor."

After the ceremony, Gao Lishi took a red scroll from an attendant and presented it to the emperor. The prime minister and the three duchesses had come to congratulate them and had brought gifts; they were waiting outside the palace.

Li Longji said, "Give them our thanks. The prime minister need not stand on ceremony and should return to his office to attend to affairs of state. The three duchesses may wait and feast with us later in the palace."

After he sent Gao Lishi away, another eunuch entered and reported that the lichees from Fuzhou and Hainan had arrived. Li Longji gave an order that they be brought in at once. At this a eunuch presented a large plate of lichees covered with a piece of yellow silk. Li Longji passed a sprig to Yang Yuhuan and said, "I know your fondness for them. I ordered the local authorities to sent them here posthaste and they have arrived on time for your feast. For this I have to drink to you." Yang Yuhuan could

不一会儿,阁上十番乐器 —— 笛、管、箫、弦、提琴、云锣、汤锣、木鱼、檀板、大鼓齐鸣,悠扬的歌声渐起,如同迸散的骊珠,大珠、小珠先后击落玉盘,铮铮琮琮,沁人心脾,恍然凝神,听了一遍,便有会于心,取出袖中铁笛,轻轻和奏。李暮何等聪慧,和过一遍,便已掌握要领,不禁暗自庆幸,这曲子如敲秋竹,如裂春冰,分明是天上所有、人间所无。沉吟良久,眼见阁上灯熄、人散,残月西斜,夜已深沉,便喜孜孜的离开宫墙而回。

李暮偷得新曲,宫中尚无人知觉。杨玉环还准备在自家生日这一天以此新曲呈献圣上哩。且说李隆基已在长生殿中坐定,随即传召贵妃娘娘。杨玉环应召,在永新、念奴的照顾下,缓缓向长生殿行来,进入殿内,拜见圣上:"臣妾杨氏见驾。愿陛下万岁,万万岁。"

"愿与妃子同享千年万年。"李隆基圣心大悦,"今日妃子诞辰,设宴庆贺,同为竟日之饮。"

"薄命生辰,荷蒙圣上宠爱。臣妾愿意先向圣上敬酒,以祝圣上千秋万岁。"太监高力士立即捧上酒来,杨玉环接过,双手呈献给李隆基。李隆基饮过,也赐妃子酒一杯。杨玉环跪下饮过,又叩头呼"万岁"为谢。行礼已罢,高力士接过小内监的红表看过,随即呈送给李隆基。原来国舅杨丞相和韩、秦、虢三位国夫人,齐来献上寿礼、贺表,在宫外伺候。

李隆基吩咐道:"多谢他们。丞相免去入内行礼,回朝去办事。三位国夫人,候朕同娘娘回宫入宴。"

这拨人才打发走,又一拨人来奏事:原来涪州和海南两处使臣已将荔枝送到骊山。李隆基命令立即取进来。内监随声而出,捧进一大果篮,掀去覆盖在上面的黄包袱,呈上。李隆基递上一枝给

only say, "Long live the emperor."

After drinking the wine she took a lichee which was red on the outside and white and fragrant when peeled; it was cool and sweet to the mouth. It was heavenly fruit and the emperor had given it to her. Lady Yang was overjoyed.

Seeing that she was in a happy mood the emperor heightened their enjoyment by saying, "Gao Lishi, order Li Guinian and his musicians to play for us."

Li Guinian and his men had waited outside for a long time. On the order he led the other musicians in and they kowtowed to the emperor and Lady Yang; they then played the Dance of the Rainbow and Feathery Garments which they had rehearsed many times.

Yang Yuhuan did her best to explain the music saying, "Every word and every note should match the dance. This part I have called light singing and graceful dancing."

"You have explained the dance very well."

Yang Yuhuan was overwhelmed with the praise and said, "I have had an emerald disk made and I would like to dance on it for Your Majesty's amusement."

"I have never seen you dance. It must be an entrancing sight. Yongxin and Niannu, Zheng Guanyin and Xie Aman, accompany Her Ladyship as she dances on the emerald disk." Li Longji's spirits were enhanced.

While Lady Yang was putting on a dancing costume, attendants prepared the emerald disk. Li Longji also changed into less formal clothes and said to Gao Lishi, "Let Li Guinian and his men play according to the score and I will beat the drum myself."

Lady Yang was helped on to the emerald disk by palace maids and, when she stood in the center, the others withdrew. She was like a red cloud descending from the sky. Gao Lishi knelt down to hold the drum and the emperor beat it to start the music. The other musicians played their own instruments. Sometimes the beat was quick and sometimes it was slow. Yang Yuhuan followed it closely changing her movements so that sometimes she was like a lotus swinging amid green leaves and at other times she whirled like the wind. The dance stopped immediately when the emperor stopped playing. Yang Yuhuan curtseyed and said again and again, "Long live the emperor!"

Li Longji rose and stepped forward to take Yang Yuhuan's hand. He said, "That was an exquisite dance and proves that there is no end to

杨玉环，不无取悦地说："妃子，朕因你爱吃此果，特命地方飞驰进贡。今日寿宴初开，佳果又及时送到。当为妃子再进一杯。"杨玉环无从表达此时的感激，只能口呼"万岁"而已。

杨玉环饮过李隆基所赐佳酒，又接过荔枝在手，先观赏一遍，只见其皮壳鲜红似染，掀去薄薄的皮壳，其肉又洁白晶莹；拿在手里一股清芬香气，送入口中齿颊既甘且凉，真是天上方才有的佳果，而皇上却将它赐给自己，不禁喜形于色，神采飞扬。

李隆基见杨玉环兴致正高，又进一步取悦于她："高力士，即刻传李龟年带梨园弟子上殿伺候。"

李龟年已先得旨意，哪敢怠慢？早在殿外等候传召。一声旨下，他即刻带领乐工上殿叩见万岁、娘娘，并奉命将事先不断演习过的《霓裳羽衣曲》演奏一遍，真是乐声悠扬，声情俊爽。

杨玉环也打起精神来说明："这一声一字，都与舞态配合，所谓缓歌曼舞相生也。"

"妃子所言，真是曲尽歌舞之蕴涵。"

得到李隆基这般称赞，杨玉环又进言说："妾还制有翠盘一面，请让臣妾在其中试舞一番，以博圣上一笑。"

"妃子妙舞，寡人倒从未见。永新、念奴，你们和郑观音、谢阿蛮一起服侍娘娘，上翠盘去。"李隆基兴致也更加浓厚。

杨玉环自去更衣，另有人陈设好翠盘。李隆基也换了便装，对高力士说："让李龟年领着梨园弟子按谱奏乐，朕亲自击鼓。"

说着，杨玉环在宫女簇拥之下，上了翠盘，众人散去。她就像一朵红云自空而降，天香四落。高力士捧着羯鼓，李隆基一声鼓响，细十番乐声随即扬起。鼓声徐急舒张，杨玉环或轻歌曼舞，宛

your charms. You were like a swallow in flight and a swimming dragon. Quite unique." He turned and called, "Maids, bring the wine! Let me offer you a cup." Li Longji took the wine from a maid, handed it to Yang Yuhuan and said, "I hope you will taste and drain this cup. This is my thanks for your dance."

"Long live the emperor!" Yang Yuhuan took the cup and was modest. "Your slave is not worthy of drinking the wine given by you."

A little drunk and affected by the allure of Yang Yuhuan's charms Li Longji said, "I shall give you ten rolls of silk and a golden headband from Jinshajiang for your dance." He took a scented pouch from his chest and gave it to Yang Yuhuan. Hand in hand they went to the sleeping palace.

如迎风荷花，飘飘在翠叶之上；或盘旋跌宕，如同天风骤起，吹得花枝招展。陡然鼓声绝响，翠盘上的舞蹈立即止住，杨玉环朝上拜谢，连呼“万岁”！

李隆基走下座来，上前携着杨玉环纤纤玉手，说道：“真好呀，你的舞蹈，真是逸态横生，浓姿百出，好像是飞燕游龙一般，真是千秋独擅哩。”回过头来说：“宫娥们，看酒来，待朕与妃子把杯。”李隆基接过宫娥捧上的酒，送给杨玉环说：“你可轻轻尝尝，但要干杯，不可剩留一点儿。这是寡人酬谢你舞蹈的酒。”

“万岁！”杨玉环接过杯来，“承陛下亲赐佳酿，妾庸劣之姿怎敢承当。”杨玉环谦恭而大方地答谢。

李隆基眼见杨玉环绝色天姿、万般风流，已有几分醉意，又慷慨表示：“朕还有上等绸缎十万尺，金沙江出的上等金头饰一件，赏赐与你。”又取出怀中的香囊送给贵妃。杨玉环接过香囊，李隆基则携着她的手同向寝宫行去。

Chapter Seven

Shift of Affection Triggers a Grudge

The deepest affection diminishes and the most profound love will brew a grudge. Although Yang Yuhuan had been in favor with Li Longji for a long time, there were three thousand beauties in the inner palace who coveted his affections and tried every means of winning his favor. Lady Plum Blossom, Jiang Caiping, had been Li Longji's favorite, but she accidentally offended him and was moved to the east wing. She would not give up and Yang Yuhuan did all that she could to guard against her. The emperor, however, still had feelings for her. Jiang was extremely clever and she would surely find a way to get back to the emperor. Yang Yuhuan knew very well that she and Jiang Caiping were incompatible, like fire and water. It was not that she could not tolerate Jiang; she was afraid that Jiang could not tolerate her. As a result she was often on tenterhooks.

One day the emperor did not return to Lady Yang's palace after attending the morning court. At dusk she was very worried and sent Yongxin and Niannu to find out what had happened. The two maids did not return for some time and Yang Yuhuan sat alone in the palace feeling wretched. Normally the emperor would have returned long before and the two would have sat together holding each other's hand chatting merrily. She had no idea why he had not returned that day. Just then there was a cry, "The emperor is here!" She got up at once, but there was no one. It was a parrot that had learnt the phrase. She stood by the rails looking around, helpless; it was already dark. Worried, she paced up and down. Suddenly she heard footsteps approaching; it was Yongxin coming back to report. "Your Ladyship, His Majesty is sleeping in the Emerald Pavilion tonight."

"Ah, can it be true?" she exclaimed. Tears rolled down her cheeks. "How shallow is the emperor's love! I wait to chat with him and he suddenly neglects me!"

Yongxin consoled her, "It is by chance that His Majesty hasn't come,

第七章
情移生怨

情到浓时转生薄,宠到极时自生嫌。杨玉环虽然得宠日久,但后宫佳丽三千,无时不在窥测,千方百计想求得李隆基的垂顾。何况梅妃江采苹,原就是李隆基的爱妃,只因偶然触怒皇上,方才被迁置东楼。但江采萍绝不会自甘罢休,杨玉环虽然处处提防,但皇上对她的旧情并未全然断绝,加之梅妃聪敏过人,自然要设巧计以挽回上心。杨玉环深知,自己的地位与梅妃的处境形同水火,势不两立。因此,她也是经常悬着心过日子。

今早李隆基上朝,直到天色已暮还未曾回宫,杨玉环心中十分不安,派永新、念奴去打听。杨玉环独自一人坐在冷清清的宫中,思绪万千,忐忑不安。换在平日,李隆基早已回宫,但今日不知何故却未见圣上人影,她正在疑惑不定,忽然一声:“呀,圣上来了!”她连忙立起身来,哪见圣上?原来是鹦哥学舌!无奈何,只得立在画栏前向外张望。忽然,宫外脚步声自远而近,原来是永新打听圣上消息赶回来禀报:“启禀娘娘,万岁爷今晚在翠华西阁宿息。”

“呀,有这样事!”出乎杨玉环意外,不免惊呼,同时两行泪水沿颊而下。

宫女永新劝慰道:“万岁爷今夜偶然不进宫,也可能并不是有

my lady. He can't be staying away deliberately. Don't be sad, Your Ladyship."

"If his affections have not shifted how could he sleep alone in another palace? The emperor never passes a night alone; can it be no one lies by his side tonight?" Lady Yang was not simple and did not believe what Yongxin said to console her. Just then Niannu returned and said, "Your Ladyship, I have found out the truth."

"What is it?"

"Your Ladyship, I heard that His Majesty secretly ordered a eunuch to fetch someone."

"Fetch whom?"

"Lady Plum Blossom, Jiang Caiping."

"Ah, so it is Lady Plum Blossom, the devil!" Her worst fears had come true. But she was still in doubt and said, "Are you certain of what you are saying?"

"Quite certain."

"Ah, heaven. Is that devil Lady Plum Blossom in favor again?" She sat silently wiping her tears.

Yongxin and Niannu said, "Don't be distressed, Your Ladyship."

Lady Yang said with feeling, "How can I not be sad or tremble at the news?" She wiped her tears away but they came again. She gave a long sigh and said, "My love and favor have turned to tears today. On other days, he loved me so dearly, but his heart has suddenly changed. If I had done wrong, he should have told me and pointed out my faults! After all the time he has been here his heart has gone to another. He has deceived me for I am simple and innocent."

Niannu told her what she knew. "My lady, a eunuch told me that yesterday the emperor sent a parcel of pearls to Lady Plum Blossom from the Blooming Flower Pavilion. She wouldn't accept them and sent them back with a poem saying that since her dismissal she had not dressed her hair and that pearls would not console her in her grief. That accounts for what has happened tonight."

"So that is it! How could I know?"

Yongxin advised her to accept the emperor's wish and pleaded the case for Lady Plum Blossom's return. This would please His Majesty and Lady Plum Blossom would be grateful. But how could Yang Yuhuan tolerate someone else? She said no and asked the pair to go to the Emerald Pavilion with her.

意疏远,娘娘不要伤怀。”

“若不是感情迁移,圣上怎能独宿别宫?何况皇上从不独眠,难道今夜竟然甘愿冷冷清清,不要人陪宿?”杨玉环并非糊涂人,不信永新好心劝慰。正当其时,念奴也回来了:“娘娘,奴婢打听清楚了。”

“怎说?”

“娘娘听启,奴婢刚才打听到,有密旨给小太监召人。”

“召哪一个?”

“梅妃江采苹。”

“呀,居然是梅精!”杨玉环终日担心的事果真发生了,但仍不放心地追问:“此话果真?”

“果真不假。”

“唉,天哪,梅精又被宠幸了?”说着,无力坐下,不断拭泪。

永新、念奴在一边劝说道:“娘娘,请不要愁闷。”

杨玉环怨恨地诉说道:“听见这话,怎不伤心?”拭了泪水,乃作长叹:“从前的蜜意恩眷,都变成今朝的泪水。唉,想从前那般恩爱,今朝陡然变心,总是奴家不对,但也该说出奴家有哪样罪名呀!”

念奴索性将打听来的消息一骨脑儿倒了出来:“娘娘还不知道,奴婢听小太监说,昨天万岁爷在华萼楼上取了一斛珍珠赐给梅妃,她不肯收,回献一诗,说什么‘长门自是无梳洗,何必珍珠慰寂寥’,所以才有今夜的事儿发生。”

“哦,原来如此,我哪里知道!”

永新劝说杨娘娘干脆做好人,不如迎合圣上之意,让皇上召回梅妃,万岁爷也高兴,料想梅妃也不敢忘恩。但杨玉环岂能容得他人?自是不允,并且吩咐她们两个随她到翠华阁去。

Niannu panicked and said, "Why do you want to go there, my lady?"

"I'll see what magic she uses, what spell she casts to charm my lord and how she so fascinates the emperor."

Niannu was even more worried and said, "The emperor doesn't want you to know what has happened tonight, my lady, and it is now nearly midnight; His Majesty will be asleep. If Your Ladyship suddenly arrived there, it may embarrass him. You had better rest and deal with the matter tomorrow."

Although Lady Yang wanted to go to the Emerald Pavilion to vent her anger, what Niannu said was reasonable. If she went there now, it would certainly enrage the emperor. She wept and sighed. "Very well. I won't go ... but what sleep will I get tonight?"

After a sleepless night, she went to the Emerald Pavilion alone the following morning.

Lady Plum Blossom was there with the emperor. Her real name was Jiang Caiping, but Li Longji had granted her the title Lady Plum Blossom because she liked plum blossom. She had taken the emperor's fancy in the past. After Lady Yang's arrival, she fell from favor and His Majesty had her moved to the east pavilion of the Shangyang Palace. The night before, however, the emperor had pretended to be sick and slept in the Emerald Pavilion. Secretly he sent a eunuch to summon Lady Plum Blossom. The maids had been told not to let Lady Yang know about this and Gao Lishi was ordered to stand guard outside the pavilion; he was to allow no one in.

Lady Yang came looking for the emperor and when Gao Lishi saw her from a distance he was taken aback. Lady Plum Blossom was still in the pavilion. What could he do?

Before he had decided Yang Yuhuan arrived and said, "Gao Lishi, where is His Majesty?"

"In the pavilion, my lady."

"And who is with him?"

"No one."

"Open the door and let me see for myself."

Even though he was experienced in handling such things, he was still at a loss and said, "Please take a seat, Your Ladyship. His Majesty was busy with state affairs. He felt a little tired and took a rest here. I was ordered to guard the door so that no one went in."

"Very well! How long will you keep up this farce? I know you fix

念奴有些慌了:“娘娘去干什么?”

“我到那里,看看梅妃如何逞媚术,把皇上搞得颠颠倒倒。”

念奴更担心了:“奴婢想今夜翠华阁的事儿,原就怕娘娘知道。此时夜深,万岁爷必然已经安寝,娘娘突然走去,恐有不便。不如娘娘先行安歇,明天再作商量。”

杨玉环虽然在气头上要去翠华阁问个究竟,但仔细想来,念奴的话确有道理。自家此时前去,必定会触怒皇上,因此只得掩泪叹息:“唉,算了算了,就不去吧 —— 只是今夜教我如何睡得着呀!”

她果然彻夜未眠。次日清晨,也不带宫女,独自一个人到翠华阁去。梅妃果然在阁中承幸哩。这梅妃并不姓梅,原名叫江采苹,只因性爱梅花,被皇上赐号梅妃。起初万岁爷对她十分宠幸,但自从杨玉环入宫后,李隆基对她的宠爱日疏,竟然将她迁置在上阳宫东楼。昨夜皇上忽然称病,在翠华西阁宿息,让小内监密召她来侍应,并告诫宫人,不得让杨娘娘知道。

杨玉环依然寻迹追踪而来,高力士远远看见,吃惊不小,心想梅娘娘还在阁中,此事如何是好?未待高力士拿定主意,杨玉环已走到阁前,开口便问:“高力士,万岁爷在哪里?”

“在阁中,回娘娘的话。”

“阁中还有何人?”

“没有。”

“你开了阁门,待我进去看看。”

高力士再老练,也未免有几分慌张,连忙说道:“娘娘请坐。万岁爷忙于朝事,有些疲乏,在此休息,不让闲杂人等入内。”

“好呀!你在我面前还玩花招?我知道你呀,巴结上得势的人,

your hopes on someone who is on the way up and insult me now that I am out of luck. Very well! I shall have to knock at the door myself." Gao Lishi had no choice and called out, "Lady Yang is here! Quickly open the door!" This warned the couple inside and the startled Li Longji immediately hid Lady Plum Blossom behind a curtain and lay on the bed pretending to be asleep.

Lady Yang entered the inner room directly through the opened door. When she saw the emperor she said, "I heard that you were unwell, Your Majesty, and have come to ask about your health."

"I was feeling slightly indisposed, so I did not go to the palace. But why should you take the trouble of coming here so early?" Li Longji acted as if nothing had happened.

"I think I can guess the reason for Your Majesty's sickness."

The emperor could only laugh and say, "What do you guess?"

Lady Yang said that it was because of Lady Plum Blossom; Li Longji denied it. Yang Yuhuan did not believe him and looked down to see a pair of women's slippers. Li Longji lowered his head, pretending to look for something and an emerald trinket fell from his chest. When Yang Yuhuan saw this, she pressed for an answer.

Gao Lishi saw what was going on and at once ordered a eunuch to take Lady Plum Blossom through a gap in the wall at the back and then to the east pavilion. Lady Yang thought that Lady Plum Blossom was still in the pavilion and said, "The sun is high in the sky. Why hasn't Your Majesty gone to court? Those who do not know what is happening will think that I, the ugly imperial concubine, have kept you back. I shall wait here till you return." Li Longji was worried about Lady Plum Blossom and used every means to delay having to go. "I am not feeling well today; I shall not go to court."

When he got the opportunity Gao Lishi discretely whispered to the emperor that Lady Plum Blossom had gone. Lady Yang kept urging him to go and Li Longji nodded and said, "Since Lady Yang wishes me to go, I will make the effort." He had nothing to worry about and left. Lady Yang found nothing and vented her anger upon Gao Lishi, "Gao Lishi, a fine trick you played behind my back. Now tell me where did the slippers and trinket come from?"

Gao Lishi explained truthfully, "Your Ladyship, His Majesty's love for you is unparalleled; he tries at all times to please you. As for these slippers and trinket, you would do well to say nothing of Lady Plum

欺负我倒运的人！也罢，待我自行敲门。”高力士混也混不过，拦也拦不住，只得高声向内传报：“杨娘娘来了！”李隆基闻言，一时手脚无措，赶紧将梅妃藏在夹幕中，自己则躺在床上装睡。

内侍开了门，杨玉环直入内室，见了李隆基，说：“妾闻圣体欠佳，特来问安。”

“寡人偶然有些不舒服，未能进宫，何劳妃子清晨来此。”李隆基装作无事的样子，说道。

“陛下生病的缘故，妾倒猜着几分了。”

李隆基只能笑着问道：“妃子猜到什么缘故了？”

杨玉环便直截了当地说出为了梅妃，李隆基一再否认。杨玉环怎么相信？低头细看，床下分明一双女鞋，李隆基装着低头寻找什么，不料怀中又掉下一朵翠钿，杨玉环见了，更是追问不已。

高力士见状，连忙吩咐小内监将梅妃从阁后越墙送走。杨玉环以为梅妃定藏在阁中，振振有辞地对李隆基说：“已日高三竿，皇上怎不临朝？外人不知道呵，还以为是我这庸姿劣貌的妃子将皇上留滞——请皇上坐朝去，妾在此候皇上退朝一同回宫。”李隆基牵挂梅妃，一再推托，勉强说道：“寡人今日有疾，不能坐朝。”

高力士见机行事，趁杨玉环不注意时，对皇上低声说梅妃已经送走。李隆基在杨玉环一再催促下，便有气无力地点头道：“既然妃子劝寡人上朝，只得勉强去了。”说罢，摆驾出宫，放心上朝而去。杨玉环自然一无所得，就向高力士大发脾气：“高力士，你瞒着我做得好事！我问你，这凤鞋、翠钿从何处而来？”

高力士索性说破：“告知娘娘，你可不要烦恼。奴才看万岁爷与娘娘百从千随，感情真好。这两件东西么，不要说是旧好梅妃

Blossom, the emperor's former favorite or even of some new beauties. Don't blame me for speaking out of turn. Even high officials have concubines so why cannot the emperor have one night of pleasure?"

Lady Yang could not refute him and gave a weak excuse for her behavior. "I do not begrudge him sharing his bed with someone else, but I hate the others play tricks on me."

Yongxin arrived and Gao Lishi asked her to persuade Her Ladyship to return and not be distressed. Before Lady Yang had taken a step, Li Longji came back from the court. He was embarrassed and tried to please Lady Yang by asking her to go to the Blooming Flower Pavilion to view flowers. Lady Yang was not in the mood and said, "Are the flowers there as lovely as those in the east pavilion? Since the plum tree is the first to flower in the spring, you don't need the clinging willow." (The Chinese for willow is "yang.")

Li Longji knew what she implied and said, "I love you truly. Don't you know where my true love lies?"

Lady Yang became coy and even asked the emperor to send her back. She took out the hairpin and jewel box and gave them to him. In the emperor's eyes she was demure and lovely and he again explained, "My love, how can you speak like this? We will love each other for a hundred years and still that will not be enough. Why should you speak of parting? It is my fault and I beg you not to be angry." Then he smiled and said, "When you shed tears and frown you are doubly charming. My love, put away the hairpin and box. We will go to the west palace where I have something to tell you." He held her hand and walked slowly.

The emperor had admitted that he was wrong and Yang Yuhuan realized that she had gone far enough. "If Your Majesty really wants me to stay, what more can I say?" Side by side, they walked to the west palace.

的,就是新知宫妃的,娘娘也不可多计较。不是奴才多嘴,如今满朝臣子,哪一个没有三妻四妾?更何况贵为天子,就不能有一宵之欢!”

杨玉环被说得无由反驳,只是有气无力地辩解:“不是我气量小,只恨他们做成圈套,将她假抛真招。”

正当此时,永新赶来了,高力士乃让她劝娘娘回宫去,不要再为此事苦恼。杨玉环尚未移步,李隆基已罢朝赶了回来,自觉惭愧,又来笼络杨玉环,要与她去华萼楼看花。杨玉环此时无此心情,说道:“华萼楼前的花怕不如东楼上的花好,有‘梅’枝儿占春先,又何需绿‘杨’牵绕?”

李隆基自然听出她话中的醋意,解释说:“寡人一片真心待你,难道妃子还不知道?”

杨玉环只是撒娇卖痴,甚至要皇上将她斥退,又将当年皇上赐她的钗、盒取出交还与他。李隆基见她娇声滴滴,颇为不忍,扶着她再次表白:“妃子啊,你怎说出这样话来?朕和你两人恩情如海,纵使百年到老还嫌不够,怎平白无故地要分开?——总是朕的错,请妃子不要烦恼。”又微笑着说:“看见你这样皱着眉头,淌着眼泪,模样特别发娇。妃子,你把钗、盒装好,朕和你到西宫说话去。”说罢,他搀着杨玉环的手,缓缓前行。

杨玉环见皇上已认错,不能过分,见好就收,答道:“陛下既然不抛弃妾,妾又还能说什么?”也就肩并肩地与李隆基回西宫去了。

Chapter Eight

Peeping a Bath and Secret Vow

It was mid-summer and extremely hot. Li Longji decided to take Lady Yang to bathe in the Huaqing Pool. Eunuchs and maids busied themselves to prepare after the order was given.

The Huaqing Pool was at the foot of Mount Lishan and the people who worked there had been at the imperial palace but had been sent there for various reasons. For instance, one of the two maids now on duty had a loud voice and was plain, stout, clumsy and unfit for singing and dancing. The other had waited on Lady Plum Blossom who had been angry after she returned from the Emerald Pavilion and became ill and died. So they were sent here. Usually there was little to do there but today everyone as busy because the emperor and Lady Yang were coming to bathe in the spring. After cleaning the palace and the pool, the maids had changed the beds and as everything was ready they were waiting outside.

Mount Lishan was on the outskirts of Chang'an. The scenery there was unique and from a distance it could be seen that it was surrounded by green trees. A red wall had been built round the Huaqing Pool and the Hot-Spring Pavilion so ordinary people could not see inside.

Inside there were gardens, carved beams, painted pillars, bead curtains, covered corridors and a spring. It was an ideal place for bathing in the summer.

Li Longji and Yang Yuhuan arrived surrounded by eunuchs and maids, then headed for the Hot-Spring Palace and the Huaqing Pool. In the palace Li Longji dismissed the eunuchs and all the maids except Yongxin and Niannu.

The others left and Li Longji said to Yang Yuhuan, "My love, the clear spring water ripples in the pool. It is soothing to the skin, fragrant and soft. Let us bathe here."

Yongxin and Niannu heard this and helped them take off their outer garments. The pearl-bright, jade-fine beauty of Lady Yang was at once

第八章
窥浴密誓

盛夏已至,酷热难当,李隆基与杨玉环去华清池共浴。

华清池远在骊山脚下，打发到这里来当差的宫女、太监总是在宫中遭到冷遇的角色。且说近来当值的两个宫女吧，一个是因为面容丑陋、身材粗大，喉咙太响，动作笨拙，被撵出梨园不得学戏,发配到温泉骊山殿中当差。一个是梅妃娘娘的宫人,梅妃自从翠阁事发后气愤交加,一病而亡,这个宫人失了依靠,也就被打发到此处来承值了。今日听说皇上要与娘娘前来共洗温泉，不免手忙脚乱起来,打扫宫殿,清洗浴池,换上崭新的铺陈。

骊山在长安城外,远远望去,一片青苍,景色幽奇。自从修建了华清池、温泉殿，又筑起一带红墙，平常百姓休想窥见园中奥秘。园中雕梁画栋,珠帘飞卷,修廊曼接翠微,温泉曲通玉池,正是沐浴避暑的好去处。

李隆基与杨玉环在一批太监、宫女前呼后拥中来到骊山，进了温泉殿，李隆基便吩咐内侍退去，只留永新、念奴几个老成宫女侍候。李隆基见内侍尽行外出后,便对杨玉环说:“妃子,你看一股清泉流入池中,纹漪洄溢,香气四溢,正宜沐浴。朕同你一同去洗沐来 。”

永新等宫女闻言,便轻步上前,为他们二人解去衣裳,杨玉环

revealed and Li Longji could not help murmuring, "My love, I cannot help feasting my eyes on you or stop loving, caressing, and cherishing you."

He held her arm and they walked into the pool. A screen separated them from the maids and Yongxin said to Niannu, "Look, how fond the emperor and Lady Yang are of each other. Don't you envy them?"

"Yes, I do."

"They caress each other among the flowers by day and lie together under the moonlight at night; they taste all the joys of love."

Yongxin suddenly added, "We have waited on Lady Yang for several years and see her each day; yet we have never seen her naked. Shall we peep through the curtain?"

"Yes, let's."

Despite the possible anger of the emperor and Lady Yang, the two took a furtive look. Yang Yuhuan's slender body floated like a lotus on the waves. She was lovely with a slim waist, alluring breasts, light arms and snow white skin. Niannu spoke in a low voice. "Look, how the emperor ogles her with a smirk on his face as if he had taken leave of his senses."

Yongxin said, "Look, the emperor holds her tight and kisses her again and again."

While they were peeping two other maids who were carrying out their chores came in and said, "You are having fun. Let us have a look too."

Startled, Yongxin and Niannu retorted, "We are just waiting on Lady Yang while she takes her bath. What is there to see?"

The other two were not satisfied by this and said, "You are not just waiting on Lady Yang, you're taking a good look at the emperor too."

"Pah, Pah, nonsense!"

While they were bickering, Li Longji helped Yang Yuhuan out of the water and called out, "Yongxin, Niannu."

At once the pair emerged from behind the screen. Lady Yang came from the spring looking fresh and radiant with her dark hair lying disheveled on her shoulder. The two maids at once supported her to a couch. They helped her to dry her body and put on her clothes. Yongxin went out to call eunuchs to come with a carriage and said, "May it please Your Majesty, the carriage to take you and Her Ladyship back to the palace is here."

Li Longji was in high spirits and said to the eunuchs, "Let the carriage follow us. We'll take it when we are tired." To Yang Yuhuan he said, "Let

雪白肌肤顿时毫无遮掩地呈现在李隆基眼前，他忍不住喃喃自语：“唉，妃子，怎能让我不爱你、抚你、看你、怜你！”说罢，便扶着杨玉环手臂，一同步入池中，一道屏风隔开，两个宫女留在屏风之外。

永新悄悄对念奴说：“万岁爷与娘娘这般恩爱，真令人羡慕啊。”

念奴也感叹地附合：“正是啊。”

忽而，永新又对念奴说：“我与你服侍娘娘多年，虽然天天见到娘娘的容颜，但从未看到她的玉体。今日何不在屏风缝隙中瞧瞧，如何？”“好呀！”念奴欣然同意。

两个宫女也不怕皇上和娘娘嗔怒，居然在两张屏风之间结合处，偷偷窥视，只见娘娘亭亭玉体，好似一朵睡莲浮在池面，双臂轻盈，柳腰一掬，肌肤雪白，胸脯酥透。念奴忍禁不住，低低对永新说道：“姐姐，你看，万岁爷盯着娘娘看哩，笑迷迷的，好似痴呆了。”

正当她们聚精会神地偷偷窥视，不提防两个做粗活的宫女突然从身后走过来，说道：“两个姐姐看得高兴啊，也让我们看看。”

永新、念奴吓了一跳，连忙分辩：“两位姐姐，我们正在伺候娘娘洗浴，有什么‘高兴’不‘高兴’！”

两个粗使宫女也不是好打发的角色，顶嘴道：“只怕两位姐姐不是伺候娘娘，倒是偷看万岁爷哩。”

“呀，呀，啐，啐，休要胡说！”正在他们斗嘴时，李隆基已扶着杨玉环走出水池，并呼叫着：“永新，念奴！”

两个宫女应声转过屏风，只见贵妃娘娘新出温泉，玉容更增光丽，只是一头乌发零乱地披着，一副娇怯无力的模样，两人赶紧上前扶着，给她揩抹身体，穿上衣衫。之后，招呼小内监推一辆如意小车来，禀奏皇上道：“请万岁爷和娘娘上车，回华清宫去休憩。”

us saunter slowly together, hand in hand and shoulder to shoulder in the cool breeze."

Ever since the day they had bathed in the Huaqing Pool, Li Longji's love for Yang Yuhuan had grown stronger. Yang Yuhuan, however, was uneasy after what had happened to Lady Plum Blossom. As the saying goes, "Being close to a tiger is like being close to an emperor." No one knew how it would end. In the palace it was quite common for someone to be quite happy one day and discarded the next. Whenever she thought about it, she was deeply worried and tried her best to keep in favor with the emperor.

The seventh day of the seventh lunar month was approaching. Legend has it that the Cowherd and the Weaving Maid, two stars in the heavens, though a couple, are only allowed to meet that night each year. The Weaving Maid walks across the Milky Way over a bridge formed by magpies. This beautiful legend has intrigued men of letters and encouraged enthusiastic young people who have left behind many moving stories, excellent articles and poems. The most popular verses handed down from generation to generation are "The rendezvous of gold phoenix and dew fare better than mortal lovers for all their meetings," and "When love is true, it makes no difference how seldom lovers meet," written by a poet of the Song Dynasty. Yang Yuhuan, of course, knew these verses. The Double Seventh was near she would do something to celebrate it.

When she did, her activities attracted the attention of the Cowherd and the Weaving Maid in the heavens. The Weaving Maid had just crossed the Milky Way and, when she saw a wisp of smoke from burning incense rising high in the sky, she asked a fairy maid, "Where does it come from?"

The fairy maid looked around and replied, "Your Ladyship, it is Lady Yang, concubine of the Tang emperor, who is in the palace praying for happiness on this Double Seventh night." Since the story of the Cowherd and the Weaving Maid had spread among people on earth, women had prayed in courtyards for skill and happiness on the night of the Double Seventh.

"She is so reverent," the Weaving Maid said with a smile, "Let us go and have a look." They drifted to the sky above the Tang court.

The conversation and laughter of mortals not only reached heavens, but it was also heard by Li Longji, who was resting in a side hall. He spoke to the eunuch standing by. "Who is laughing and talking there?"

The eunuch called to a eunuch outside. "His Majesty asks who is

李隆基此时兴致很高，对两个小内监说道："你们推着车儿跟在后面，朕和娘娘累了再乘。"又回过头来对杨玉环说："朕和你手搀手，肩并肩，慢慢迎着这阵凉风走回去。"

自从华清池共浴温泉以后，李隆基对杨玉环更是宠爱万分，但杨玉环遭遇过因梅妃而生出的波折后，心中总不踏实，俗话说："伴君如伴虎"，谁也不知道今后的结局。

眼看七夕就到了，民间传说，牛郎织女虽为夫妇，但每年只有七月初七(农历)之夜，方能在天河相会，由喜鹊牵丝搭桥，让织女渡过银河与牛郎相聚。"金凤玉露一相逢，便胜却人间无数"，"两情若是久长时，又岂在朝朝暮暮"。多么深沉的感情，多么执着的热恋！眼见七夕来临，杨玉环怎能不好好利用这一佳节哩！她的活动又怎能瞒住上天的织女牛郎哩！

且说渡过银河的织女，已隐隐看到下界一簇香烟，摇摇直上，袅袅腾空，便问仙女道："那是何处？"

仙女凝神细看了一会儿，回禀道："娘娘，那是唐天子的贵妃杨玉环在宫中乞巧哩。"

"难得她一片诚心。"织女回过头来含笑地对牛郎说："咱们去看看吧。"说罢，双双飘至唐宫上空。

下界的人欢语笑，不但传入上天牛郎织女之耳，也让正在别殿休憩的李隆基隐约有闻，不禁向立在身边的内侍问："是哪里这般笑语？"

内侍又高声问殿外的太监："万岁爷问，是哪里这般笑语？"承值的太监高声禀道："是杨娘娘到长生殿去乞巧哩。"

不待内侍转述，李隆基已经听得分明，忙对内侍说："不要传

laughing and talking there?" The eunuch on duty replied, "Lady Yang is going to the Palace of Eternal Youth to pray for happiness."

Li Longji heard this and said to the eunuch, "You don't have to relay this to me, and don't light the lantern. I will go there quietly." He left the side hall followed by eunuchs.

Yongxin and Niannu had already made the arrangements in the hall. Displayed on the table were a golden basin, a silver vase with fresh flowers, fruit and burning incense; candles lit up the hall. Li Longji looked on quietly and listened attentively as Lady Yang held burning incense and prayed. "I, Yang Yuhuan, reverently burn this incense, the offering of a true heart, as I pray to the twin stars above. May our love pledged by a hairpin and jewel box last forever and I am not be cast off like a fan when autumn comes."

While Her Ladyship was praying, Yongxin and Niannu looked around and suddenly saw the emperor. They cried in astonishment, "Ah, His Majesty is here!" Lady Yang turned hastily to kneel to him.

"What are you doing here, my love?"

"It is the evening of the seventh day of the seventh moon, so I prepared some fruit and was praying to the Cowherd and the Weaving Maid for grace and skill."

The emperor made fun of her. "You are already cleverer than any heavenly weaving maid. What more do you have to ask for? My love, look at the Cowherd and the Weaving Maid. Separated by the Milky Way they can only meet one night each year. How they must long for each other!"

"When you speak of the twin stars' grief at separating, sire, it makes me sad. It is a pity we mortals do not know what happens in heaven. They must be lovesick too." She wiped away tears.

"Ah, darling, why are you weeping?"

"Though the Cowherd and the Weaving Maid meet only once a year, their love will endure for all eternity. But our love, I am afraid, will not last as long."

"Why should you say that, my love?" He moved close to her and whispered, "Can the stars enjoy the same pleasure as us?"

"Your Majesty has been very kind to me, but there is something I beg to be allowed to say tonight...."

"Don't hesitate. What is it?"

Sobbing, Yang Yuhuan said, "Now I am the most favored of all

报，也不要张灯，待朕悄悄前去看个究竟。”说罢，乃跨出殿去，自有内侍跟随身后。

长生殿中早有永新、念奴两个宫女布置整齐，案上燃着沉香，摆设着金盘、银瓶，陈列着瓜果、鲜花，四周烛光掩映。李隆基悄悄观看，只见贵妃娘娘手拈燃香，低声祷告。他便凝神谛听，原来她说道：“妾身杨玉环，虔诚燃香，拜告牛郎、织女双星，伏祈保佑咱家钗盒情缘绵延不断，莫让咱秋扇见弃。”

永新、念奴在娘娘祷告之际，却放眼四顾，突然瞥见皇上，惊呼道：“万岁爷来了。”杨玉环闻声立即转过身来，拜倒在李隆基面前。

“妃子在此，作何消遣？”

“今天是七夕佳节，陈设一些瓜果，向牛郎织女乞巧。”

李隆基打趣道：“妃子巧夺天工，何须再乞巧。朕想这牛郎织女，被银河隔断，一年才能相会一次，这相思真令人难熬呀。”

“陛下说起这两颗星座的别离之恨，妾便感到凄然。只可惜人间不知天上的事。他们也一定会为相思不已而病的。”说罢，泪水不觉地淌下来。

“呀，妃子为何掉泪？”

“妾想牛郎和织女，虽然一年只见一次，但却是地久天长。只恐怕陛下与妾的恩情，倒不能像他们那样长远。”

“妃子，你说到哪里去了？”李隆基移步向前，紧紧傍住杨玉环，悄悄说道：“那双星，怎比得上我和你！”

“臣妾受恩深重，今夜有句话儿……”

“妃子有话，但说不妨。”

杨玉环抽抽答答地说道：“妾蒙陛下宠爱，六宫佳丽无人能

Your Majesty's servants. But I am afraid that as time passes you will stop loving me. I will be forsaken and we will not live together till our hair turns white. If only our love would endure, I would die content." Her tears streamed down.

Li Longji wiped them away with his sleeve and said, "Don't be so sad, my darling. Ours is no common love."

"If you love me so much, sire, I beg you to vow under the twin stars to make our love eternal."

Li Longji promised and said, "Let us go then to offer incense and make a vow together." He took her hand and they walked together. The emperor offered incense and bowed with Yang Yuhuan, "May the twin stars in the heavens be our witness! We, Li Longji and Yang Yuhuan, love each other so dearly that we wish to be husband and wife in every new life and never be parted." Li Longji raised his hands and bowed, saying, "In the sky we will be two love birds, flying together." Yang Yuhuan bowed and responded. "On earth we will be twin branches on one tree." Together they said, "Though heaven and earth may end, may this vow last for ever and for ever." Yang Yuhuan turned and thanked Li Longji, saying, "I thank the emperor from the bottom of my heart. I shall remain true to this vow in life and death." She asked Li Longji, "Who will be our witness tonight?"

Li Longji thought a while and pointed to the sky, "The Cowherd and the Weaving Maid that shine beside the Milky Way can be our witnesses."

Moved by this the Cowherd said to the Weaving Maid, "See, my lady, how devoted the Tang emperor and Lady Yang are to each other. We lovers in heaven should watch over lovers on earth as we are entrusted to do. As they have asked us to witness their secret vow of love, we should protect them."

"There is a sad fate ahead of them; they will soon be separated by death. If they remain true, we can bring them together again."

"You are right. But now the night is nearly done and we must go back to our palace." The Cowherd and the Weaving Maid left hand in hand.

比。只怕日久恩疏，难偕白头到老。若能长久，死也值得。”泪水不断落下。

李隆基举起衣袖为她擦干泪水，说道：“妃子，不要伤感。朕与你的恩情，岂是一般等闲能比的！”

“既蒙陛下如此情深，不如趁此七夕之夜，就在双星之下，赐给盟约，以坚终始之念。”

李隆基倒也爽快应允：“朕和你焚香立誓去。”说着，牵着杨玉环走向案前。李隆基上了一炷香，与杨玉环同时拜了一拜：“双星在上，我李隆基与杨玉环，情重恩深，愿世世生生共为夫妇，永不相离，如背此盟，双星鉴之。”盟罢，李隆基又作一揖，说道：“在天愿为比翼鸟。”杨玉环拜了一拜，应道：“在地愿为连理枝。”两人又同声道：“天长地久有时尽，此恨绵绵无绝期。”杨玉环又转身向李隆基拜谢：“深感陛下情重，今夕之盟，妾生死都要坚守。”继而又问李隆基：“今夕之盟有谁可以作证？”

李隆基沉思一番，指着上苍：“银河两岸的牛郎、织女双星可证。”

牛郎闻言，不禁十分感动，对织女说：“你看唐天子与杨娘娘，好不恩爱，我与你既然缔结天上良缘，又专司人间爱恋，他们两个既向我们设盟，须要保佑他们。”

“只是他们两个将要遭逢一场劫难，免不了生离死别。若果他们不背今日之盟，咱们一定要让他们重聚。”

“言之有理。你看，夜色将尽，我们回斗牛宫去吧。”牛郎说罢，便与织女携手同下。

Chapter Nine

Fanyang Rebellion

An Lushan, prince of Dongping Prefecture, was made military governor of Fanyang and left the capital after the emperor mediated in a dispute between him and the prime minister, Yang Guozhong. The two, one a civil and the other a military official, were incompatible.

Though appointed a prince, An Lushan had started his career as a military man and felt constrained in the capital where he was unable to realize his ambitions. Now at the frontier, far from the court, he could act independently and do as he wished — plot to seize the throne.

There were 32 districts under the jurisdiction of the Fanyang military governor. Half the district commanders had been Hans and the others were Tartars. As the two nationalities had different characteristics, An Lushan found it hard to work with them and he presented a memorial to the emperor asking if he could substitute Tartar chiefs for the Chinese generals. Li Longji approved his request. Now An Lushan had under him Tartar chiefs and generals and they had become his confidants.

Of the 32 generals the fiercest were He Qiannian in the east, Cui Qianyou in the west, Gao Xiuyan in the south, and Shi Siming in the north and they were the closest to An Lushan. When autumn came and the men and the horses were fit, it was time to drill and train. An Lushan ordered the four generals to take their men hunting and they followed his command.

Did An Lushan actually send them hunting? No. It was a pretext for drilling and training his men. He inspected his troops and would launch the rebellion when the time came. Naturally the four generals knew what was on his mind and each trained his men to be like fierce tigers and brave dragons. An Lushan was happy to see this and knew that he was prepared and that he could accomplish what he wanted. He murmured to himself, "Tang emperor, Tang emperor, there is no way that you could stop my men and horses!"

第九章
范阳叛变

东平郡王安禄山因与丞相杨国忠积不相能，形同水火。李隆基为了调处文武，将他放出朝去，任范阳节度使。安禄山本是武弁出身，在朝中虽身为王爵，但终觉平生抱负未能大展，事事遇到掣肘，处处受到拘束。如今远离朝廷，终算跳出樊笼，可任意行事。

范阳节度使下辖三十二路将官，原来一半是汉人，一半为番人。安禄山不能完全将他们倚为腹心，寄以重任。因此，他奏请李隆基，准他将三十二路将官一律改由番人充任，李隆基居然允其所请。如今大小将官全都是番人，也都成为他的心腹爪牙了。在这三十二路将官中，尤其以范阳镇东路将官何千年、西路将官崔乾祐、南路将官高秀岩、北路将官史思明最是凶猛勇武，也最是安禄山倚为重镇的心腹将领。如今秋高气爽，人强马壮，正好演习武艺。安禄山乃吩咐这四路将官召集各路兵丁，前往沙地，围场角猎一番。

其实，安禄山这厮哪里是围捕野兽？无非是借口捕猎，实则操练人马，检阅自家实力，待机发动叛乱而已。这四大将领，自然知道安禄山的心事，在角猎中无不尽力亮相，各逞其能。安禄山看了他们的表现，不禁心花怒放，知道自家的羽翼已丰，大事可图，暗自念叨："唐天子，唐天子，你怎挡得住俺的兵马哩！"

As the saying goes, if you don't wish anyone to know what you've done, it is better not to have done it in the first place. Someone was aware of An Lushan's activity. It was Guo Ziyi, the newly-appointed governor of Lingwu. When he had first met An Lushan in the capital, he realized that he was a rebel and harbored ill intent. The emperor, however, trusted him and made him military governor of Fanyang, which was like letting the tiger return to the mountain. Guo Ziyi was even more worried when he learned that Tartar generals had been appointed. After he took up his new post, Guo Ziyi became aware that Lingwu was a place of great strategic importance and should be well defended. In the meantime he sent scouts to Fanyang to find out what was happening so that he could take precautions.

Guo Ziyi was sitting in the hall thinking when an attendant reported the return of a scout. He summoned him in at once and said, "Scout, you've been back there?"

"Yes, governor. I gathered a great amount of important information and returned as quickly as possible to report to you."

Discreetly, Guo Ziyi asked his attendants to close the door and said, "Step forward. Tell me, what is An Lushan's military strength? How powerful is his army?"

"My lord, when I reached Fanyang, I found a host of army tents, numerous spears and swords, and military curfew is strictly observed."

Guo Ziyi interrupted him, "What is An Lushan doing now?"

"He has dismissed his Chinese generals and appointed Tartars in their places. Pretending to hunt each day, they in fact improve their horsemanship."

"What else?" Guo Ziyi knew about this and was anxious to find out what new moves An Lushan had made.

"You would scarcely suspect such treacherous behavior. By underhand and sinister means he has rallied the barbarians and secretly gathered outlaws and criminals; many are hiding in his lair."

This surprised Guo Ziyi, who said, "Ah! Indeed! But has no one informed the government of this?"

"I heard that a month ago someone in the capital accused him of plotting rebellion and the emperor secretly sent a eunuch to Fanyang to watch him. But when An Lushan met the envoy, he pretended to be stupid and behaved politely, bribing him to say nothing. The eunuch was happy. He returned to court and completely cleared An Lushan of every charge.

俗话说得好，若要人不知，除非己莫为。安禄山的一举一动，也有人注意。这就是新任灵武太守郭子仪。以前在长安，初次看见安禄山时，郭子仪就认为此人生就一副反相，而所作所为又显然包藏祸心。偏偏圣上相信他，命他出任范阳节度使，无异是放虎归山。郭子仪自升任新职以来，每每想到灵武地方，乃是军事重镇，宜严密防守。同时不断派出精细的哨卒，前往范阳打听消息，以作未雨绸缪之计，免得变生肘腋，措手无及。正当郭子仪坐在大堂上沉思之际，忽报探子已回来，他立即召见："探子，你回来了么？"

"是，回禀大人，小的打听了许多重要消息。"

郭子仪处事谨慎，听说有重大消息，立即吩咐左右侍从将仪门关了，然后方对探子说："把你探得的安禄山军情说给俺听。"

"禀告老爷，范阳到处是营帐，密密麻麻，刀枪弓箭，号令不断。"

"那安禄山在边关，近日做何勾当？"郭子仪直截了当地问道。

"他裁去了汉将，任用了番人。每天都在跃马弯刀，说是打猎，看样子是在操练兵马。"

"还有什么举动？"郭子仪原就知道这些，迫不及待地要了解安禄山最近的动静。

"他的贼心真难逆料，心肠又极为歹毒。除了诱使番将成为心腹以处，还招买四方亡命之徒，藏在营帐中。"

郭子仪吃了一惊："有这样的事！难道朝臣中没有一人奏告么？"

"听说一个月之前，京中有人告称安禄山有谋反之意，万岁爷暗中派了一个太监到范阳察看他的动静。那安禄山见了这钦命太监，礼数周到，小心伺候，假装痴呆，虚作老实；又把大量的金银财宝送给太监，不惜工本贿赂收买，那个太监十分高兴，回朝奏道安

Now the emperor trusts him implicitly and had the informer sent to An's camp as punishment. Who dares to breathe a word against him any more?"

Guo Ziyi sighed and said, "What will this lead to?"

"Recently the prime minister presented a memorial to the throne, which declared that An Lushan's treason was obvious and asked His Majesty to have him executed. An Lushan heard of it and was a bit worried. But the emperor declared that he was loyal and told the prime minister to stop suspecting him. When An Lushan heard of it, he laughed aloud and said he would destroy the all powerful minister."

Guo Ziyi said, "So he wants to destroy the prime minister! That means he is ready to rebel. How is it that I have never seen the memorial from the prime minister in the bulletin?"

The scout said, "It was marked confidential and was not published in the bulletin; the prime minister had a copy sent to An Lushan to goad him into revolting."

This made Guo Ziyi angry and he said, "A rebellious general at the frontier and a treacherous prime minister at the court! My anger is hard to contain!"

The scout added, "An Lushan has another scheme of presenting horses which is even more dastardly.

Guo Ziyi said, "How? Explain it to me."

"An Lushan sent his general, He Qiannian, with a memorial to the throne asking to be allowed to present three thousand horses, each of which would be accompanied by two armed guards, two trainers and one groom; that amounts to fifteen thousand men taking the horses to the capital. It would cause a huge disturbance along the way and ordinary people will suffer. Who could check them? Once these troops and horses reach Chang'an, they will cause much trouble."

Startled, Guo Ziyi said, "Ah, if he succeeds in this plan, the capital will be in danger."

"The memorial has just been sent but the emperor has not yet agreed to his request. It is obvious that An Lushan is plotting against the throne." The scout told Guo Ziyi all that he knew.

Guo Ziyi rewarded him with a jar of wine, one sheep and fifty taels of silver, as well as a month's leave. He then ordered manoeuvres the following day.

Guo Ziyi's careful defensive measures did not stop An Lushan's plot to overthrow the Tang Dynasty. To further his ambitions, An Lushan

禄山并无谋反之意。万岁爷因此深信不疑。甚至反把告奏的人，送到安禄山帐前治罪。从此哪有人再敢出首奏告？”

郭子仪听罢，只能长吁短叹：“唉，如此怎么是好！”

“前日杨丞相又上一本，说安禄山叛迹十分明显，请皇上赶紧加以处决。那安禄山知有这一奏本，倒也有些害怕。哪曾想到圣上却说他为人诚实，要丞相不必疑他。安禄山知圣意如此，便哈哈大笑，大骂这些谗臣，咬牙切齿地说一定要清除皇帝身边的奸邪。”

郭子仪更是吃惊：“呀，他要清君之侧，这不是造反又是为何？杨丞相的奏本，朝报上怎没有见到？”

探子答道：“杨丞相的奏本，是密本，原不在朝报上登载的。只因杨丞相要激反安禄山，特命人抄送给他的。”

郭子仪闻言大怒：“唉，外有造反的藩将，内有奸诈的丞相，真令人怒发冲冠！”

探子继续报告：“小人还打听得这安禄山近日还有献马一事！”

“什么献马？你快明白说来。”

“安禄山派何千年进表，奏称向朝廷献马三千匹，每一匹有武装士兵二人，骑兵二人，供给牧草的士兵一人，三千匹马就有一万五千人护送入京。如此计施行，一旦入了京城，不把朝廷闹翻了天！”

郭子仪大惊失色：“呀，此事如行，京城危急了！”

“这本方才奏进，圣旨未下。只是从这事件也不难看出安禄山这家伙的狼子野心。”探子一口气把打听到的军情细细禀报。

郭子仪一面犒赏他一坛酒、一头羊，五十两银子，着他休息一月；一面吩咐中军官，传令众军士，明日教场操练。

尽管郭子仪用心防守，也阻扼不住安禄山吞并李唐王朝的野

had entered into a league with the tribes of the north and rallied outlaws and vagabonds from all parts of the empire. He gave them military training and waited for the time. As Li Longji had always trusted him, he intended to revolt only after his death. Yang Guozhong kept warning the emperor saying that he was disloyal and asked to have him executed. Although the emperor did not listen to Yang Guozhong, An was vulnerable because he was far away at the frontier while Yang was present at the court. For this reason An could not postpone the revolt too long, as sooner or later he would be stabbed in the back. Acting on this An Lushan ordered his troops to march on the capital, regardless of the consequences.

At first An Lushan dared not show his hand and employed deception by forging a decree in the emperor's name. The decree ordered him to march secretly to the capital with his army and kill the prime minister. By this means he would seize the capital and ordinary people would not realize that his ambition was to overthrow the Tang Dynasty.

The situation in the frontier was critical, and urgent memorials about An Lushan's rebellion were detained by ministers in power. The country had been at peace for a long time and civil officials had become indolent and officers frivolous. When war suddenly broke out, no one knew how to deal with it properly, and in a hurry, Geshu Han, a retired general, once working as a military general in Hexi and Longyou, was appointed deputy marshal and was responsible for the defence of Tongguan Pass, a place of strategic importance as it guarded the route to the capital.

Although a deputy marshal, Geshu Han could not make independent decisions; he had to listen to a eunuch appointed as an army inspector and sent by the court. When An Lushan's army arrived at the Pass they were opposed by a weak Tang force. The rebellious army was large and strong and under the circumstances Geshu Han thought it the best to defend the city by closing the city gates which would make it impossible for it to be taken quickly or easily. But the army inspector insisted that they fight and Geshu Han had no choice but to go out and fight as best he could. They were no match and An's officers captured him after a few skirmishes. As a result of the surrender Tongguan Pass was lost. Ecstatic An Lushan led his irresistible force on towards Chang'an.

The love between Li Longji and Yang Yuhuan deepened after that day they bathed together in the Huaqing Pool and later made a secret vow in the Palace of Eternal Youth. The emperor completely neglected state

心。为了实现此愿,安禄山先后联络塞上诸少数民族部落,招纳天下亡命之徒,练兵百万,待时而动。只因李隆基对他十分信任,又极为看重，他想待李隆基身后再起兵举事，哪知丞相杨国忠屡次揭露他的叛迹,要皇上立即加以诛戮。天子虽然未听从,但自家在边关,杨国忠却在朝内,若不早早起兵,迟早免不了要受到暗算。因此,安禄山便不顾一切地立即起兵向京城进发。

起始，安禄山并未公然打出反唐旗号，他假造了皇上给他的敕书,号称奉有密旨,入朝除去君王之侧的奸佞杨国忠。其实,他是借此掩饰自已反唐之心，同时欺骗天下百姓，好让他趁机攻入长安,夺取唐室江山。

边关形势急转直下，封封告急文书，均被截留在朝廷大臣手中。由于太平时久,文恬武嬉,突然乱起,措手不及,一时也派遣不出精兵勇将来,拣来挑去,只有做过河西、陇右两镇节度使的哥舒翰可以充任。不过他早已年老多病,在家休养。只因军情危急,便又重新起用他为兵马副元帅,率领一支军队防守入京咽喉之地潼关。

哥舒翰虽被授命为副帅,但却有内侍为监军,事事掣肘,处处作梗,事权不专,难有作为。不日之间,安禄山叛军已打到潼关之下。哥舒翰主张闭关自守,安禄山急攻,一时也破不了关。可是内侍却主张出关逐敌，逼着哥舒翰出战。哥舒翰无奈，只得拼死迎敌，他这个老将哪是安禄山帐前凶猛如虎的众将军的对手？不消几个回合,就被擒拿。哥舒翰乃献关投降,安禄山大喜过望,挥动大小三军,势如破竹,一路杀奔长安而来。

李隆基自从与杨玉环于华清池共浴，在长生殿订盟以后，感

affairs and knew nothing of the seizure of the Tongguan Pass by An Lushan. He just spent the days and nights with Lady Yang.

Autumn comes when summer goes. Autumn painted the imperial garden in many colors; willow leaves turned yellow, the duckweed grew less green and the red lotus shed all of its petals. The cassia flowers were in bloom. Clouds drifted across the blue sky and high up wild geese were flying. It was a time to appreciate natural scenery and the emperor ordered Gao Lishi to prepare a small feast in the imperial garden. He and Lady Yang visited it.

They arrived holding each others' hand in a carriage pushed by eunuchs. Gao Lishi was waiting to greet them at the west gate and said, "May it please Your Majesty and Your Ladyship to alight here." He helped them down and withdrew as there were no new orders from the emperor.

"My love, let's take a walk."

"As you wish."

Hand in hand they wandered among flowers and trees. There was a cool gust of wind and a row of trees cast long shadows by the railings. Swallows still lingered by their nests, and a duck and a drake slept on the pond. They walked slowly, the only people in the garden.

"Gao Lishi, bring wine! I shall drink a few cups with Her Ladyship."

Gao Lishi came at once and said, "The feast is already spread and ready in the pavilion. Please step over there."

They forwent the sumptuous food that was usually cooked in the imperial garden and Li Longji ordered a simple meal of vegetables and fruit. He dismissed the imperial musicians and asked Lady Yang to sing a song composed by Li Bai, while he accompanied her on the flute. It was a small feast; they did as they liked without ceremony.

In a while, words from the song, "Her dress is like a brilliant cloud ..." could be heard. The couple came to the part, "The famous flower and the beauty are delighted, and the emperor enjoys the scene with a smile," and they gazed at each other; Lady Yang was grateful for the thoughtful arrangement. She drank a few more cups and was intoxicated, intoxicated by wine and affection. She looked so lovely in that state that Li Longji could not take his eyes off her; he was drunk himself.

But extreme joy begets sorrow. The sound of drum could be heard and Gao Lishi and some eunuchs came running. The drum woke Li Longji and he said, "Where did the sound of drum come from?" No one answered. The prime minister, Yang Guozhong, rushed in, saw Gao Lishi and asked

情日渐深笃，朝政全然荒废，安禄山攻破潼关的消息，他竟然毫不知晓，依然与贵妃日夕嬉戏。

夏去秋来，御花园中秋色斑斓，柳叶添黄，苹叶减绿，红莲脱瓣，桂子初绽，长空新雁，天淡云闲，正是赏秋佳日。李隆基吩咐高力士在花园中安排小宴，要与杨玉环同游。他们俩手携手上了如意小车，被内监轻轻推向御花园。高力士早已在园门口侍候，“请万岁爷和娘娘下车。”说着，将他们扶下车来，退立一旁。

“妃子，朕与你散步一回。”“陛下请。”

李隆基便携着杨玉环同向花间树丛漫步，微风过处，凉意顿生，一廊桐阴，碧沉沉地护着回栏，树上秋燕依人，池中鸳鸯双宿，园中一片静悄悄，寂无人声，只有他们两个信步漫游。

“高力士，拿酒来，朕与娘娘小饮数杯。”

高力士闻声而上：“宴席在亭子中，请万岁爷和娘娘上宴。”

小宴全然排除了往日御厨中供应的烹龙炮凤，李隆基只点了几味脆生生的蔬菜和水果，他也不要梨园旧曲，只要妃子为他清唱李白写词、李龟年谱曲的《清平调》，自己吹笛伴奏。两人一唱一吹，纯然是清游、小宴，任性而为，不讲排场。

一时，“云想衣裳花想容……”歌声曼长，笛声悠扬，待唱至“名花倾园两相欢，长得君王带笑看”之际，两人四目彼此注视，特别是杨玉环，眼波流动着无限深情，为皇上的这种精心安排而感激不已，不禁多饮了几杯，沉醉了，沉醉于美酒，也沉醉于纯情，醉态可掬，娇怯衤伕，益发动人，李隆基观赏再三，也不禁沉醉了。

真是乐极生悲，正当他们沉浸在黑甜梦乡中，忽然宫中传来一阵急切的击鼓声，高力士带着内监赶了出来。李隆基自然也被

loudly, "Where is the emperor?"

"In the imperial garden."

Yang Guozhong continued walking and said, "The situation is serious. I must go straight in." Gao Lishi followed him and as soon as Yang Guozhong saw Li Longji he said, "Your Majesty, I have had bad news! An Lushan has revolted and his army has entered the Tongguan Pass. He is marching on the capital."

Li Longji was alarmed and said, "What of the troops defending the Pass?"

"General Geshu Han was defeated and has surrendered to the rebels."

Li Longji did not know what to do and stammered, "Ah, ah, ah, Geshu Han has been defeated. How is it that An Lushan has rebelled? He must have left Fanyang, taken Luoyang rapidly and then marched on to Tongguan Pass. The news strikes dread into my heart and I quake with fear.... What plans do you have to resist them?"

Yang Guozhong had calmed down and said, "In the past I repeatedly warned Your Majesty that An would rebel, but you would not listen to me. Now what I predicted has happened. At the moment we are powerless to resist him. For the time being Your Majesty should go to western Sichuan and wait there until the generals from the provinces rally to defend the throne."

Li Longji had nothing to contribute himself and said, "Very well, very well. I'll do as you say. Put out the order for all princes and ministers to prepare to accompany me." Yang Guozhong left and Li Longji spoke to Gao Lishi. "Quickly order Chen Yuanli, Commander of the Imperial Guards, to muster three thousand men to escort us." Gao Lishi left.

A eunuch spoke out, "May it please Your Majesty to return to the palace for a rest?" Li Longji paced forward and murmured, "While we were feasting merrily in the garden, I had no idea that this would happen. What shall I do? Maids, has Lady Yang slept?"

"Yes, she is fast asleep."

"Do not wake her. We shall wake her when we leave at dawn tomorrow. Ah, heaven, how unfortunate I am to be overtaken by such a disaster and how distressing it is to think of her taking to the road with her flower like beauty!"

Early in the morning Li Longji, Yang Yuhuan and many eunuchs and palace maids left the palace. Ministers including Yang Guozhong went

鼓声惊醒:“何处鼓声如此急迫?”左右也无人答话。丞相杨国忠一头闯进来,迎面碰上高力士,便高声问道:“万岁爷在哪里?”

“在御花园内。”

杨国忠边走边说:“军情紧急,只得直接进内禀报。”高力士也只能随着他一同入内。李隆基迎了出来,杨国忠一见皇上,立即禀告:“陛下,不好了。安禄山起兵造反,杀进潼关,不日就到长安了。”

李隆基大为惊异,问道:“守关将士何在?”

“哥舒翰兵败,已投降贼人了。”

李隆基闻知,顿时失了主意,结结巴巴地说:“呀,呀,呀,哥舒翰也打败了,那,那安禄山怎的顿时发了兵,占了洛阳,又破了潼关。爱卿,你,你有何退兵之策?”

杨国忠此时反倒镇静下来:“当日臣再三启奏皇上,安禄山这厮必然反叛,陛下不听,今日果应臣言。事发突然,怎能抵挡,不如圣驾暂时去西川避一避,召请各路将领前来护驾平贼。”

李隆基此刻哪有什么主意?“好,好,好,就依卿所奏,快快传旨,诸王百官,即时随朕去西川。”杨国忠领了旨意去宣颁了。李隆基又吩咐高力士:“你快传旨,令右龙武将军陈元礼,统领三千人护驾同行。”高力士奉旨去办了。

内侍趁机进言:“万岁爷先回宫休息。”李隆基边走边叹,自言自语地说道:“唉,正玩得高兴,哪知有此事变,怎么办呢——宫娥们,杨娘娘可曾睡了?”“已睡熟了。”

“不要惊醒她,等明日天亮再叫醒她同行。唉,天啊,寡人不幸,遭此播迁,连累她这般花容月貌,也要跋山涉水,真令人痛心!”

次日凌晨,李隆基挈带着贵妃杨玉环,还有许多太监、宫女紧

with the emperor and they traveled day and night heading for western Sichuan. As the capital became more and more distant they saw mountains and rivers and deserted houses with broken tiles and withered crops. There was chaos everywhere, totally unlike the Kaiyuan period. Li Longji was sad to see it.

Gao Lishi suddenly arrived. "Your Majesty, we are at Mawei Station. Would you please take a rest here." He helped Li Longji and Lady Yang alight and went inside. Li Longji spoke to Lady Yang. "I was wrong in believing the scoundrel An who has forced us to make this move. There is no point in regretting it. The only thing I feel sorry about is that you, my love, have to take this hard journey with me. There is nothing else I can do."

Although tired and not properly dressed, Lady Yang kept up proprieties and said, "I, your servant, shall follow you and not shrink from any hardship. I only hope that the rebels will soon be defeated so that Your Majesty can return to the capital."

Let us leave the pair pitying and consoling each other. The three thousand imperial guards led by Commander Chen Yuanli had enjoyed a good position and had lived in comfort. Now that they experienced hardships they complained and grumbled. At Mawei Station they ran about shouting and sighing and plotting in groups. Finally the general cry was that An Lushan's rebellion and the flight of the emperor from the capital were all Yang Guozhong's fault. If the treacherous minister was not put to death they would not escort His Majesty even if he threatened to kill them.

Chen Yuanli heard the commotion and came out of his quarters and said at the top of his voice, "Stop shouting and pitch camp quietly. I shall report to the emperor and ask for his orders." The commotion died down but soon started again.

Before Chen Yuanli had reported to the emperor, small groups of soldiers carrying swords were searching for Yang Guozhong. They shouted out that he had been the cause of the trouble and was now secretly scheming with western tribesmen. They vowed to kill him. The leader of the group cried out, "Whoever wants to kill Yang Guozhong join us!"

Yang Guozhong ran but the guards surrounded him and there was nowhere to hide. Before you could drink a cup of tea he was arrested and without any further ado his head was chopped off.

In the inner room the roaring startled the emperor. He called out, "Gao Lishi, who is shouting outside? Call Commander Chen here at once."

紧跟随离宫出行。一班大臣如丞相杨国忠也随驾西迁。跋山涉水，日夜兼程，向西川进发，行了一程又一程，渐渐地远离长安了。但成都仍远，一路上只见剩山残水，空舍崩瓦，人烟稀少，庄稼枯萎，一派纷乱，哪有开元盛世景象！李隆基睹此现实，也不免怅然。

高力士忽然上前奏道："此处已是马嵬坡，请万岁爷在此暂住休憩。"奏罢，就侍候李隆基与杨玉环下马，走进驿舍。坐下后，李隆基关心地对杨玉环说："寡人不道，误宠逆臣，以致有这次迁徙，后悔也来不及了。妃子，只是带累你一路劳顿，颇觉不安，又无可奈何！"

杨玉环虽然劳累之极，衣冠不整，钗横鬓乱，但仍不失礼仪，回答道："臣妾此际自应随驾而行，怎敢辞劳。只愿早早破贼，皇上能及时还都便好。"

不说这两人你怜我惜，诉说心思。那右龙武将军陈元礼率领的三千禁军，昔日在京城养尊处优，何等威风，哪曾受过这般苦楚？早已军心浮动，怨言四出了。到了马嵬坡驻扎下来后，更是彼此叹息，四处串联，终于闹将起来，一呼众应，齐声吼道："安禄山造反，万岁爷西迁，都是杨国忠弄权激成的，假若不斩此贼，我等死不护驾！"

陈元礼听到鼓噪之声，立即出帐询问究竟，大声安抚道："众军不要吼叫，暂时进营休息。待我奏过圣上，自有主张。"鼓噪之声倒暂时停止，但不一会儿又高涨起来。

陈元礼还未及进内奏禀圣上，早有许多军士提着刀，到处搜寻，一批批地进入营帐，又三五成群地走出，七嘴八舌地高声谈论、叫喊："杨国忠专权误国，如今又与吐蕃勾结，我等与他誓不两立。"为头的军士招呼众人道："要杀杨国忠的，快跟我们前去！"

Gao Lishi met Chen Yuanli at the door. Chen knelt before the emperor and said, "Long live the emperor!"

"Why are the soldiers shouting?" The emperor was apprehensive.

Chen Yuanli spoke truthfully. "Your Majesty, by trying to take over the reins and usurp all power Yang Guozhong endangered the state. When the guards discovered that he had been secretly negotiating with western tribesmen, they were indignant and killed him."

"What!" Li Longji panicked and could not utter a word. When Lady Yang heard it she turned her head to wipe the tears away. Li Longji thought for a moment. He had to accept what had happened and said to Chen Yuanli, "Very well. Give orders to resume our journey." He knew that it was most important that they reached western Sichuan in time.

Chen Yuanli came out and announced, "His Majesty pardons the guards for killing the prime minister and orders you to set out once again."

杨国忠抱头鼠窜，但在众军士包围之下，无处藏身，一时成为过街老鼠，人人喊打。不到一杯茶时间，他就被捉住，不容他狡辩，“咔嚓”一刀下去，他的人头落地。

李隆基在后室，也听到喧哗之声，大惊失色：“高力士，外面为什么事如此喧嚷？快宣陈元礼进来问个明白！”

高力士领旨，走出外屋，正好陈元礼进来，叩见皇上：“臣陈元礼见驾。”

“众军士为何事呐喊？”李隆基心有疑惧地问道。

陈元礼毫不掩饰地奏道：“臣启陛下，杨国忠专权误国，造成此次变乱，又与吐蕃勾结，因此激怒六军战士，他们竟自将杨国忠杀了。”

“呀，有这样的事！”李隆基惊恐交加，一时说不出话来。那杨玉环闻知兄长被害，顿时悲痛万分，转过身去，不断拭泪。李隆基思索片刻，只得承认已成的事实，吩咐陈元礼说：“此事就罢了。传旨赶快起驾赶路。”他知道，眼下最重要的是尽快到达成都。

陈元礼奉命出来宣旨：“众军士听着：圣旨下了，赦你们擅自诛杀杨国忠之罪，赶快起行。”

馬嵬坡

Chapter Ten

Death at Mawei Station

Li Longji had misread the situation. After killing Yang Guozhong he thought that the soldiers would be pacified; he had pardoned them. The soldiers, however, were restless and called out together, "Though Yang Guozhong is dead, his cousin Lady Yang is still with the emperor. Until she is killed, we will not go a step further!"

Chen Yuanli had to make a report to Li Longji. He knew that the soldiers were afraid that Lady Yang would later take revenge for Yang Guozhong's death. He advised the emperor, "I hope Your Majesty will put aside your love of Lady Yang and have her executed to satisfy the guards."

"Aya! How could they request this?" Li Longji was thoroughly alarmed. Yang Yuhuan grieved; she shivered and tugged the emperor's sleeve. Li Longji said indignantly, "If Yang Guozhong was guilty, he has already paid with his life. But his cousin only served in the inner palace. What can the army suspect her of?"

Chen Yuanli could only say, "Your Majesty is right. Yet the troops are in an ugly mood. What can we do?"

Yang Yuhuan listened attentively and was sad and frightened. She said, "Your Majesty, this has taken me by surprise and I feel distressed. As I grieve for my cousin's death, I find that I too am involved. I must have been fated to suffer. I beg you, sire, give me up at once." She was choking and could say nothing.

Helpless, Li Longji consoled her, "My love, don't be sad...." From outside the cry came, "We shall not move a step unless Lady Yang is executed!"

Chen Yuanli knew that the situation was urgent and said, "Though Lady Yang is innocent, Your Majesty, she is the prime minister's cousin. As long as she is at your side the troops will feel unsafe. Only when the troops feel safe will your own safety be assured. I hope Your Majesty will

第十章
马嵬死别

李隆基对形势的估计仍是不足，以为赦免了众军士诛杀杨国忠之罪后，便可稳定军心。哪知众军士仍不放心，齐声呐喊："国忠虽诛，但贵妃还在。不杀贵妃，誓不护驾。"陈元礼只得入内见皇上，如实禀报，其实他也知道众军士是担心杨贵妃事后算帐，他劝皇上说："望陛下割去一时私恩，将娘娘正法，以慰军心。"

李隆基大感意外，杨玉环更是慌张得牵着李隆基衣袖，吓得簌簌直抖。李隆基不无气愤地辩解道："杨国忠即使有罪，如今已被劫杀。妃子一直在深宫随驾，又有什么事会使众军士怀疑？"

陈元礼说："圣上的话极其明白，只是军心已变，也无良策！"

杨玉环听到此际，既伤心，又惊恐，"陛下，这桩事太意外，臣妾兄长遭了劫杀，未曾想到又牵连臣妾。想来此事是前生所定，臣妾薄命，应受此罚。望皇上就舍弃臣妾吧，……"说到此际，已泣不成声。

李隆基只能无力地劝慰："妃子，你先不要悲伤……"一句话未了，外面又传来："不杀贵妃，死不护驾"的叫喊。

陈元礼知道事情紧迫，不能不将此事说得更彻底些："臣启禀陛下，贵妃虽然无罪，杨国忠是其亲兄，今在陛下左右，军心不安。如军心安，则陛下也安。这道理，愿陛下三思。"

consider this carefully."

Li Longji's mind was in a muddle and for a moment he was unable to say anything. Yang Yuhuan clung to his robes crying sadly, "I can't bear to leave Your Majesty.... I never expected them to be so cruel!" Li Longji sobbed and the shouts outside became louder. He took hold of her and said, "My love, I don't know what to do."

Seeing that nothing had happened the soldiers surrounded the station making an uproar. Gao Lishi had to urge the emperor. "Your Majesty, the troops have besieged the station. If we hesitate, they may become desperate. What is to be done?"

Li Longji knew that there was no other avenue for him to explore. He could only save the situation by giving up Lady Yang and he said, "Chen Yuanli, quickly pacify the troops while I find a way out."

After Chen Yuanli left Li Longji and Yang Yuhuan clung to each other and cried; both knew that it was time for them to part forever. Li Longji sighed and said, "It would have been better for you to have loved an ordinary person rather than an emperor. Then you could have lived till your hair turned white. How can we abandon the love between us so suddenly?"

Yang Yuhuan shared his feelings but the situation forced her to choose death. So she knelt down and said, "Your Majesty has shown me so much favor that even if I kill myself I cannot repay your kindness. The situation is desperate and I beg you to allow me to commit suicide to pacify the troops. Then you will arrive at western Sichuan safely and I shall die comforted." She fell to the ground weeping.

Sorely afflicted Li Longji held her to his bosom. He said, "How can you say that, my love? If you die, what are my throne and empire to me? I would rather lose my empire than abandon you."

"I will never forget Your Majesty's kindness. But things have come to such a pass that there is no other way out. If I hesitate any longer we may all be destroyed and then my guilt will be greater. Please give me up and preserve your empire."

Hearing what they said Gao Lishi sobbed in sympathy, but under the circumstances he had to remind the emperor of his duties. Kneeling he said, "Since Lady Yang shows such spirit and wishes to sacrifice herself, I beg Your Majesty to think of the empire and force yourself to agree to her request."

The cries outside became louder and louder and Li Longji knew

李隆基此刻心乱如麻，一时也说不出话来，杨玉环则牵衣痛哭："叫臣妾怎舍得皇上呀……真未想到这样的强霸！"李隆基也不禁抽泣。外边军士叫喊之声，声声刺耳，他一把抱住杨玉环："妃子，这形势真叫我难以招架啊！"

外面军士见内里一直无动静，更加浮躁不安，蠢蠢欲动，将驿舍围得个密不透风。高力士见状，也不得不进言了："万岁爷，外面军士已把驿亭包围了，若再拖延，恐有他变，怎么办？"

李隆基知今日不抛弃杨玉环，不能解脱危境，遂道："陈元礼，你快去安抚众军，朕自有道理。"

当陈元礼出外后，李隆基与杨玉环抱头痛哭，双方都知道死别之期已至，李隆基不禁叹息道："你爱上个堂堂天子，倒不如爱上个老百姓，那样还能白头偕老！咱们的恩义，怎能霎时抛去？"

杨玉环自然也有同感，但有鉴于眼前局势，不能不选择一死，乃跪在李隆基面前，说道："臣妾受皇上深恩，杀身难报。今事势危急，望皇上赐妾自尽，以定军心，妾死犹生啊！"说罢，又哭倒在地。

李隆基伤心至极，一把将她搂在怀中："妃子，说哪里话！你若死去，朕虽有天子之尊、四海之富，要它有什么用！宁可国破家亡，决不舍弃你！"

"陛下，你对臣妾的恩重，令臣妾难忘。但事情到此地步，无路求生，倘若再留恋，玉石俱焚。望陛下舍弃臣妾，以保天下。"

高力士听了两人的哭泣诉说，也不禁一洒同情之泪。但事已至此，他不能不提醒皇上，便跪下进言道："娘娘既然自愿慷慨捐生，望万岁爷以天下社稷为重，勉强割恩罢。"

驿外此刻呐喊之声更加紧急，李隆基也深知只有此路可行

that this was the only thing that they could do. He sobbed, stamped heavily and said, "Well, well, so be it then! If she insists, I cannot forbid her. Let Her Ladyship do as she thinks right!" Weeping he went to another room and covered his face.

Although she had made up her mind to die, when Yang Yuhuan heard this she was sad and cried out bitterly, "Long live the emperor," before falling to the ground. Gao Lishi shouted to the soldiers outside, "Listen men! His Majesty has ordered Lady Yang to commit suicide."

"Long live the emperor! Long, long live the emperor!" The troops were relieved.

After calming the troops Gao Lishi helped Yang Yuhuan to rise. She murmured sadly, "I thought that we would live till we were old. Who would have expected that soon we will be parted forever or that I was going to die for the emperor?" When they walked past a shrine she wanted to go in and pray. Gao Lishi did not have the heart to refuse the request of a person about to die. Kneeling before the image of Buddha Lady Yang said, "Great Buddha! My sins are many; have mercy on my soul!" She wept openly.

Gao Lishi knelt down and said, "May Your Ladyship enter paradise! Have you any last commands for me?"

"Gao Lishi, the emperor is growing old. When I am dead, you will be the only one who can understand him. You must look after him and tell him not to think of me any more."

Her sincerity moved Gao Lishi and he said, "I will, my lady."

"Gao Lishi, there is something else." She unfastened the hairpin from her hair and took out the jewelry box. She said, "The emperor gave me these to pledge his love. Bury them with my body and be sure not to forget!"

Gao Lishi took them and said, "Yes, my lady."

She knew that the time for death was near and wept again. Chen Yuanli and a few soldiers arrived. He ignored her distress and said, "Lady Yang has been ordered to commit suicide. Why is she still here delaying His Majesty's journey?" The soldiers pressed forward and Gao Lishi who stretched out his hand to stop them said, "Keep back! Lady Yang is about to die."

Yang Yuhuan was angry and said, "Ah, Chen Yuanli! Why don't you pitch yourself against the rebels instead of against me?" The soldiers pushed forward and Gao Lishi did his best to stop them.

了，痛哭，顿足，近乎吼道：“妃子既然执意如此，朕也做不得主了。高力士，只听娘娘的主意吧！”说罢，掩面抽泣，转身向别屋走去。

杨玉环虽说决心一死，但乍听到李隆基竟然同意，也十分伤心，一面口称‘万岁’谢恩，一面哭倒在地。高力士对驿亭外高声叫道：“众军士听着，万岁爷已有旨，赐娘娘自尽了！”“万岁，万岁，万万岁！”众军士顿时感到压在心头的一块巨石已被搬去。

高力士安抚住军心，就扶着杨玉环向里屋走去，杨玉环仍然伤心地自言自语地诉说：“原以为可以百年偕好，哪知死别就在眼前，臣妾为君王尽命了。”不觉已走进佛堂，跪倒在佛像之前：“佛爷，佛爷！你念杨玉环罪孽深重，望我佛超度！”拜罢，又放声痛哭。

高力士跪下说：“愿娘娘好好升天，有什么话儿，就吩咐奴才。”

“高力士，圣上年事已高，我死之后，只有你是旧人，能体会他的心意，须小心奉侍他。再请代为转奏圣上，今后不要再记念我了。”

这番深情厚义的话，倒说得高力士伤心，答道：“奴才知道了。”

“高力士，我还有一句话，”说着，她卸下头上的金钗，取出怀中的钿盒，递与他：“这一对金钗，一枚钿盒，是圣上定情所赐。你拿它为我殉葬，万万不可遗失。”高力士接过钗、盒，答道：“奴才晓得。”

诸事交待已毕，杨玉环知道绝命之期已至，不禁又放声痛哭。陈元礼不管这些，领了几个军士走来问道：“贵妃既奉旨赐死，怎么如此不决断，影响圣驾上路！”身后的军士蜂涌向前，高力士赶紧伸手拦阻：“众军士不得无礼，杨娘娘即刻归天。”

杨玉环不禁有些气愤，有气无力地说道：“唉，陈元礼，陈元礼，你的兵威为什么不指向逆寇，却用来逼奴自杀！”众军士听了又欲上前。高力士有些招架不住，但仍尽力维持。

Yang Yuhuan looked round. There was a pear tree. She removed her white silk belt and sighed, "I will end my life here with the pear tree." She bowed to heaven and said, "Yang Yuhuan thanks the emperor for his past kindness; we shall never meet again. Although my body will lie in the earth, my spirit will follow the imperial pennants!" She then hung herself.

Chen Yuanli shouted to the soldiers, "Lady Yang has died, men, withdraw!"

Gao Lishi took down the silk belt which Lady Yang had used to hang herself with and took it to Li Longji. "Your Majesty, Lady Yang is dead."

Li Longji looked dazed and said nothing. Gao Lishi tried again. "Lady Yang is dead, sire. Here is the silk belt with which she hanged herself." Only then did Li Longji accept the fact and he cried bitterly, "Aya, my love! my love! How can I bear this?" He slumped onto a chair and said, "She was like a peach blossom, but now...."

Gao Lishi showed him the hairpin and the box and said, "Her Ladyship asked me to bury these two articles with her." Li Longji looked at them and recalled the pledge of love they made in the Palace of Eternal Youth. He cried aloud.

"Your Majesty, where shall we find a coffin at such a time?"

"Never mind that. Wrap her in a silk quilt and bury her deeply for the time being. Mark the place well so that we can remove her body later. The hairpin and the box can be fastened to her clothes." He covered his face and cried out, "I shall never see her again in this life."

Gao Lishi made these arrangements. Chen Yuanli entered and knelt down. "May it please Your Majesty, your horse is ready."

Li Longji stamped and said bitterly, "What do I care if I never reach western Sichuan?"

Outside trumpets sounded, men cried out and horses neighed; the troops were ready to go west. Gao Lishi knew that although the emperor was disconsolate he had to move on to western Sichuan. He came in quietly, advised him and helped him mount his horse. Along the road they encountered thick mists, cold winds and yellow dust which together with the long distances compounded Li Longji's sorrow and bitterness.

After Yang Yuhuan hung herself General Chen Yuanli led the guards to escort Li Longji to go to western Sichuan. They were worn out many

杨玉环看到庭边一棵梨树，便从腰间取出一条白绸，叹道：“罢,罢,这一株梨树,便是我杨玉环结果之处了。”说罢,又深深一拜:“臣妾杨玉环叩谢圣恩,从今不再相见了,我将命丧黄泉,但妾的灵魂只依傍着圣上啊！”哭罢,投环自缢而死。陈元礼见杨玉环已死,转身对众军士高呼道:“贵妃已死,众军速速退出！”

高力士取下杨贵妃自缢的白绸，边哭边走，见了李隆基回禀道:“启禀万岁爷,杨娘娘归天了。”李隆基怔怔地盯住他,说不出话来,高力士再禀奏道:“杨娘娘归天了。自缢的白绸在此。”李隆基这才醒悟过来,失声高呼:“哎哟,妃子,妃子,这不痛煞寡人！”倒在椅上抽抽答答地说道:“唉,当年桃花般的美貌,如今……”

高力士取出金钗、钿盒说道：“这两件东西，是娘娘吩咐殉葬的。”李隆基睹物伤情,情不自禁地又痛哭起来。

“陛下,这军马仓猝之间,如何准备衣棺？”

“也只得从权处理，可用一床绸被将杨娘娘包裹好，需要深埋,记好地点,以待日后改葬。这两件钗、盒就系在娘娘衣上吧。”交待完毕,掩面失声:“今生今世又怎能再见她！”

高力士去处置娘娘后事了，陈元礼进来禀道：“请陛下起驾西行。”李隆基顿足,恨恨地说:“咳,我便不去西川也算不得什么！”

驿外军号声声,人声嘈杂,马声嘶吼,都准备起行了。高力士知道李隆基发狠归发狠，西川还是要去的，便悄悄地进来，劝说一番后,扶他上了马,一齐向成都进发。一路上只见长空塞雾,寒风吹旋,黄尘扑面,路途遥远,更增加李隆基的愁思与悲苦。

杨玉环自缢马嵬坡后，右龙武将军陈元礼率领六军扈从李隆

days in the hard journey. Li Longji complained and yearned desperately for Lady Yang. At times he thought of himself as the cruelest man in the world. He was an emperor and had been unable to protect his beloved imperial concubine.

The guards marched slowly on and arrived at Fufeng where Li Longji rested in the Fengyi Palace while the soldiers camped around it.

Incessant wars in the past had emptied almost all the houses; deserted fields produced no grain. The soldiers plundered and looted all the way so that there was practically nothing left when they passed. At Fufeng no one had anything to eat. That included Li Longji.

An old peasant arrived shivering and carrying a bowl of oatmeal. He said to Gao Lishi, who was guarding the gate, "Please, sir, would you let His Majesty know that the peasant Guo Congjin has come to present oatmeal."

Gao Lishi was overjoyed; he had sent eunuchs to seek out food some time ago and they had not returned. He had been worried that the emperor would be angry. He told Guo Congjin to wait there and reported it straight away to emperor. Li Longji said at once, "Let him come in."

Guo Congjin followed Gao Lishi into the hall and he kowtowed to the emperor, saying, "Your humble subject Guo Congjin salutes Your Majesty."

"Where are you from?" asked the emperor.

"I live here, Your Majesty."

"How do you make a living?"

"I tilled the land and was happy to live here when times were peaceful; harvests were good, I had enough to eat and was clothed. Now there has been a sudden rebellion at Fanyang and I am much afraid. I heard that Your Majesty was flying to the west and feared that there was nothing for you to eat in this desolate place. I still have some oats at home, so I present you a bowl of oatmeal and hope that you will not find our simple country fare too rough or coarse."

Li Longji was moved and he was hungry. He said, "Thank you. Bring it to me, Gao Lishi."

Gao Lishi took the bowl from Guo Congjin and presented it to the emperor.

Inside the bowl was a yellow and white gruel and though the emperor was hungry he did not eat. His thoughts flew elsewhere and he murmured, "Ah, after living in luxury in the palace all these years I have never tasted

基向西川进发,仆仆风尘已非一日。李隆基一路上自怨自艾,悲苦愁思不绝于怀,有时甚至认为自家白白做了一朝天子,竟然不能保护心爱的妃子免于一死,成为千古无情之人。不管李隆基愁苦欲绝,六军将士依然继续前进,到了扶风地面。此处有座皇家别宫凤仪宫,李隆基便住进宫中休憩,六军将士各自在凤仪宫附近扎下营寨。

连年战乱,十室九空,田野荒芜,粮食无收,大军过处,更是抢掠净尽。上自皇上,下自士卒,住定下来后,无不钻头觅缝寻找可以填饱饥肠的食物。正当其时,有个老汉抖抖索索地捧了一碗麦饭,说道:“公公,烦请转奏皇上,说扶风野人郭从谨特来进饭。”

高力士闻言,欣喜异常,正是踏破铁鞋无觅处,得来全不费工夫。他一面招呼郭从谨稍待,一面三步变两步地进宫面奏,李隆基更不迟疑:“召他进来。”

紧跟着高力士,郭从谨小心翼翼地跨进宫来,拜见皇上,“草民郭从谨见驾。”“你是哪里人?”“小民自幼生在扶风,为此地人。”“何以为生?”“小民耕田为业,幸亏遭逢太平盛世,岁岁丰收,衣食不愁,岂料范阳之变骤然爆发,无限惊惶。又听说圣上西巡,心想一路上村野残破,怕圣上无食充饥,小民家中尚有稻麦半升,将它煮了一钵麦饭,特来呈献,望圣上不以野民所供粗粝怪罪。”

李隆基听了这番言语,倒也着实感动,再说腹中空空,饥肠辘辘,早已难耐,便也爽快地接受:“这倒要谢谢你了,高力士,取上来。”高力士奉命从郭从谨手中接过瓦钵,呈给李隆基。

李隆基接过瓦钵,只见钵中不干不稀、黄白相间的一大碗麦饭,尽管饥饿难耐,却未即刻吞食,而是低头沉思,又自言自语地说道:“唉,寡人长年住在深宫后殿,哪曾尝过这样的饭食!想当

anything like this. I had more than one hundred dishes of rare delicacies and fresh vegetables and fruit each day and yet I often thought them ill prepared. Who would have thought that I would have to satisfy my hunger with this? How can I swallow it?" He ate a little, sighed and put down the bowl.

Seeing that he could not eat the oatmeal, Guo Congjin said, "Your Majesty, who do you consider responsible for the trouble we are in today?"

"Who would you say?" Li Longji was surprised by the question.

"I hope you will forgive me if I speak frankly." Guo Congjin was persistent and seemed to have made up his mind.

"Don't hesitate. Go on."

"It was Yang Guozhong's fault. He relied on his relationship with Your Majesty to accept bribes and strengthen his evil power until he had corrupted the whole empire. For many years he waged a feud with An Lushan and eventually provoked An Lushan to revolt."

Li Longji defended himself saying, "How could I know of Yang Guozhong's challenge and An Lushan's rebellion?"

"An Lushan has been planning to revolt for a long time and everyone knew of his treason. Last year when someone informed on him Your Majesty had the informer put to death. After that who would risk his life to warn you?"

Li Longji had to admit to his faults and said, "Yes, I bear much of the blame. I remember when Yao Chong and Song Jing were ministers of state they gave me such good advice that I felt that my subjects from all over the country were before me and that I could see them. After they died the new ministers simply tried to seize power or curry favor with me. They were not like you, a loyal citizen."

"But if Your Majesty had not come here, what chance would I have of seeing you?"

Li Longji sighed and nodded. "I profusely regret it."

Guo Congjin saw that the emperor felt remorse and said no more. He gave a few words of consolation and took his leave.

Just then an envoy with one hundred thousand rolls of silk tribute, which had been sent by the military governor of western Sichuan and was on its way capital, arrived at Fufeng. When the envoy heard that the emperor was at Fufeng he asked Gao Lishi to report his presence to the emperor.

年，御膳房的太监，每天烹调的家荤野腥、进供的时鲜果蔬，何止百样之数！每餐要摆满一张大餐桌！还拣三挑四，嫌他调和不当。哪曾想到有今天，居然将这种麦麸用来充饥，这种饭食如何下咽！”吃了一口便丢在一旁，兀自叹息不已。

郭从谨见圣上难以下咽，便开口问道：“陛下，您可知道今日之祸落得这般下场，是谁造成的？”

“你说是谁造成的？”李隆基不免有几分诧异。

“陛下若赦臣无罪，草民当冒死直言。”郭从谨似乎早有准备，颇有几分破釜沉舟的气概。“但说不妨。”

“还不是那杨国忠！他倚恃国舅身份，纳贿招权，猖狂专断，受他祸害的遍及天壤。他与安禄山长年争斗，越演越烈，以致激反安禄山呵！”郭从谨毫无顾忌，一诉积闷。

李隆基不无辩解地说道：“杨国忠挑衅，安禄山谋反，寡人哪里知道。”“安禄山那家伙包藏祸心，天下之人无不知晓。去年有人上书揭发，陛下反将此人诛杀，谁肯再冒死进谏！”

李隆基也不得不承认：“这总怪朕的糊涂，以致如此。唉，朕记得姚崇、宋璟作丞相时，敢于直言进谏，天下民情，朝堂明白。哪知姚、宋之后，满朝臣宰，只知讨好固宠，倒不如你郭从谨一片忠心！”

“若不是陛下西行到此，敝老汉哪里能见到皇上！”

李隆基叹息，点头：“想起来真叫人后悔莫及。”

郭从谨见李隆基已极其懊悔，便不再多说，告退出来。

正当此际，西川节度使派了使臣进贡十万匹彩缎进京，闻知皇上驾幸扶风，就转到此处，来至凤仪宫前，先找到高力士，请他向皇上奏报。

Li Longji told Gao Lishi to accept the rolls of silk and sent the envoy back. He then said to Gao Lishi, "Order the guards to gather. I have something to say to them."

Chen Yuanli went inside the hall while the guards gathered outside the palace. Li Longji asked Chen Yuanli to pass a message onto the guards and he addressed them, "Soldiers, listen to me. The Fanyang rebellion was unexpected. We have traveled far to western Sichuan to avoid attacks and I thank you for your escort. Today, however, I have a proposition."

"What are Your Majesty's orders?"

Li Longji showed his human side and said, "I know that while you have been on the road to western Sichuan and you have been longing for your parents, wives and children. The journey is arduous and the road is as hard as the road to heaven. We are going to a remote destination; you are cold and hungry and have experienced every kind of hardship. I have thought about this for some time. I cannot settle with you as I am not in the capital and I have no money. Today an envoy from western Sichuan brought a hundred thousand rolls of silk tribute and I want to distribute it among you in lieu of a salary so that you can go home and be reunited with your families."

"Then what about Your Majesty?"

"I have decided to proceed slowly to western Sichuan with the eunuchs and young princes."

Li Longji was surprised at the reaction. After they had heard what he had said, the guards said in a chorus, "We are heart-broken at Your Majesty's words. Soldiers are trained for crises but after receiving our salary we proved useless and could not destroy the foe. We want to follow you to western Sichuan. As for the silk, we would not dare accept it; please use it for rewards when the rebellion is suppressed. Your Majesty, if we do not mean it, heaven will punish us."

Li Longji was deeply moved and said, "You are so loyal that I will always remember you, but I cannot bear to keep you for too long. You must go home."

"Can it be that Your Majesty suspects us of being disloyal because of Lady Yang's death?"

"No, that is not the reason. But the citizens of Chang'an are concerned about us. Go back and tell them that I am safe and well."

The guards did not waver and said that they wanted to follow the

李隆基闻奏后，吩咐高力士去处理，十万匹彩缎全部收下，打发使臣回去。待高力士处理好交接手续，又吩咐道："高力士，你召集六军将士，朕对他们当面有话说。"

不一会儿，六军将士齐集凤仪宫外，只有右龙武将军陈元礼一人上殿来，李隆基让陈元礼传话出去："将士们，朕有话说。此次范阳之变，事出突然。为避兵戈之扰，远来西川，劳动将士仓猝之间随朕西巡。今天呵，朕有个主意与大家商量。"

"不知万岁爷有何主意？"

李隆基此刻倒似乎颇通人情地说道："朕知道众将士都随朕西行多日，无不思念家乡、父母、妻子、儿女。何况蜀道之难难于上青天，道路崎岖，程途遥远，饥寒交迫，辛苦劳累。朕于心不忍，总想找一个好办法安置大伙儿。但朕出巡在外，没有银两分给众将士，今早成都使臣送到彩缎十万匹，就将此分给各将士，权充粮饷，大伙儿分得一份，也可还乡，与父母、妻子早早团圆。"

"那么皇上怎么办？"

"朕已有所考虑，只带着子孙，由内监相伴，慢慢捱到蜀中去。"

李隆基未曾想到这番言语倒收到了意外的效果，众军士见皇上如此体恤士卒，反倒不愿离去，齐声高呼："万岁爷这番话语，令臣等将士寸心如割。自古道，养军千日，用在一朝。只怪臣等无能，空领粮饷，未能剿灭叛贼，今日生死随行，护送万岁爷直到西川。这彩缎，臣等将士也断断不敢受收，皇上还是将它收下，留待他日臣等平叛后论功行赏。皇上呵，咱们若有违心，皇天后土绝不饶过咱们！"

李隆基也不无感动地劝道："你们的忠义，朕难以忘怀，长年拖累你们，朕心实有不忍，大伙儿还是还乡吧。"

emperor to western Sichuan. They would return to the capital together when the rebels were swept away. Only then did Li Longji give his consent and said, "It is getting late; we will spend the night here, and start early tomorrow."

“呀,万岁爷,莫不是因贵妃娘娘之死,疑惑俺们不忠?”

“不是呀, 只是念你们家乡父老记挂你们 —— 你们还乡吧,告诉长安父老,说朕平安无事。”

众军士依然表示情愿随驾西行,决无二心,待扫净叛贼,一同返回长安。李隆基至此方允将士所请,让大伙儿今夜好好休息,明日早早出发。

Chapter Eleven

The Spirit Followed

After Yang Yuhuan hung herself at Mawei Station, her spirit drifted from the station and followed Li Longji to western Sichuan.

Moved by Li Longji's attempt at distributing the silk tribute the guards pledged to accompany him to western Sichuan. They walked slowly; they had traveled a long time, the road was desolate and they had little food. Yang Yuhuan's spirit drifted with the wind and soon caught up with them. It saw the banners fluttering from the imperial canopy and when it approached it wanted to cling to the robe of Li Longji. A drum sounded, the spirit was startled and stopped. A black wind covered the road and when it died Li Longji had gone. The spirit could only return amidst the dust.

In a while Yang Yuhuan's spirit saw the ghost of the Duchess of Guo coming her way. It was being beaten by two devils who were taking her to the City of Avenging Spirits. There was another ghost, a male dripping with blood and running. Yang Yuhuan's spirit looked at it and saw that it was her cousin, Yang Guozhong, who was being dragged by two devils to the Forest of the Hills of Swords and Knives in Fengdu, a city of ghosts. The spirit of Yang Yuhuan thought of her sister in the Pei Family who had enjoyed every luxury in her life and of her cousin Guozhong who had seized power and ruined the state; they had both come to this end. If this was the case with her sister and cousin, she must be guilty too. The future looked bleak; what would her end be? She had no option but to return to Mawei Station and repent.

At the time the Tutelary God of Mawei Station had been summoned by the God of the Eastern Mountain and told to watch over the body and spirit of Lady Yang. In a former life she had been a fairy on the fairy mountain and had died in his territory; he had to wait for further orders from heaven. The Tutelary God went to inspect the place where Yang Yuhuan had been buried.

第十一章
死不泯情

且说杨玉环自缢马嵬坡驿舍，身虽死而情不泯，魂灵儿守情不散，忽忽悠悠地飘来飘去，终于离开了驿舍，追逐李隆基前往西川。

虽然李隆基拟分彩缎给士兵之举赢得军心，表示要齐心协力护送他到西川，然而这队人马毕竟离乡日久，供给不足，行动甚是迟缓。杨玉环之魂乘风驾云，不多时便赶了上来，到了车乘之旁，正待拽住李隆基的黄龙袍，突然"铛"的一声锣响，将她吓得停在半空，顿时黑风阵阵，遮断前路，待到黑风过去，已不见了李隆基形影。

片刻之后，在愁云苦雾之中，她见虢国夫人披头散发而来，两个鬼卒一边拽一边打，促她去枉死城中。紧接着那边又来了一个满身血污的男子，盯睛一看，原来是自家兄长杨国忠，同样有两个鬼卒拽他去酆都城上刀山剑树。她不由不想到：裴家姐姐生前享尽荣华，国忠哥哥在世擅权误国，如今都得了这般结局！姐姐、哥哥如此，自家岂能没有罪殃？想来想去，还是返回驿舍去忏悔罪孽吧。

正当其时，马嵬坡的土地公公被东岳帝君召去，告诉他这贵妃杨玉环原系上界蓬莱仙子，如今死在咱的神界之内，须要保护好她的肉身、安顿好她的魂魄，等待天帝玉旨。土地公公奉了这训谕，忙着去杨玉环葬身处察看。

Yang Yuhuan's spirit drifted back to Mawei Station and hovered above the pear tree where she had hung herself. There was some writing on it — Lady Yang lies here. Was it not the writing of Gao Lishi? So she was buried there! Ah, Yang Yuhuan, Yang Yuhuan, in the past you lived such a life of luxury and pleasure. Now you are lonely; a covering of yellow earth instead of silks and brocades. It is very sad! Where are the hairpin and the jewelry box you asked Gao Lishi to bury with you? Did he do what you asked, or did he just throw them away. If he threw them away, how could you prove your love? But it is meaningless; even if he had buried them, how could your decayed body reunite with the emperor? The spirit wept sadly.

The Tutelary God who had just arrived heard her weeping, "Is that the ghost of Lady Yang crying there?"

"Yes. What god are you? Please pardon me for being here."

"I am the Tutelary God of Mawei."

"I beg you to help me."

The Tutelary God told her about his instructions from the God of the Eastern Mountain. "You were formerly a fairy on the fairy mountain; you were sent to earth to expiate some faults. And now, though you have ended your span of life on earth, you are not permitted to return to heaven yet." He unfastened the white belt she used to hang herself and said, "By the order of the God of the Eastern Mountain, I deliver you from your sins to save you from hell."

"I thank you. May I ask if I will ever meet the emperor again?"

"That I do not know. For the time being you may stay at the station and wait for an order from heaven. I shall be leaving you now." The god suddenly disappeared. After what he had told her the spirit of Yang Yuhuan had no choice but to stay.

The Tutelary God left but he frequently came and went on his rounds. The local temple had been prosperous. After An Lushan rebelled the local people ran away; now it was deserted and no more incense burned there. Many wandering spirits roamed around nowadays so he had to make more inspection tours and see to it that everything was all right. One night when he arrived at the station on an inspection tour he saw the spirit of Yang Yuhuan sitting, weeping alone on the tomb and murmuring under the pale moon and cold stars. He hid and listened to what she said.

The spirit of Yang Yuhuan sighed and said, "In life I enjoyed great favor and honor and took pleasure with the emperor in the west palace.

杨玉环的魂灵儿已飘飘悠悠地回到驿舍，也寻到自家缢死的梨树，绕着梨树往返看视，突然发现一行小字“贵妃杨娘娘葬此”。这不正是高力士的手笔么？啊，俺原来就埋在此处！唉，杨玉环呀杨玉环，你当年何等风流，如今这般冷落，呀，皇上赐我的金钗、钿盒，俺曾吩咐高力士与我殉葬，不知他是否将它们埋下？唉，就是埋下了又有什么意思！俺这残尸败身，又岂是能与皇上重结同心？想到这里，不禁凄凄哀哀地哭泣起来。

“喂，喂，那哭哭啼啼的，可是贵妃杨玉环的鬼魂么？”土地公公刚刚来到驿舍，就听见这哭泣之声，不禁上前查问。

“奴家正是。你是哪位尊神？请恕我冒犯。”

“吾神乃马嵬坡土地。”

“啊呀，望尊神与奴家做主。”杨玉环魂灵儿好似找到救命菩萨似地祈求着。

土地公公便转告她东岳帝君所说：“你本是蓬莱仙子，因有小过被罚落尘世，如今虽是期限已满，但一时还不能回到上天。”说着，解去她颈子上还系着的自缢用的白绸，又说：“吾奉东岳帝君之命，解除你的冤结，可免你沉沦。”

“多谢尊神了，只是不知道奴家与皇上还有相见之日么？”

“此事非吾神所能知晓。你还是暂时安住在驿中，以待天命吧，吾神去也。”说罢，陡然不见踪迹。杨玉环也只能在此栖息。

当年这座土地庙香火颇盛，只因安禄山造反，本境人尽都逃散，以致庙宇荒败，香火断绝。目今野鬼又大大多过往昔，更要加紧巡看，以免生出事端。今晚土地公公又来到驿舍，见杨玉环魂魄独坐坟头，对着淡月寒星，且泣且诉，便藏在一边，听她诉说些什么。

Now my corpse is buried in the ground and I am sad. Who would recognize this ghost as the former Yang Yuhuan!" The spirit took the hairpin and the jewelry box out from her sleeve and gazed at them murmuring, "These pledges of love taken from the grave were given to me by the emperor. I feel sad when I see them. I thought that our love would remain as solid as them, but it has been severed just as a thread is snapped. If I had known that our love would end like this, I would never have kept them. I remember the jewelry box giving off a fragrance at night and the hairpin glittering in the morning mirror. What joy and love we had. When I think of our former love, how can I bear to close my eyes in death?"

The spirit was lost in thought and repented murmuring, "Ah, Yang Yuhuan, although I died a sad death, all that I did in my life was bad; the crimes that my cousin and sisters committed in their greed for power will be laid at my door. How can I be forgiven? The Tutelary God said that I was once a fairy on the fairy mountain but since I have been so sinful I have no hope of rejoining the fairies. All I ask for is to return to my former lover, then I will be content."

When the Tutelary God saw that she was sincerely repentant he showed himself and said, "Lady Yang' I am here."

Startled, the spirit said, "So the Tutelary God is here."

"I heard you repenting. Your penitence will move the gods on high to pardon you and restore your love."

"Thank you for your sympathy. But I fear my faults were too many and that I cannot be pardoned. It makes me sad."

"Do not be sad. I will give you a travel permit allowing you to wander around at will for a hundred miles. However, I must remind you that you were once an immortal and that you were sent to earth for minor faults. When you went to the palace you were led astray by love which led to this catastrophe. Now that you have repented and awoken from your dream, I hope that you will forsake your old ways and return to heaven as soon as possible."

Yang Yuhuan's spirit was pleased to hear that she would receive a permit. But how could she, an unhappy ghost, go to heaven? With the travel permit she could travel at night and vanish by day; guided by the moon and stars she could find her former love.

The Tutelary God did not know what was on her mind and gave her the permit before leaving.

The spirit of Yang Yuhuan rose from the grave and hovered around

杨玉环魂魄叹息道："想俺生前与皇上在西宫行乐，何等荣宠！今日白骨荒坟，这般凄惨！"停了半晌，从袖中摸出金钗、钿盒，盯着这两件信物自言自语道："这两件东西就是当年皇上定情之物，如今已从墓中取得，看了这定情之物更令人伤心，实指望两情坚固如金钗，哪知却变成断绳头！想当年，钿盒香气满双枕，金钗光辉跃明镜，多么恩爱！提起这恩情，教我黄泉之下又怎能瞑目！"

不一会儿，陷入沉思的杨玉环又自言自语地忏悔道："想我半生所为，哪椿不是罪孽，兄弟姊妹，挟势弄权，罪恶滔天，皆由我而起。我的罪孽怎能忏悔将尽！那日土地公公说俺原是蓬莱仙子，我这般罪孽，哪还敢再回仙境，只愿与我那个人儿呀能再相逢匹配！也就心满意足了！"土地公公听至此处，知她真诚悔过，便显出身来："贵妃，吾神在此。"

杨玉环倒吓了一跳："啊，原来是土地尊神。"

"吾神见你深自谴责，真诚悔过。你这忏悔必能感动天庭，总会让你来日重圆旧盟。"

"多蒙尊神鉴谅，只怕奴家罪孽太重，难以超拔！"

"贵妃不必悲伤，我今发给你一张路条，千里之内任你魂游何处。你原籍蓬莱，因有小过罚至人间。入了宫廷后又欢娱过头，乃有此难。还算你能悔过自新，盼你切莫贪恋迷途，及早回归仙班！"

杨玉环魂灵儿闻知土地公公要发给她自由通行的路条，也颇为欣喜。自忖一介怨鬼，岂能升天成仙？不过有了路条，可随风而行，荡荡悠悠，日隐夜出，依月傍星，重寻往日金钗钿盒之盟，不也可好！土地公公也不知她此刻想些什么，交了一张路条给她，便飘然而去。

杨玉环魂灵儿从坟头立了起来，又绕着梨树徘徊，想起那天

the pear tree. It thought about the day that she had been forced to hang herself and again wept sadly.

The Weaving Maid from heaven passed by on her way to present silk to the Heavenly Palace. When she saw a gloomy aura rising to the sky she said to the angels, "Do you see that sad and foggy atmosphere? What place is that down below?"

"That is Mawei Station, my lady."

"Tell the carriage to stop, and summon the Tutelary God of Mawei."

The Tutelary God arrived, kowtowed to the Weaving Maid and said, "The Tutelary God of Mawei greets you, my lady. May you be blessed for ever."

"God of Mawei, as I passed by I noticed a sad atmosphere from your territory penetrating to the sky. What is the cause?"

"I will tell you, my lady. That was Yang Yuhuan, the concubine of the Tang emperor, who was lamenting her death on her grave."

"So it is Yang Yuhuan. I remember the evening in the tenth year of the Tianbao period; she and the Tang emperor swore to be husband and wife all their future lives at the Palace of Eternal Youth. But now, poor thing, she is an unhappy spirit. Tell me how she died."

The Tutelary God told her the whole story, including the mutiny of the guards and the suicide of Lady Yang. After hearing the story, the Weaving Maid felt sympathetic and said, "Though she was to blame for her own death, the Tang emperor, the son of heaven, was unable to protect a woman. What of his pledge at the Palace of Eternal Youth? How heartless he is!"

"My lady, Lady Yang does not blame the emperor. She was thinking about how she could renew her union with her lover."

"Even when she is in such a state she still remembers the pledge in the Palace of Eternal Youth. I find this very touching."

"She has repented her former sins too, my lady."

"Well, if she repents all her sins she could be forgiven. I shall speak for her in heaven and have her restored to her position among the fairies."

The Tutelary God said, "My lady, even if you restore her to her old position, she will not renounce her pledge to the Tang emperor."

This touched the Weaving Maid and she said, "Well, she is very steadfast in her love." She added, "You may go back to your post now. I shall see to this." She ordered the angels to drive her carriage to the heavenly palace.

受逼自缢，又凄凄惶惶地哭泣起来。

正当此际，织女为了呈献天锦给天帝，经过此地，只见下界一股怨气直冲云层，便开口问侍从的仙女道："这道非烟非雾的怨气直逼过来，你看下界是何处？""启禀娘娘，下界是马嵬坡地方。"

织女吩咐仙女："暂且停下云车，宣召马嵬坡土地前来。"

土地公公应召而来，上前叩见。"土地，我路经此地，见你界上有怨气一道，直冲云汉，是何缘故？"

"这是下界唐天子贵妃杨玉环，如今在黄土坟头抱怨自己屈死。"

"呀，原来就是杨玉环！记得天宝十年七夕之夜，她与唐天子在长生殿上，盟誓永为夫妇。想不到如今已成怨鬼，太可怜了！土地，你将她死时光景说与我听。"

土地乃奉命将当年六军不发、贵妃自缢的情况告诉织女。织女听说后十分同情，说道："虽是杨玉环自取罪孽，但以天下之主，不能庇护一个妇人，长生殿中的誓言何在？李隆基也未免太薄情了！"

"娘娘呀，那杨玉环倒未埋怨唐天子无情，只是心心念念想着与李隆基重寻旧盟。"

"到了这地步，还记得长生殿中誓言。有这般真情，也叫人不能不怜悯。"

"启禀娘娘，杨玉环近来又痛自忏悔生前罪孽。"

织女闻言，点头说道："能忏悔自家罪孽，便能自新。吾当保奏天庭，令她重新回到仙班中来。"土地又进言道："娘娘呵，她即使回到仙班，仍不会忘记与唐天子之盟约。"

织女心中未免有所触动，赞叹道："好一个情痴！"继而吩咐道："你且回去，我自有道理。"随即吩咐仙女，驱动云车，向天庭驰去。

Chapter Twelve

Hearing Bells and Mourning the Image

After Li Longji left Mawei Station, there was no beautiful Lady Yang to accompany him. He rode on horseback closely followed by Gao Lishi. The guards marched westward in front of him day after day past mountains, gorges, empty houses and deserted fields. Poplar leaves rustled in the autumn wind and sometimes one or two lonely geese lamented overhead. It all increased Li Longji's sorrow.

After Yang Yuhuan committed suicide Li Longji lost interest in life. He and his government faced a hopeless exile and an arduous journey as a result of the rebellion of An Lushan. He thought the matter over and decided to cede the throne to Li Heng, the crown prince, leaving him to restore peace.

The procession had gone on and on for a whole month and was nearing western Sichuan. As the crown prince was now the ruler, Li Longji ordered Gao Lishi to go slowly. But it was autumn and the mountains, water and fallen leaves on either side of the road made him sad and he sighed often.

Gao Lishi worried about this and frequently offered advice. "Your Majesty, you are tired after the long journey and the weather is cold. You must not grieve, but keep up your spirits."

"Ah, Gao Lishi, you know that Her Ladyship and I always sat together and walked shoulder to shoulder; we were never apart. Now the westward exodus has killed her and I cannot but think of her." He sobbed as he spoke of her death and murmured, "It makes me sad to think of the past and I feel hatred when I look back towards Mawei Station."

The guards were just ahead and Gao Lishi thought it improper to mention the subject. He said, "Your Majesty, the path ahead is steep. Keep a firm grip on your reins, sire, and ride slowly."

Li Longji realized what he implied and knew that he had been careless. He said no more, held the reins tight and moved on slowly.

第十二章
闻铃哭像

李隆基离开马嵬坡驿舍之后，孤孤零零地骑在马上，高力士紧跟在身后，六军战士在前，终日穿山过峡，向西川前进。自从杨玉环自缢身死，李隆基顿然失去生活乐趣，加上安禄山叛乱，朝廷迁徙，万民流亡，面对残局，无力收拾。他思前虑后，决定将皇位传给太子李亨，由新皇帝去重造太平了。

行行重行行，这队人马走了整整一个月，已距成都不远。既然皇位传给太子，身上重担也卸了下来，李隆基便吩咐高力士缓缓而行。沿路所见，无非是残山剩水，无边落木，令人伤情，不免长吁短叹。高力士见状，十分担忧，不时劝说道："万岁爷，路途劳顿，风寒霜重，望皇上善自排遣，不要过分悲伤。"

"唉，高力士啊，你是见到的，朕与妃子，坐则同凳，行则比肩，哪曾分开过？如今这般结果，教寡人如何撇得下去！"说到伤心处，不觉抽泣起来。

高力士知道六军战士在前，李隆基这一话题不能再让他说下去，便岔开道："前面就是栈道了，请万岁爷挽紧缰绳，缓缓前进。"

李隆基也领会到高力士的用心，知自己失言，便刹住这一话题，把缰绳紧紧挽住，坐骑也就自然放缓。他便留意起四周令人惊

Looking around he saw horses and men picking their way along a path beneath towering and precipitous mountains that almost touched the sky while monkeys and wild birds wailed in the background. Dark clouds gathered, engulfing the mountains; the wind was cold and the sky dark. It was a frightful scene.

"It is going to rain, sire. Will you go into the Jian Pavilion to take shelter?" Gao Lishi got down first and helped Li Longji to dismount and walk up to the pavilion. After Li Longji sat down, Gao Lishi told the soldiers to take shelter as well.

Li Longji sat for a while in the pavilion then stood up and looked at the scene around them. He improvised a poem and recited to himself:

I walk here alone in my grief,
My sorrow as endless as the hills and streams.
The wind has driven storm clouds over,
Rain falling endlessly makes me sick at heart.

He spoke to Gao Lishi, "Where does that irritating sound come from? Find out what is causing it."

Gao Lishi walked to the railings and looked around. "Your Majesty, it is the rain in the forest and the bells hanging from eaves; they make a noise in the wind."

"The dripping of the rain and the tinkling of the bells are dismal and frightening. And the glowworms in the wet grass disturbed by the wind are like spirit lights. Ah, It is I who did my love sit alone on the empty mountain unable to be with my love. The raindrops and the bells have rekindled my sadness...."

Gao Lishi had to distract him. He saw that the rain had stopped and said, "Your Majesty, do not grieve. The rain has ended. Will you come down now?"

When Li Longji left the pavilion and mounted his horse, Gao Lishi called out, "Guards! To horse. The emperor is on the horseback." The procession continued along the narrow mountain track now green after the rain.

The day that Li Longji entered western Sichuan he learned that Guo Ziyi had been victorious and would soon suppress the rebellion. Since he was no longer in charge of state affairs, he just passed the day mourning over his love. It was just like the poem that reads:

怕的景色：两边峰峦高插入云，山壁如削，猿声哀鸣，子规啼血，不时阴云四合，山谷里天昏地暗，冷风阵阵侵袭，令人不寒而栗。

“唉呀，雨来了，请万岁爷登上剑阁，避开这阵雨。”高力士先跳下马来，搀扶李隆基下马、登阁。坐定之后，又吩咐军士们驻扎避雨。

李隆基登上剑阁，坐了一会儿又立起身来，向阁外四顾，不禁点头自语：

独自登临意转伤，蜀山蜀水恨茫茫。

不知何处风吹雨，点点声声迸断肠。

随后，又向高力士问道：“你听那边什么东西不住的响，吵得好不心烦。”

高力士走到栏杆前，四周张望后对李隆基说：“圣上，是雨打树声、风吹檐前铃铎声。”

“呀，这雨声、这铃声好不做美呀！淅淅零零，高响低鸣，让人心惊！你看，高力士，那白杨林中，风狂雨骤，湿萤乱飞，鬼火闪灭。哎呀，是我辜负了卿卿，俺独坐空山，不能早晚与卿卿相伴，令人恸绝，这阵阵雨声、铃声，惊醒俺一腔愁恨，叫人难以平息！”

高力士不能再任他发泄，看看阁外，阵雨已停，便趁机奏道：“万岁爷，不要愁烦了。雨停了，请下阁赶路吧。”

待到李隆基走下阁来，上了坐骑，高力士才招呼军士：“军士们，上前去，起驾了！”一行人马又继续在雨后青山夹峙中向前行去。

不日，李隆基一行进了成都，闻知郭子仪兵威大振，近日即将荡平叛贼。何况已传位太子，不再过问朝政，每日更是思念妃子，正是：

Green the hills and streams of Sichuan,
Where day and night I mourn.
I should never have given up my love,
Not though she cost me my empire.

Li Longji ordered the authorities to build a temple in Chengdu and sought out skilled artisans to make a life-size image of Lady Yang sitting down. When it was finished he told Gao Lishi to bring it to the palace; he would escort it to the temple himself.

While he waited he thought of Lady Yang and blamed himself for breaking their pledge. He had promised to become her husband all their future lives, but he had deserted her on the road. He hated An Lushan who rebelled and forced him to go westward; he hated the imperial guards who had pressed him hard and had drawn their swords and spears at Mawei Station just after they had left the western gate of the palace; he also hated Chen Yuanli, the general of the imperial guards, who forced him, a powerless emperor, to give her up. All of them were hateful. He blamed himself for losing his head. Had he shielded her with his body, they might never have dared to attack the emperor. Suppose they had struck him down, what would it have mattered? They should be together at least in the nether world. Now he lived on alone and his life had no meaning. He had nothing to do all the day, but pine with endless tears and infinite sorrow. "Ah, my darling, whether I'm on earth or in heaven, this sorrow will never end!"

"May it please Your Majesty, Lady Yang's image has arrived." Gao Lishi's words awoke Li Longji from his reverie but he was still confused. When he saw the wooden image, he immediately stood up and cried, "My darling. We've been apart for some time. I am glad that you have come today. Let me tell you all about my sorrow...." He approached the image and said, "My love, why don't you answer me...." He stretched his hand and when he realized it was an image he gave out a cry.

"The carriage is ready, Your Majesty, for you to escort Her Ladyship to the temple." Gao Lishi reported.

"Very well," said Li Longji. "Give the order that my horse goes to the left of the carriage carrying the image so that we can proceed side by side." On the road, when he thought of their past pleasure trips and how they contrasted with the sorrowful procession today, he was sad.

蜀江水碧蜀山青，赢得朝朝暮暮情。

但恨佳人难再得，岂知倾国与倾城。

近日又命成都府建庙一座，请能工巧匠用檀香雕成妃子坐像，吩咐高力士先行将坐像抬进宫来，让他亲自护送入庙供养。

李隆基坐在宫中等待时，又想起妃子杨玉环来，深自谴责自己背誓负盟，当年也表示要与她生生世世比翼齐飞，何曾想到半路上将她抛弃！他又恨安禄山起兵叛乱，逼得自家不得不离京西巡；又恨三千羽林军才出皇宫西门就沸沸扬扬起哄，到了马嵬坡终于动了刀枪；又恨陈元礼趁势威逼手中无权的君王，终于让她被害。想起这些，真是好恨哟！怪自己全无主张。当时自家若将自身去抵挡，那些乱军未见得敢冒犯君王；呀，纵然冒犯我，又有何妨！倒与她能在黄泉相依相伴！不像今日自家虽然无恙，但独自一人活着还有什么风光！整日哀愁不断，眼泪不干！唉，我的妃子哟，人间天上，咱俩个此恨此愁如何能偿！

“启奏万岁爷，杨娘娘的宝像迎到了！”高力士一声禀报，将李隆基从自怨自悔的沉思中唤醒过来，蓦然见了杨玉环坐像，忽地立起身来，放声痛哭：“呀，我那妃子呵，一向别离，今日你却突然来临，待寡人与你好好细诉冤情，痛说愁肠……”他直向坐像走去，边诉边问：“妃子呀，妃子，你怎么不答应……”伸手去搀扶，才知道原来是檀香木雕成的神像！不禁失声痛哭。

“车驾备好啦，请万岁爷上马，送娘娘入庙。”高力士禀报道。

“那就起驾吧！”李隆基又吩咐高力士：“你去传旨：马儿在左，车儿在右，朕与娘娘并驾而行。”一路上，他想到当年曾与妃子夫唱妇随，并骑游赏，如今却落得这般模样，一阵愁云又涌上心头。

"We have reached the temple. Will Your Majesty alight?" asked Gao Lishi. Eunuchs and maids escorted the image into the temple.

After a while Gao Lishi reported, "The auspicious hour has come. Your Majesty, we are waiting for your order to carry Her Ladyship to her throne." Maids placed the image to the throne and when everything was ready Li Longji stood up and stepped forward. He took incense from Gao Lishi but before he burned it in front of the image, his thoughts turned to the pledge made before the Cowherd and the Weaving Maid on the night of the seventh day of the seventh lunar month at the Palace of Eternal Youth. Who would think of the broken incense-stick today? Tears coursed down his cheeks; he trembled as he stood before the image.

"The first libation." Gao Lishi appeared to remind the emperor, who recovered and took the goblet from a eunuch saying, "May your spirit come to the libation. You were buried in haste and at a time of confusion at Mawei Station. No sacrifice was offered at your grave."

"The second libation."

"I offer you this cup. I hope to move your grave back to the imperial mausoleum one day and we'll be buried together."

"The third libation."

"Now the libation is over, but there is no end to my sorrow. Why do you not move or say something? My heart seems slashed with a knife and my entrails burn with fire."

Gao Lishi, the maids and the eunuchs all wept when they heard this. When Li Longji stopped crying, he looked at the image and gave a cry. "Look, Gao Lishi! Are those not tears on her face?"

The maids and Gao Lishi looked at the image and actually saw tears falling down the cheeks of the image. They all knelt and cried, "Her Ladyship!" After a long pause Gao Lishi said, "Will it please Your Majesty to burn the sacrificial paper money?"

Li Longji burned the paper money handed to him by Gao Lishi, took another cup of wine from him and poured the final libation.

"It is growing late, Your Majesty. Will you return to the palace?" Gao asked.

Li Longji knew it was time to leave. He looked again at the image and ordered the maids to lower the curtain. He then mounted his horse and left the temple but his sorrow undiminished.

高力士趋前禀报:“到庙中了,请万岁爷下马。”妃子坐像自有仪从抬进庙去。不一会儿,高力士又禀报道:“吉时已到,万岁爷,请下旨让娘娘升座。”自有宫女扶像上座。李隆基离座上前,接过宝香,想起当年七夕,长生殿中,与妃子拈香对牛郎织女盟誓,如今却拈着一把断头香！刹时凄惶万端,泪水汩汩涌出,颤巍巍地立在像前。

“初赐酒！”高力士似乎在提醒圣上。李隆基明白过来,便接过内侍递过的酒杯,说道:“这一杯盼你前来享用,马嵬坡上匆忙下葬,不曾用半碗凉浆祭奠你。”

“再赐酒！”

“这一杯再献你,盼来日正式安葬皇陵,我当与你同穴合葬！”

“终赐酒！”

“呀,妃子,这一杯,礼已尽,寡人的话儿未完,你怎的不动声色不搭腔,好不令朕伤心,痛煞肝肠！”

听了李隆基如此沉痛的话语,高力士和两旁宫女无不痛哭失声,随后又是一片抽泣。李隆基哭罢,又盯着杨玉环坐像呆看,忽然惊呼道:“呀,高力士,高力士,你看娘娘的脸上,不是流出泪来了！”

众宫女和高力士应声看去,果见坐像流泪,个个双膝跪地,齐齐向娘娘叩拜,口呼娘娘不断。好一会儿,高力士方不得不开口:“请万岁爷与娘娘焚帛烧纸。”

李隆基点燃高力士捧的纸、帛,又接过一杯酒,倾洒于坐像前。

“天色已晚,请万岁爷回宫。”高力士促驾返回。

李隆基也知道不可再逗留庙中,便又仔细看了几眼,吩咐宫娥将娘娘坐像前的神帐放下来,然后才走出庙门,上马回宫,一路哀愁,自不必言。

Chapter Thirteen

The Reburial on the Way Back

After An Lushan took Tongguan Pass, he marched straight to Chang'an, the capital. Li Longji and Yang Yuhuan had left for western Sichuan, and the ordinary people of the capital were under the boot of An Lushan's soldiers who had burned and looted everywhere they went. Palace maids and musicians from the Pear Garden Conservatory fled.

Yongxin and Niannu, personal maids of Yang Yuhuan, fled the palace and followed a group of refugees. They arrived at Jinling (Nanjing today) after crossing the Yellow and Yangtze rivers. There they became nuns in a Taoist temple and settled down. Li Guinian, the orchestra leader, also went south with his lute and made a living singing in the streets and lanes of Jinling. Fairs were held in front of the famous Vulture Peak Monastery on the riverside and Li Guinian often sang songs about Li Longji and Yang Yuhuan to the ordinary people. His songs also expressed his yearning for the capital and his native place.

Lei Haiqing, the famous lute player from the Pear Garden Conservatory, stayed in the capital. He became angry when he saw the court officials who had received high positions and huge salaries. Their sons and wives had also been given titles but they now feared death and forgot their gratitude to the former emperor. They had all surrendered to the rebels and thought only of their present comfort. They did not care for history's verdict. To him this was shameful and disgusting. Though he was only a musician, he would not loose his self respect as they had.

An Lushan appreciated imperial music and kept a large number of musicians to play for him. He decided to celebrate his victory and feast with the traitors at the Frozen Azure Pool. There was to be music and Lei Haiqing was naturally among the musicians summoned.

An Lushan gave an audience to the officials in the inner court. Those who waited outside the palace were his former colleagues; they were now his subjects. When they were told to go in, they vied with other to be first

第十三章
归途改葬

安禄山破了潼关之后,直指长安。京城里留下的百姓,尽受安禄山一伙的烧杀抢劫,百般蹂躏。宫中侍女、梨园弟子也四散逃亡。

那杨玉环的贴身宫女永新、念奴逃离宫廷,渡黄河、过长江,来到金陵(今南京),在女贞观中做了女道士。乐工李龟年也流浪江南,在金陵城中大街小巷抱着一面琵琶奏曲糊口。南京青溪之傍,有座有名得鹫峰寺,每逢庙会之日,李龟年就将李隆基与杨玉环的故事,在庙前广场弹唱给士民听,借此倾泻自己的故国之思。

梨园之中赫赫有名的琵琶圣手雷海青,仍留在京城。他冷眼观察,那班平日受到唐天子宠爱的文武百官,如今却个个贪生怕死,背义忘恩,纷纷投降。雷海青为之气愤填膺,心想自己只是一个乐工,却有自己的气节,那些没廉耻的勾当,绝不会做出来的。

安禄山这家伙倒垂涎于宫廷音乐,拘留了大批乐工,以供自己享乐。他决定在凝碧池做个太平筵席,既为自己庆功,又安抚降顺的逆子贰臣。为此,他传集梨园弟子前往奏乐助兴。雷海青也自然在被传集之列。

安禄山内殿命内监宣百官进见。那批早在殿外伺候多时的文武百官,原先都是安禄山的同僚,如今则成为他的臣属,你先我后

and knelt down, saying, "Long live the emperor, long, long live the emperor!"

An Lushan was happy and said, "You may rise. Today I have a little leisure and invite you to feast at the Frozen Azure Pool to celebrate the pacification of the empire." The officials thanked him and followed their new master to the feast.

Proudly An Lushan sat at the table, while the officials flattered him by kneeling and offering him wine. He was in an ecstatic mood and ordered music. The Dance of the Rainbow and Feathery Garments, Li Longji and Yang Yuhuan's music, was soon heard. An Lushan was pleased to hear it and said, "Bravo! Well played!" The puppet officials said, "The Tang emperor went to great pains to have this dance rehearsed, but it is now played for the pleasure of Your Majesty. Your Majesty is indeed favored by heaven!" The flattery went to An Lushan's head and he said, "True. More wine!"

Suddenly the noise of weeping was heard at the convivial gathering. Both the emperor and the officials were surprised and listened. Someone was not only weeping but singing also. "While the rebellion began at Fanyang, the beacon fires are gleaming. Thousand of homesteads lie in waste and the people are in utter misery." Another verse of the song asked, "Emperor of Tainbao, where are the former officials now?" An Lushan became angry and said, "Who is that crying out there?"

"It is the musician Lei Haiqing."

"Bring him in."

When the guards brought Lei Haiqing in, An Lushan shouted, "Lei Haiqing, we are drinking here to celebrate peace. How dare you be so woeful out there?"

"Ah, An Lushan!" Lei Haiqing stood there fearlessly and berated him. "An Lushan, you were an officer who was defeated in battle and you should have been sentenced to death; yet the emperor was merciful and spared your life. He even made you a prince! Instead of trying to serve the government well, you rebelled with your army. You have befouled the capital and forced the emperor to flee. You are an arch criminal who will soon be put to the sword when the imperial army returns. Who are you to talk of feasts and pacification?"

"Aya!" An Lushan had not expected this and he was furious. "What insolence! Since I ascended the throne, no one has disobeyed me. How dare you, a common musician, defy me? Men, draw your swords." The

地跪了一地，你起我落地口呼："万岁，愿主上万岁，万万岁！"

安禄山见状，好不得意地说："众卿起来。孤家今日政务稍闲，特设宴在凝碧池上，与你们共享太平！"

安禄山大刺刺地坐在上席，那班无耻伪官，争先恐后地上前，下跪，献酒，谗媚阿谀之态可掬，安禄山心花怒放，吩咐内侍传梨园弟子奏乐。霎时，《霓裳羽衣曲》随着阵阵香风传来。当年李隆基与杨玉环宴筵间的情景突然重现，安禄山不禁赞道："奏得好。"那班伪官深知安禄山心思，讨好地说："臣等心想当年天宝皇帝，不知费了多少心力，才教成此曲，今日却留给主人受用，真是主上洪福齐天。"安禄山兴高采烈地高呼道："众卿说得有理，再上酒来。"

正当新主、伪官欢乐之际，忽然传来一阵哭泣之声，君臣凝神细听，哭泣又变成低吟："范阳兵起，四野烽烟，万户遭殃，生民涂炭"；"天宝皇帝，昔日百官，今又何在？"安禄山不禁大怒："呀，什么人在那儿啼哭？"

"是乐工雷海青。"

"拿上来。"

雷海青顿时被扯了进殿。安禄山劈头大骂："雷海青！你好大胆，孤家在此设太平之宴，你竟然哭泣嚎叫！"

"咳，安禄山！"雷海青毫无惧怕之色，痛骂起来："安禄山，你原本是一个败将，论罪应斩。侥幸得到皇上恩典，赦你大罪，封你为王。你不思报效朝廷，反敢起兵作乱，占据京城，逼走皇上。你的罪恶满盈，不日天兵到来，必将你这家伙诛杀，你还饮什么太平之筵！"

"呀，呀，呀！"安禄山哪曾料到有此一骂，气得满口吐沫，吼道："唉，有这样事！孤家入登皇帝大位，臣下无人敢不顺从。量你

guards took out their swords but they were no threat to Lei Haiqing for he had made up his mind to die. He went even further, cursing and pointing at An Lushan, "An Lushan, you are a heartless monster and a beast with a human face! Though I am only a common musician, I am not as shameless as these turncoat officials. An Lushan! You have defied the will of heaven, you will soon fall, a corpse bespattered with blood!" He threw his lute at An Lushan; it was seized by the guards.

An Lushan roared, "Take him and kill him quickly!" The guards dragged Lei Haiqing off. An Lushan was still angry when the puppet officials came forward to say, "Do not be angry, Your Majesty. Why pay any attention to a foolish musician?"

"My pleasure is spoiled. You may leave."

"Your Majesty's orders shall be obeyed. Let us see the emperor back to the palace." They knelt.

An Lushan left in a towering rage. The officials at once rose, all talking. "That musician deserved to be killed. Fancy a musician posing as a patriot! What's wrong with us coming to the feast? He positively tried to put us in the wrong! All of us simply acting a part; how much, after all, is a loyal minister worth? Lei Haiqing, Lei Haiqing, you were foolish because you have never been an official!"

Although An had seized the throne, people like Lei Haiqing had not accepted him and generals of the Tang empire still fought against him. He was in a difficult situation.

After Li Heng ascended the throne in Lingwu, he struggled to restore the Tang empire. He made Guo Ziyi Military Governor of the Northern Circuit and ordered him to lead his troops in the fight against the rebels. Guo Ziyi had defeated Shi Siming and Hou Qiannian, An's generals, and was advancing on Chang'an. The great Yan empire of An Lushan had not only been defeated militarily, but there were also conflicts in the inner court. An Lushan's favorite concubine Lady Duan had wanted to make her son, An Qing'en, the crown prince, which enraged An Qingxu, An Lushan's elder son. He colluded with Pigsy Li, An Lushan's favorite general, and had An Lushan killed.

The puppet empire collapsed soon after An Lushan died and Guo Ziyi and his troops marched into Chang'an. Guo Ziyi made the office of the imperial guards his temporary headquarters. When Guo Ziyi had entered the capital, he saw the desolate scenes and remembered how it had been. It made him sad. He suddenly recalled the restaurant and the

这个小小的乐工,怎敢如此无礼! 军士,看刀伺候! ”两旁的侍军,立即拔出刀来,但这吓不倒雷海青,他又上前一步,指着安禄山大骂:“你这个忘恩负义的家伙,完全是人面兽心! 我虽然是个微不足道的伶工,却不会像那班无耻的朝臣,靦颜事敌!我却要指斥权奸! 安禄山,你少不得尸横血溅,没有好下场! ”言罢,飞手将一面铁拨琵琶朝安禄山掷去,被侍军及时挡住,安禄山气得暴跳如雷:“快把这家伙拿出去砍了! ”

众军士横拖竖拽地将雷海青架走,安禄山还在气恼,一班伪官赶紧上前劝慰:“主上息怒,无知乐工,不必介意。”

“孤家心上不快,众卿且退。”

“领旨,臣等恭送主上回宫。”又齐臻臻地跪了一地。

待安禄山悻悻离开后,这班伪官儿方才立了起来,七嘴八舌地说:“杀得好,杀得好。一个乐工也要当起忠臣来,难道我们吃太平宴的,倒错了不成! ”

再说安禄山窃得皇位,不但内有雷海青这般忠义之士的斥责,而且外有大唐各路勤王军将的反攻,也不好应付这一局面哩。

李亨即位灵武后,便积极谋思平叛之计。任命郭子仪为朔方节度使,领了大军征剿安禄山。先后战胜了自称大燕皇帝安禄山手下大将史思明、何千年,直奔长安而来。大燕皇帝好景不长,不但连连兵败,宫闱之间也发生变故,安禄山宠爱段夫人,要立她的儿子安庆恩为太子,长子安庆绪心怀怨怼,勾结安禄山宠将李猪儿,半夜将安禄山刺杀。

安禄山一死,伪朝立即土崩瓦解,郭子仪部将长驱直入,大小三军,浩浩荡荡,来到京城地面,暂时驻扎在龙虎卫衙门。郭子仪

poem written on the wall. He said to his generals, "When I first came here there were lines written by Li Xiazhou, a fortune-teller, on the wall of restaurant. I did not understand them then but realize now that all his prophecies have come true."

The generals asked him to explain the meaning of Li Xiazhou's poem and Guo Ziyi said, "An Lushan led all the troops from the north against the capital. That explains the meaning of 'When the northern town is deserted'. Then General Geshu Han was defeated at the Tongguan Pass which explains 'And no horse returned from the Pass'. The third line, 'He comes to the ghost beneath the hill' refers to Mawei Station, while the fourth line 'And there hangs a silken dress on the ring' predicted how Lady Yang would die."

"So that's it. But thanks to your might the capital has been recovered; that was a wonderful achievement," the generals said.

Although the victory made Guo Ziyi happy, the job was not finished. He said to the generals, "The capital has been recovered, but the reigning emperor is still at Lingwu and the old emperor is far away in western Sichuan; ministers have fled and citizens dare not return to their homes. We must clean up the palace and sweep the imperial tombs so that the reigning emperor and the old emperor can return." The generals bowed and said, "Yes". Guo Ziyi gave an order asking the refugees to return and take up their former tasks. He also called on the former officials to work together for reconstruction. A general was appointed to lead five thousand fully equipped imperial guards to Lingwu and escort His Majesty, Suzong, back to the capital. Obeying an order of the new emperor, Guo Ziyi himself went to western Sichuan to welcome Li Longji, the old emperor, back.

Li Longji had been in western Sichuan for more than a year before Emperor Suzong had suppressed the rebellion and sent someone to welcome him back to Chang'an. He had arrived at western Sichuan in haste and distress but the procession that left was leisurely.

Very soon they arrived at Fufeng where they stayed in Fengyi, the pleasure palace. Li Longji recalled that this was where an old peasant had offered him a bowl of oatmeal. He stood quietly in the dusk; the palace looked desolate and he was gloomy.

It was getting dark and Gao Lishi advised him to enter and have a rest. Li Longji paid no attention to this and said, "How far is it to Mawei, Gao Lishi?"

重入京城，不胜感慨，想起当年一派太平景象，如今山河破碎，满腹悲凉，陡然又想起当年新丰酒楼上的题诗，对身边将领说："那年入京，见到酒楼上李遐周的题诗，不知其意，如今倒句句应验了。"

诸将不知此诗如何，请郭子仪讲述一番。"那诗上说'燕市人皆去'，不正是说安禄山入侵西京；'函关马不归'正是哥舒翰兵败潼关；'若逢山下鬼'者指'嵬'也，'环上系罗衣'之'环'乃贵妃娘娘之名，这两句不正说马嵬赐缢之事么？"

"原来如此——今仗元帅洪威，重新收复宫阙，此乃不世功勋啊！"

郭子仪却不敢为眼前的胜利自喜，任重而道远哩，他对诸将说："唉，京城虽然收复，但是圣上还在灵武，上皇远在成都，千官尚流散各地，百姓也未回乡归里。如今首先要将宫廷收拾好，以便上皇归来，圣上回殿。"诸将听了，一齐弯腰称"是"。同时郭子仪又命人招集流民，重安故业；罗致旧臣，共图新政。然后，又命一军将率领龙虎军五千人，准备好仪仗队，前往灵武，迎接当今皇帝回京，并听从肃宗旨意，亲自去成都迎接上皇李隆基回宫。

李隆基避难四川一年有余，安史之乱终于平息，被肃宗派员迎回。一行人离开成都，从容行路，不像当年来川时那般匆忙、狼狈。

不日已进入扶风境内，还是在凤仪宫内驻跸。李隆基想到去年此时，有老汉献麦饭。如今回到此处，只见这离宫十分寂寥，暮色沉沉，一派苍凉景象，不由得不伤感起来。

高力士见天色已晚，劝李隆基早早安歇，他并不答理，反倒问道："高力士，此去马嵬坡，还有多少路？"

"Only a few dozen miles."

"I have ordered the local authorities to make a proper grave for Lady Yang. Go there at once and see that the work is done quickly. When I arrive, the reburial can take place."

Gao Lishi had left and there was no one close talk to him; Li Longji was doubly sad. Although it was dark and quiet, he did not feel like sleeping. He stepped down to the courtyard and raised his head to see the moon. It was rising slowly and light from it fell on the green grass on a corner of the wall. He felt lonely; there was no one to share the view with. He was heart-broken.

He thought of Yang Yuhuan lying cold in her lonely grave. In the past if he had left her even for a moment it was hard to bear; now death separated them forever. How sad it was! When they pledged their love with the hairpin and the jewelry box, little had he thought that they would buried with her. Thinking about this, he cried aloud, "Ah, my darling. How shall I ever forget you looked and spoke?" He thought of how she was not only lovely when she was happy; she was also charming when she was angry with tears in her eyes. No other woman had understood or delighted him so much. They loved each other and there was no other beauty who could compare with her. She was dead. He too was more dead than alive. If he could meet her after death, he would rather die than continue living alone. He wanted to leave this world and enter the nether regions to rejoin her under the earth.

He looked up and saw the moon high in the sky. He remembered how they prayed to the Cowherd and the Weaving Maid on the seventh day of the seventh moon and made a secret vow. Now he was alone beneath the moonlight! Ah! Circumstances changed so quickly. "Ah, Moon! When we made our vow, you must have heard it too; you were there by the Milky Way. I hope you will not deny it and persuade the Cowherd and the Weaving Maid to help make our pledge of love come true."

It was cold and late. After experiencing wars and parting from Yang Yuhuan, Li Longji was becoming old and frail. He was tired and went into the palace.

The master of Mawei Station after receiving the imperial order was busy with preparations. He went from door to door finding people to tidy the house and the yard and make a new grave for Lady Yang. While he was bustling round, Gao Lishi came to oversee his efforts which made him work harder. The imperial order stated that Lady Yang's body was

“只有一百多里了。”

“前次已传旨下去,命令该地方官为妃子造一座新坟,你可连夜赶去,催督工程,不可拖延,待朕到时便行改葬。”

高力士领旨而去，李隆基身边更无亲近之人可以谈心，自然更无人劝慰,不免倍感愁苦。虽然暮色四合,庭院寂静,但他仍不想就眠。独自步下台阶,只见墙头冉冉升起一轮月华,渐渐照遍台阶墙角,洒向碧草青苔,院中并无可以共赏之人,更觉伤心!

由自身的寂寞,不由想起杨玉环的孤独,想当年,两人偶然离开一时半刻,也令人难捱难耐;如今却是阴阳两分开,怎不教人痛煞愁怀!当年咱用金钗、钿盒与你永订白首之盟,这两件信物哪是用来殉葬之物?他深自悔恨,妃子既死,咱不也是虽生犹死;倘若死后能够重逢,不也强过独生!唉,咱不如早早赴黄泉,也好和她在地下结成连理并开蒂!

偶一抬头,只见明月当空,不禁又想到:当年七夕,与妃子在长生殿中同向织女牛郎祝祷,密誓百年,岂知今日月下,单单留下独自一人!唉,唉,时移境易,人变事迁,月呀,月呀,我想当年密誓之时,你当时也在银河之畔,自然是个见证。如果你不赖账,你也应该在织女牛郎耳边多说好话，怂恿织女牛郎帮咱们完成金、钿之盟,让咱们再续前缘。

夜深了,凉气侵人,李隆基毕竟饱经乱离忧患,年事已高,此时不免阵阵倦意袭来,也支撑不住了,只得回室内休歇去。

且说马嵬坡驿臣自从上次接到旨意后，就匆忙准备起来。挨家逐户传唤各色工匠，先把驿舍房屋收拾一番，又将院落打扫干净,再将娘娘故茔建造。正当他忙得不可开交之际,高力士奉旨前

not be seen by any men so the station master had to get four hundred women to work as grave diggers. He and his men had spent a whole day conscripting four hundred women. But they did not know how to use a hoe or pick so they had to be trained during the night.

Li Longji arrived in a carriage escorted by eunuchs and imperial guards the following day. Gao Lishi, the master of Mawei Station and other officials waited on the road to welcome him. He sat down in the hall and they withdrew to wait outside.

It was late in the afternoon and after resting Li Longji walked past the Buddhist shrine. It was silent, no one chanted scriptures there. The pear tree on which Lady Yang had hung herself was still there covered with green leaves which made it look sombre. Sombre thoughts came into Li Longji's mind. "The surroundings are unchanged, but you are dead. All my sighs are useless. The nights are long but you have never appeared in my dreams. Your face was as fresh as spring but where will I see it again?"

"As Your Majesty directed, I have superintended the work on a new grave for Lady Yang. Now everything is ready for you to begin the ceremony whenever it pleases you." Gao Lishi woke Li Longji who had not slept properly the whole night. He answered, "Order my carriage."

After a while Gao Lishi said, "Your Majesty, it was under this poplar tree that Lady Yang was buried."

Li Longji looked around and said sadly, "Ah, the weeds have grown rank and the wind sighs. Take pity my darling, I am most wretched!"

The women workers who had been gathered by the master of the station appeared and Gao Lishi said at once, "The women workers have come." Li Longji ordered that the guards be withdrawn and asked Gao Lishi to inspect their work.

Gao Lishi passed on the order. The guards marched out and the women started to dig. With great care they removed the grass and earth from the top, but when they reached the depths, there was no sign of Lady Yang's body. The women were surprised and spoke among themselves. Suddenly one of them found a pouch and cried, "Oh, look! It is a scented pouch."

"Bring it to me," Gao Lishi ordered and the woman handed it to him. When Gao Lishi saw it he cried out, "Alas, My Lady." But he stopped for it was an inappropriate time for him to show emotion. He ordered the woman worker to withdraw and reported the find to Li Longji. "Your

来督工,他更不敢有丝毫懈怠。又听说,圣上恐怕男的民工窥见娘娘玉体,有不恭不雅之举,要另选四百名女工掘坟开棺。他不得不吩咐驿卒分头去征调,忙了一整天,总算调齐了四百名女工。

此日,在不多的军士护行之下,李隆基一众人马渐渐来到马嵬坡,早有驿卒报知高力士。高力士招呼着驿丞一同出外迎驾,接进驿舍中来,安顿好上皇歇息,便退出在院外侍候。

时近黄昏,李隆基休息片刻后,便步近佛堂,庭前那一株梨树犹自绿叶成荫,却又显得一片阴凄。唉,当年妃子就在此树自缢,树犹在,人已亡,令人长吁又短叹,长夜愁苦谁人知!

“奴才奉旨,督造娘娘新坟,万事齐备,恭请万岁爷亲临启墓。”高力士的禀报,惊动了一夜未眠的李隆基,立即吩咐高力士:“传旨起驾。”到了坟场,高力士上前禀奏:“启奏万岁爷,这棵白杨树下,就是娘娘埋藏之处了。”

女工们此刻已在驿丞驱使下,从四方走来,高力士连忙招呼,并向李隆基禀告:“女工到齐了。”李隆基便吩咐高力士,让军士回避,要高力士亲自监督女工小心开掘。

高力士遵旨照办,让护驾军士,立即离开坟场,指挥女工围着白杨散开,让她们在坟堆四周轻轻下锹。坟头渐渐被挖平,再向下掘去,渐挖渐深。打开墓穴,一无所获,并未见到杨玉环的尸体,众女工不免有些诧异,七嘴八舌地小声议论着。突然一个女工在墓穴中发现一个香囊,不禁叫道:“呀,是一个香囊!”

“快送过来!”高力士命令道。女工敢不应命。高力士接过一看,确是娘娘之物,掩面大哭,呼叫道:“我的娘娘呀”顿时又刹住,心想此刻还不是他这个太监奴才哭的时候,便吩咐女工退去一

Majesty, the grave has been opened, but it is empty. Even the silk quilt wrapped round the body and the gold hairpin and the jewelry box that were buried with her have disappeared. There is nothing left but this scented pouch." He presented it to Li Longji. They had no idea that the heavenly emperor had made Lady Yang a fairy and raised her to heaven.

"How could that be?" Li Longji took the pouch from Gao Lishi and cried out, "I gave her this pouch on her birthday, after she performed the Dance of the Rainbow and Feathery Garments at the Palace of Eternal Youth. Where are you now, my darling?"

His head was lowered in thought and suddenly he raised it. "Could you be mistaken, Gao Lishi?"

"That day I peeled off part of the bark on the poplar and wrote on the tree to mark the place. How could I mistake it?"

"Could her body have been exhumed?"

"If that were the case, why would the scented pouch have been left?" Li Longji thought this reasonable and reflected in silence.

"There have been many cases, sire, of immortals who were raised from the dead. Perhaps Her Ladyship has attained immortality. Since this pouch was worn by Her Ladyship when she died, if we bury it in the new grave it will serve the same purpose."

"You are right. Wrap this scented pouch in the pearl-decked garments, put them in the marble casket and let the burial take place with due ceremony."

Gao Lishi was capable. He placed the pouch in the casket, ordered the women to put the casket in the grave and sealed up the tomb. He then gave them a string of cash apiece as a reward and sent them away. Only Mistress Wang, a woman worker, was still there, and Gao Lishi asked why she did not go. The woman said that she had picked up one of Lady Yang's silk stockings the previous year and wanted to present it to the old emperor. Gao Lishi reported this at once to Li Longji and took her to see him. When Li Longji examined it he realized that it actually was one of Lady Yang's stockings. He wept and ordered Gao Lishi to give the woman five thousand strings of cash as a reward and allowed her to stay watching over Lady Yang's grave.

Gao Lishi tried to console Li Longji who was still lamenting when envoys sent by the reigning emperor arrived. Commander Guo Ziyi and four soldiers kowtowed to Li Longji. "Your subject, Guo Ziyi, Military Governor of the Northern Circuit, has come on His Majesty's command.

边，转身走上几步，向李隆基禀道："启禀万岁爷，墓已开启，却是一座空穴，连裹身的锦褥和殉葬的金钗钿盒都不见了，只有一个香囊在此。"说罢，双手递上香囊 —— 他们当然不知道天帝早已让织女娘娘传旨，命蓬莱仙子杨玉环炼形尸解升仙去了。

"呀，有这等事！"李隆基接过香囊大哭道："这香囊乃是当日妃子生辰，在长生殿上试舞《霓裳羽衣曲》时朕赐给她的。我的妃子呀，你如今却在哪里？你怎的化去不留痕迹！"

李隆基问道："高力士，你有没有记错地方？"

"万岁爷，奴才当年曾削下杨树半边，题字为记，不会记错的。"

"怕不被人挖掘了？"

"不会，若是被掘，怎么还会留下香囊？"李隆基听了这般解释，也觉得有理，但仍旧不解。

"奴才想来，自古神仙多有尸解之事，娘娘不是凡人，定然也成仙了，这香囊原是娘娘所佩之物，将它葬入新坟之中，不也可以？"

"说的有理。高力士，就着你将这香囊用珠缎裹好，放在玉匣中，依礼安葬便了。"

高力士极会办事，不一会儿就吩咐女工将已经盛在玉匣中的香囊放入墓中、封土为坟，并赏女工每人一贯钱，将她们遣散回去。惟有一个叫王嬷嬷的女工未曾退去，高力士问她何故不回，她说当年曾拾得杨娘娘遗袜一双，要献给万岁爷。高力士不敢怠慢，连忙奏知万岁爷，并将王嬷嬷带进去。李隆基接过高力士双手奉上的锦袜，仔细看过，果然是妃子遗物，睹物伤情，泪珠不淌自流，继而吩咐高力士赏王嬷嬷五千贯钱，让她在此看守贵妃坟墓。

正当李隆基仍在伤心堕泪、高力士不断解说劝慰之际，当今

We have an escort for your welcome return, sire."

Li Longji at once wiped away his tears and replied, "Yours was a truly remarkable achievement, my lord. You succeeded in wiping out the rebels and recovering the capital so that the imperial sacrifice could be renewed and the empire rebuilt."

Guo Ziyi replied humbly, "I was late in crushing the rebels, therefore, I deserve punishment and can claim no credit."

"No one could say that, my lord. Gao Lishi, order the carriage to proceed."

In no time Gao Lishi had arranged everything. Led by Guo Ziyi and other officials, and escorted by soldiers, Li Longji returned to the capital in a carriage.

皇上所派前来迎返太上皇的大臣已到了驿舍。守门军士进来禀报，紧跟着进来四名军士、一名武将，见过太上皇李隆基，禀报道："臣朔方节度使郭子仪，今奉上命，带领仪从，恭迎太上皇圣驾返京。"

李隆基赶紧拭泪止悲，答道："卿荡平叛逆，收复京城，宗庙重新，乾坤再造，真不世之功也。"

郭子仪却谦恭地答道："臣枉为大帅，破贼已迟，负罪不浅，哪有功荣！"

"卿说哪里话来 —— 高力士，咱们就起驾返京吧。"

不到一盏茶时间，高力士已安排好一切，郭子仪率众在前引路，众军士在四周护送，太上皇李隆基便也不失风光地回京城而去。

CHAPTER FOURTEEN

Making Amends and the Lover's Reunion

After the trials of a long and arduous journey, Li Longji finally returned to Chang'an, the capital. He took no part in affairs of state and just stayed in the southern part of the western palace where he spent his time in leisure. However, he found it hard to cope with leisure and thought of Yang Yuhuan all the time. On some particular rainy nights, when leaves fell from the plane trees and the wind moaned, grief overcame him.

On one such night, when rain drops were beating against the windows, Li Longji sat alone by a lamp; Gao Lishi was in the other room. Li Longji was lost in thought. He had hoped to see his darling one more at Mawei, but the grave had been empty except for her scented pouch. He did not know if she had been carried to heaven or whether her body had decayed. Was there any way for him to see her again?

"Ah, where does the singing come from?" He was surprised to hear a melody that came from far away and went to the window. "It is sad.... Can it be one of my musicians?" He listened again and said, "Ah, it is Zhang Yehu singing." He paced a few steps and stopped. "Let me listen to his singing."

"The steep path winds across a thousand hills, and the way is rugged; when a squall of rain sweeps over the treetops, the bells on the pack-horse start ringing...." He heard the words and murmured, "That is a tune I composed called 'Bells in the Rain.' When I was traveling through the mountains I heard bells ringing in the rain and thought of her so I put the sounds into music. Hearing this reminds me of that sad journey and I feel more broken-hearted than ever." The rain outside fell fast then slow and heavier and lighter by turns. Li Longji could not sleep.

Gao Lishi did not sleep either. He listened carefully to the sounds from the inner room. Li Longji was in a sad mood again, so he entered quietly. "It is late, Your Majesty. Won't you rest?" In the distance the

第十四章
补恨重圆

经过千山万水，李隆基终于返回了京城长安。既然已经传位给太子李亨，便退居南内为太上皇，不再过问朝政。终日思念妃子杨玉环不能自已。每当梧桐叶落之日，凄风苦雨之夜，最是愁人。

又是一个风雨之夜，愁灯照壁，落叶敲窗，高力士自在外室侍候，内里就是他一人独坐。想想前时在马嵬坡改葬，原指望能一睹妃子遗容，岂料掘开坟墓，不过空穴一座，仅留得一枚香囊，不知是尸解仙去，还是肉消骨化。唉，怎么才能与她见上一面？

“呀，何处歌声？”窗外飘过一阵悠悠扬扬的乐曲，李隆基不免有些惊讶，便立起身来走近帘前仔细谛听。“呀，凄凄入耳，丝丝入扣，怕不是梨园旧人所歌？”他出神地聆听，“呀，这是梨园张野狐唱的！”

“万山蜀道，古栈岩峣，急雨催林梢，铎铃乱敲……”一阵曲辞传入耳际，李隆基不免感伤地自语道：“呀，这不是朕所作的《雨淋铃》么！当时朕在栈道，闻得铃声、雨声相应和，思念妃子，制成此曲。今夜又闻此曲，怎不令人肝肠寸断！”窗外雨声或大或小，曲声时缓时急，万种凄凉，千般愁思，缠人恼人，怎能入眠？

外间高力士也并未入眠，仔细听着内室动静，眼见上皇又动了感情，便轻轻推门进来，悄悄劝道：“夜深了，请万岁爷安息吧！”

third watch sounded. "So it is midnight already," Li Longji said. "Do you know what is on my mind? How can I sleep? Gao Lishi, arrange the couch. I will sleep on it. I only hope that I'll have a sweet dream and see Her Ladyship."

When Li Longji had fallen asleep Gao Lishi left the room quietly. Li Longji slept soundly on the couch either from tiredness or old age.

Suddenly two eunuchs entered the room; they knelt down and said, "Wake up, Your Majesty!"

"Who are you?"

"Lady Yang ordered us to invite Your Majesty to visit her."

"What? So she did not die after all!" Li Longji asked in surprise.

"The day that trouble broke out among the guards she changed her dress and slipped away through the crowd. She has been a wanderer ever since."

"So she is still alive! Where is she now?"

"She is staying in a post station for the time being. She heard that Your Majesty had been longing for her day and night, so she sent us to welcome you. She wishes to fulfill the pledge she made with Your Majesty in the seventh night of the seventh lunar month."

"So that is it! Lead me there quickly. We will bring her back to the palace this very night."

In spite of the lateness, the dew, the cold wind, and the black sky, Li Longji left his bed chamber and followed the two eunuchs to the gate. A military officer suddenly barred his way. "Your Majesty should be inside the palace. Why are you wandering out at night incognito?"

Li Longji fell into a rage and said, "Who is this rough officer who stops me so rudely?"

"I am Commander Chen Yuanli. Will it please Your Majesty to return to the palace?"

When he heard his name, Li Longji became more irate and said, "Curse you, Chen Yuanli! At Mawei Station you incited the guards and forced Lady Yang to commit suicide. Execution is too good for you. How dare you oppose me again. You ignore my authority and behave with such arrogance!"

"If Your Majesty does not go back, the troops may mutiny again."

"Curse you again! You think that I have no more authority because I have given up the throne. You rely on your troops to take such liberties. This cannot be forgiven. Attendants! Cut off this rebel's head!"

正说着,传来漏鼓三声,李隆基也有些惊讶:“呀,居然三更天了!朕在几上靠靠吧。但愿今夜做个好梦,梦见娘娘回来才好。”

眼见上皇已凭几入睡,高力士乃悄悄退出。也许多日疲惫,也许年事已高,李隆基歪在几案上居然沉沉睡去。

忽然,有两个小太监进来跪禀道:“万岁爷,请醒来!”

李隆基睁开睡眼,问道:“你二人是哪里来的?”

“奴才奉杨娘娘之命来请万岁爷的。”

“怎的?杨娘娘未死?”李隆基诧异非常。

“回万岁爷,当日乱军纷纷,娘娘换了民妆,悄悄溜出驿舍,长期流落在外,四处飘泊。”

“呀,原来杨娘娘未死!现在何处?”

“如今暂居驿舍,闻知圣上朝思暮想,因此派遣奴才前来迎驾,说要与圣上实现七夕之盟,重续前缘。”

“有这等事!你二人快随朕前去,连夜将娘娘接回大内。”

李隆基也不顾夜深人静,露凉风冷,月黑途遥,无人护驾,便随着两个小太监离了寝殿,才要迈出宫门,忽然一员武将上前拦住:“陛下已安居南内,为何深夜微行,要到哪里去?”

李隆基勃然大怒:“哪里跑来你这么一个泼官,胆敢拦驾?”

“臣乃陈元礼,陛下快请回宫。”

闻知其名,李隆基更是暴怒:“哇,你就是陈元礼!当日在马嵬坡,逼死贵妃,罪不容诛。今日又来侵犯圣驾!你也太猖狂了!”

“陛下若不回宫,只怕六军又将生变。”

“哎呀,你这个陈元礼!你欺朕退居南内,不再掌权,大逞威风,罪该万死!内侍,替朕拿下这贼臣,立即斩首!”

The two attendants immediately drew their swords and killed Chen Yuanli then led Li Longji out of the gate. After a while they said, "Your Majesty, we have reached the station. Will it please Your Majesty to enter?"

Li Longji looked around. In the wilderness stood two or three desolate houses. When he approached a gate he saw tall wild grasses and moss growing on the steps. A wind sighed and insects emitted shrill notes. Where was Lady Yang? Suddenly he seemed to be in the station or at the river bank. What a great flood! A monster was coming out of the water! It had the head of a pig and the body of a dragon. It was rushing towards him. Startled, Li Longji gave out a cry and woke from his dream. He was in a cold sweat. He sat on the couch and realized that it was a dream. He called out, "What is that noise outside, Gao Lishi?"

"It is only rain on the plane trees. It is the fourth watch now. You are awake?"

"Just now I had a dream, Gao Lishi. Two attendants came to tell me Lady Yang was in Mawei Station and wanted me to go there to fulfill our pledge. Gao Lishi, in ancient times when Emperor Wu of the Han Dynasty mourned for Lady Li, a necromancer by the name of Li Shaojun summoned her spirit for him. There must still be such necromancers. As soon as dawn breaks, try to find one to summon Lady Yang's spirits."

Gao Lishi carried out the order and posted imperial edicts in streets to summon necromancers. On the second day a necromancer who responded to the call was invited to the palace.

He was called Yang Tongyou and he came from Linqiong. He said he was able to summon the wind and rain and spirits and ghosts. The task would be a test of his magic power for he had learned that the old emperor was longing to see Lady Yang.

His magic power, however, was limited; the genies he sent all returned empty-handed. There was no other way out he told his attendant; he would have to go into a trance and complete the search himself.

After his spirit left the altar, it went directly to Fengdu. At Senlo Hall it called out in a loud voice, "Where is the officer on duty?"

"Who is making such a noise?" asked the Judge. He saw the necromancer and said politely, "What do you want here, sir?"

"I have come to search for Lady Yang's spirit."

"Please take a seat. That is easy. We have a special book for the registration of queens and court ladies." He asked the ghostly attendants to bring the book. The necromancer went through the book from beginning

两个内监抽出佩剑，将陈元礼斩杀后，便引着李隆基走出宫门。不一会儿，上前禀报："万岁爷，已到驿舍了，请万岁爷进去。"

李隆基放眼看去，只见满院荒草，阶生青苔，白杨迎风摇晃，寒蛩四角啾鸣，哪有妃子在？倏忽之间，又好像身在曲江池畔，突然一头猪龙，从水中跃出，直扑而来，李隆基大吃一惊："哎哟……"随即梦醒，身上兀自冷汗不已，索性坐了起来，定下神来，方知刚才一切情事都是梦境，不禁高声问道："高力士，外边什么声响？"

"万岁爷，是雨打梧桐声 —— 已是四更天了，圣上已醒来？"

"高力士，刚才倒打了个盹儿，不想梦见两个内侍来，说杨娘娘还在马嵬坡中，请朕过去再续前缘。高力士呀，朕想从前汉武帝思念李夫人，有个叫李少君的人，为他召来李夫人之魂，让他们相见。等天亮后，你可传旨，普天之下寻个能召来杨娘娘魂魄的方士来。"

高力士只得答允。天明后果然在通衢大道贴满聘请方士的诏书。居然有个道士揭了榜文，被请进大内来。

这个道士姓杨名通幽，四川临邛人，颇能呼风唤雨，摄鬼召魂。闻说太上皇李隆基欲召见娘娘杨玉环生魂，便应诏而来。

岂知他的法术也有限，能耐也不济，派出去的黄巾力士个个空手而回。他只得飞出元神，自去寻觅。

杨道士的元神飞出坛外，便直向酆都城而去，上了森罗殿，便大呼："值日判官何在？"

"谁人敢在此喧哗！"判官厉声喝问，及至看见来者，便又谦恭地行礼："是仙师降临！不知有何公干？"

"贫道特来寻觅大唐贵妃杨玉环之魂。"

"仙师请稍坐，此事不难，凡宫嫔妃后，地府有专册登录。"随

to end twice, page after page, but did not find Yang Yuhuan's name. He had to leave and said to the Judge, "Since she is not in hell, I must search for her in heaven."

He went to a number of places in heaven and found nothing either. Just as he was about to leave he saw the Weaving Maid and bowed, "Madam, my respects."

The Weaving Maid said, "What brings you here?"

"I am searching for Lady Yang's spirit. The old Tang emperor asked me to. She is not in hell and I came to look for her in heaven, but she is not there either.... I wonder if my lady can tell me where she is."

"Since you cannot find her, you had better go back and say that you have failed."

"Yes, my lady. Only I boasted at the court that my spirit will find the fair one in the void."

"Who told you to boast?"

"It is as if I was looking for trouble. The emperor was so constant in his love; he thought of her each day."

The Weaving Maid became a little angry when she heard this and said, "He let her die at Mawei; what love and affection can he have for her?"

"No, my lady, you wrong him. A mutiny broke out as they fled in confusion. Even though he was the Son of Heaven the guards were insolent. No one would carry out his orders and this was the cause of the tragedy."

"Now that they have been separated so long I expect the emperor feels her loss less keenly."

"Oh, no, the emperor is broken-hearted and feels bad day and night. He longs for her and wants to meet her spirit."

When she heard this the Weaving Maid recalled that the Cowherd had pleaded for Li Longji the other day. If that were so, it was a pitiful situation. The necromancer wanted to continue searching somewhere else while the Weaving Maid thought about it. Moved by the necromancer's determination she said, "Tongyou, wait. If you really want to find Yang Yuhuan, I may be able to help you."

The necromancer was astute enough to realize that the Weaving Maid could tell him where Yang Yuhuan was and he bowed at once saying, "My Lady, where is Yang Yuhuan?"

"Have you ever heard of other worlds outside this one? Well. Beyond

即命小鬼送上名册，杨道士便逐页细找，均无杨玉环之名，无可奈何地向判官告辞："既然不在地府，贫道去了，只得再上天庭寻觅。"

说罢，好个杨道士，又从地府直飞天庭。在天宫各处走了一遍，也未见有。出了天门，却顶头撞见织女娘娘，赶紧行礼："织女娘娘，小道杨通幽叩首。""通幽免礼——到此何事？"

"小道奉大唐太上皇之命，来访贵妃杨玉环之魂，先去地府求之不得，又来天宫亦是无着——对了，娘娘不知能否指示途径？"

"通幽，杨贵妃既无处可寻，你便去复旨便了。"

"娘娘，复旨不难，只是小道夸下海口，要为太上皇寻回贵妃。"

"谁教你说大话、夸海口的？"

"不是咱夸海口，只可怜老君王钟情不弃，终日思念贵妃。"

织女娘娘闻言不无怨嗔："马嵬坡下已经绝情逼死，还有什么'情'呀'意'呀！"

"呀，呀，织女娘娘，你休错怪了人。当日六军不发，兵刃相加，虽贵为天子，也无人听从号令——这才造成这椿生死两途的悲剧！"

"如今死生又隔，岁月更逝，只怕李隆基之情也渐渐淡薄了。"

"不然，那太上皇为此寝食不安，伤心病重，但求一见芳魂，诉诉哀情！"

织女娘娘听了这样的解说，想起前日牛郎也曾为李隆基辩白，看来此情是真。未免陷入沉思。杨道士只得告辞，表示仍要上天入地，寻出个究竟来。织女娘娘为杨道士精诚所动，连忙叫道："通幽，止步。你真的要寻找杨玉环，待我指出一个所在，让你去寻访。"

杨道士赶紧回身行礼："请问娘娘，杨玉环现在何处？"

"好吧！通幽，那东极巨海之外，有一座仙山，名曰蓬莱。你到那

the Eastern Ocean there is a fairy mountain named Penglai. If you go there, you will hear news of her."

"Thank you for your help. I will go there at once and find Her Ladyship." He said goodbye and flew away with the clouds.

After he had left, the Weaving Maid went into her palace and sat down. The Cowherd had asked her to assist in the reunion of Li Longji and Yang Yuhuan so that they would keep their trust in them. She had wanted to help but thought that Li Longji was hard-hearted. The Cowherd had defended him and now the necromancer was also saying that Li Longji was firm in his love and sought high and low for her spirit. It was touching, but she wanted to know what Yang Yuhuan thought before she would do anything.

She ordered her attendant to send for Lady Yang and Lady Yang arrived at Xuanji Palace in a minute.

"I am here, Your Ladyship," said Yang Yuhuan.

"Don't stand on ceremony. Please be seated."

"You sent for me, my lady. What are your instructions?"

"Yuhuan, I asked you to come just for a chat. I have never asked you to tell me your story. I would like to hear all about your love for the Tang emperor during your life on earth."

The request made Yang Yuhuan sad. She breathed in and said slowly, "Let me tell you the whole story." But before she came to the important part, she sobbed, stopped for a while and then continued, "We loved each other deeply and pledged to remain together throughout our various lives. But during the unforeseen Fanyang rebellion, I died at Mawei Station and we parted forever."

The Weaving Maid said, "I have been told that your love continues even after death. If that is so, how could he be so heartless as to give you up at the Mawei Station?"

Yang Yuhuan wept and defended Li Longji. "It was indeed sad but not because the emperor was heartless. During the mutiny swords were unsheathed and the emperor was in peril. How could he protect me at such a time? I was willing to die and the situation forced me to. It was nothing to do with him." As she cried she covered her face with her sleeve.

For a moment they looked at each other and said nothing. Yang Yuhuan then showed the Weaving Maid the hairpin and jewelry box saying,

里,便可寻访到杨贵妃的消息了!"

"多谢娘娘,小道即刻就去蓬莱。"说罢,行礼作别,踏云而去。

话说杨通幽远去寻那蓬莱仙后,织女娘娘入宫坐定,回想今年七夕之夜,牛郎一再怂恿自家去促成李隆基与杨玉环重续前缘,不要辜负他们两人对咱夫妇设盟共誓的信任。自家之所以迁延日久,乃是深怪李隆基薄情无义。不过牛郎已为他辩解,今日又从道士杨通幽口中探听确实,李隆基深情不移、悔恨不已,此情此意实在感人。但不知杨玉环意下如何,尚须问个明白,方好为他们谋求重圆。想定后,命侍儿立即召来杨玉环,探其心曲。刹时,杨玉环就来到织女娘娘璇玑宫中。"娘娘在上,杨玉环叩见。"

"玉环免礼,请坐。""蒙娘娘呼唤,不知有何法旨?"

"玉环,你生前与唐天子的恩情究竟如何,不妨向我细说一遍。"织女娘娘开门见山,直截了当地问道。

提起这事儿,杨玉环不免悲从中来,缓了一口气,细细诉说道:"娘娘,听我细说。生前他与我,你怜我爱,共誓生生死死,永不抛开。哪曾想到范阳之变,奴家惨死马嵬坡中,从此生离死别,两下里苦恨茫茫。"

织女又问道:"听说你俩旧情未断,生前死后无休无歇。既然如此,为何李隆基如此心狠,居然将你抛弃不顾?"

杨玉环闻言泪下如雨,"说来的确伤心,这事儿也不能怪他薄情!那日变乱四起,兵刃相加,朝廷西迁,君王遭难,他怎有能力庇护妾身?妾迫于形势,赴死无怨,与李隆基并无干涉!"

织女娘娘与杨玉环两人上下相对而坐,一时无语。片刻之后,

"He gave me these when we pledged our love and I had them with me when I died. I took them to the fairy mountain to keep with me forever. I long so much to resume our love, but how can it be possible?"

"That is indeed a sad story! But now that you rank as an immortal you should free yourself of earthly desires. If you allow them to entangle you, you may be banished to the world of men." The Weaving Maid wanted to know what she really thought.

"Your Ladyship, though I am ranked with the immortals, I dream all the time of the Tang palace. And come what may, my love will never die." She suddenly stood up and said, "I would gladly be banished from heaven of only we could love again."

Moved by her sincerity the Weaving Maid left her seat and touched her shoulder. "Yuhuan, be calm and sit down. The Cowherd and I have wanted to help you for a long time, but after what happened at Mawei I felt that Li Longji must be quite heartless. I just met Yang Tongyou, the necromancer, who told me that Li Longji was longing for you; he had sent him to find you under the earth or in heaven. As the emperor is still true to you, I told the necromancer to go to your fairy mountain. I also thought that you might bear some grudge against the emperor and called you here to find out what you thought. Now that I know you are both true in your love, I think that you should stay together. I shall put your case to the Heavenly Emperor and ask him to make amends for your past unhappiness by living together forever."

Yang Yuhuan was overjoyed to hear this, but she still had doubts. "I am only afraid that our sins were too great and will become a barrier that will keep us from each other. I will be content if I can just see him once more."

"Very well. I have heard that at the Mid-Autumn Festival they will be playing a new version of the Dance of the Rainbow and Feathery Garments which you composed. You will certainly be invited. On that night the emperor will leave the world of men. When you return, tell the necromancer to lead the emperor to the moon that night to meet you there. Does that suit you?"

Yang Yuhuan still found it unbelievable and said, "Are lovers' meetings allowed in the palace of the moon?'

"It can be arranged. I shall tell the mistress of the moon beforehand. By the time you meet, I shall have procured an imperial decree so that your wishes will be fulfilled."

杨玉环又从怀中掏出钗、盒递与织女娘娘："这金钗、钿盒，就是君王定情时所赐。妾被难之时，带在身边。如今携来蓬莱，朝夕把玩，只想再续前缘。但怕不能够实现美梦呵！"

"唉，这也是一椿千秋惨痛之事！只是你如今已升仙班，宜断绝情缘，若被此思念牵扯，只怕又遭磨劫。"织女娘娘仍在进一步试探。

"娘娘，杨玉环纵然列位仙班，但心思总离不开唐宫，纵使千回磨难，此情难灭！"说到此处，杨玉环突然立起身来："娘娘在上，倘若能再续前缘，情愿被仙班除名！"

织女娘娘也为此情所动，离位而下，扶着杨玉环肩头，缓缓说道："玉环，别激动，坐下，听我说 —— 牛郎与我，早就想为你重续前缘，只因为马嵬坡一事，令我深恨李隆基无情无义。方才见到道士杨通幽，说到李隆基想你念你，命他入地上天，必要把你寻到。我念他如此钟情，已指引杨通幽到蓬莱山去了。我怕你还有遗憾，所以特地先召你来询问。现在知道你们俩的真情，应该成对成双。我当奏请天庭，使你两人永远成双，以补从前离别之情。"

杨玉环闻言，喜出望外，旋又不无怀疑，说道："只怕罪孽深重，难以实现了 —— 目前只要能会上一面，也就满足了。"

"也好。听说中秋之夕，月宫要演奏你所谱的《霓裳羽衣曲》，必然邀你。恰好此夕正是李隆基飞升(亡化)之时，你可回去，令杨通幽届时引导李隆基到月宫一见，如何？"

杨玉环仍然不敢相信："只怕月宫之内，不便私会。"

"不妨，我先与嫦娥公主说明。你们相见之时，我便奏请玉帝送来玉旨，使你们情缘永续便了。"

Moved and grateful, Yang Yuhuan bowed deeply and said, "I thank Your Ladyship. I must go now."

The spirit of Yang Tongyou, the necromancer, followed the directions of the Weaving Maid and arrived at Penglai, the fairy mountain, after flying across the eastern ocean and many mountains. He walked over hills, by springs and flowers and along paths and came to a building with an inscription, *The House of Lady Yang*, carved on a board hanging above the gate. He knew that this must be the residence of Lady Yang. He took a hairpin from his hair to knock lightly on the door. No one answered. He knocked again and a fairy attendant opened the gate and asked, "Who are you?"

"I am Yang Tongyou, the necromancer. I salute you." He bowed.

"What do you want here?"

"The Tang emperor asked me to send his regards to your mistress."

"Her Ladyship has gone to Xuanji Palace. Please wait for a moment."

As an immortal, Yang Yuhuan could go anywhere at will and much faster than the necromancer. She had returned to her residence at almost the same time that Yang Tongyou arrived. When she saw the necromancer standing in the yard, she knew at once who he was, but said to the attendant, "Where does this necromancer come from?"

"I was just going to report to you, madam. He brings a message from a Tang emperor in the human world."

Yang Yuhuan walked into the hall and said, "Since he comes from the emperor, let him approach." The pair entered, the fairy attendant leading the way.

"Please be seated. May I ask the purpose of your visit?"

"On the emperor's command, I have come to bring you his regards."

"How is the old emperor?" Yang Yuhuan was anxious to know about Li Longji.

"He has become ill from thinking of you day and night."

This broke the heart of Yang Yuhuan and tears coursed down her cheeks. His love moved her deeply but as they were separated she could do nothing except ask the necromancer to send him her love.

"I will. But I beg you to give me some token."

This was reasonable and Yang Yuhuan said, "When we pledged our love, the emperor gave me a double hairpin and a jewelry box. I will give you half of the hairpin and half of the box. Please tell the emperor that if

杨玉环十分感激,深深一拜,说道:“多谢娘娘,就此告辞。”

那杨通幽自在天庭得到织女娘娘指点后,便驾云乘风,飞过东海,来到蓬莱仙山。只见山恋起伏,山泉流淌,山花幽香。越过无数山峰,终于在山之巅、云之下看到一片参差高低的建筑。走上前去,只见洞门紧闭,一块横额,题作“玉妃太真之院”。便抽下头上银簪,轻轻叩门,未见应声,又轻轻再叩,方有仙女前来开门:“你是谁人?”

“贫道杨通幽,此处有礼了。”“到此何事?”

“大唐太上皇帝,特遣贫道前来问候贵妃杨娘娘。”

“娘娘到璇玑宫中去了,啊,娘娘已经返回,请仙师稍待。”

杨玉环身为蓬莱仙子,来去自由,片刻之间,已经从璇玑宫打了一个来回,与杨通幽脚跟脚地回到院中。刚刚走进院门,就见一个道士立在台阶之上,便明知故问地问仙女道:“道士从何处来?”

“正要禀知娘娘,他是人间唐家天子太上皇所遣。”

杨玉环边走边说:“既然是太上皇使者,快请相见。”待杨通幽上得堂来,杨玉环问道:“请问仙师为何而来?”

“贫道奉太上皇之命,特来问候娘娘。”杨通幽恭谨地回答道。

“太上皇可好?”杨玉环急于知道李隆基情况。

“太上皇日夜思念娘娘,因此成疾,至今未愈。”

杨玉环听得此言,愁肠寸结,泪珠滚滚,颇为李隆基深情感动,但音容一别,无法前去侍疾,只得请杨通幽为她表达关切之情。

“贫道遵命,一定代为转达娘娘对太上皇的眷恋之情。不过空说无凭,求娘娘赐给一件物品为信。”

杨玉环觉得这要求很自然,也很合乎情理,便应允道:“好

we remain true, we shall be able to fulfill our pledge." She could now say such a thing because she had the assurance of the Weaving Maid. She then took out the hairpin and the box and divided them into two asking the attendant to give one of each half to the necromancer.

"There is still something on my mind, My Lady."

"Say it."

"These tokens were made on earth. If I give them to the emperor, how can he be sure that I received them from you? Can you tell me something which none but yourselves know?"

"You are right." She lowered her head in thought then raised it and said, "Ah, I have it! At midnight on the seventh day of the seventh moon in the tenth year of the Tianbao period, when everyone else was sleeping, the emperor and I were at the Palace of Eternal Youth. As we stood shoulder to shoulder thinking of the Cowherd and the Weaving Maid in heaven, we vowed to love each other throughout all our future lives." She wept when she spoke of this.

"With this, I can report back to the emperor. Now I must leave you."

Yang Yuhuan suddenly remembered the words of the Weaving Maid. "Wait, there is something else! On the fifteenth night of this eighth moon there will be a big celebration on the moon when the Dance of the Rainbow and Feathery Garments will be performed. That night the emperor will leave the earth. I shall wait for him on the moon. Will you please guide him there? If he misses the opportunity, he will never see me again. You must remember this."

"I shall certainly tell the emperor about this grand celebration on the fifteenth night of the eighth moon." He then took his leave.

Even though Yang Tongyou had not wasted a moment in his travels to heaven and hell, Li Longji had already become impatient. His longing made him ill and he was now afraid that the necromancer was either lying or not doing his utmost. It was late autumn. The limbs of semi bare trees bent from the wind and rain which had fallen all night. He had not slept a wink and was not sure about the future.

Just then Yang Tongyou returned and reported to him. When he said that he had not found Lady Yang in heaven or hell, Li Longji became stricken with grief and wept. "That means I will never see her again. It is sad!"

"Your Majesty, don't grieve. Listen to me. I met the Weaving Maid in front of her palace, and she told me that Lady Yang was on Penglai

吧。当年承宠之日,太上皇赐有金钗一对,钿盒一只,如今就分钗一股,劈盒一扇,烦请仙师代奏太上皇。只要两相情愿,坚定不移,自可不负从前七夕之盟。"随即,将分开的钗、盒让侍儿送给仙师。

"贫道还有个想法。""请说。"

"这金钗、钿盒乃人间常见之物,献与太上皇,恐未深信。须得当年之事,为他人所不知者,说与贫道传去,才见贫道所言是实。"

"这也说得有理。"杨玉环低头沉思,又抬起头来对杨通幽说道:"记得天宝十年七月七日之夜,深夜无人之时,太上皇与妾并肩而立,有感于织女牛郎之事,虽然一年一会,却世世不变,便向织女牛郎起誓,太上皇与妾要永为夫妇。"

"有此一事,贫道可以回覆太上皇了。就此告辞。"

杨玉环吩咐杨通幽道:"今年八月十五夜,月中大会,奏演《霓裳羽衣曲》,恰好此夕,正是太上皇飞升之时,我在那里专等,烦请仙师届时指引太上皇前往一会。""贫道领命,照办。"

"仙师,请替我再次感激太上皇的眷恋之情。"

"贫道一定向太上皇奏明八月十五日之会。"说罢,踏云归去。

太上皇李隆基已等得不可耐了。如今正是晚秋季节,叶枯条疏,光秃秃的树桠在秋风中摇摆,淅淅沥沥的秋雨一夜滴到天明,好不令人伤情,真叫人难以入眠,又感到来生未卜此生顿休!

正当他透骨相思、沉疴不起之际,杨通幽从海外仙山归来,向太上皇回话:"启禀万岁爷,贫道奉命寻找贵妃娘娘,上天入地下黄泉,岂知两处茫茫皆不见……"说到这里,李隆基大惊,痛哭,说道:"如此说来,永无再见妃子一面之期了,这不真的痛煞寡人呀!"

"万岁爷,请勿忧愁,听贫道说来。那日在天庭璇玑宫前遇到

Mountain...."

"Did you see her?" Li Longji interrupted.

"Yes. Lady Yang cried when she heard that you were ill. She asked me again and again to convey her love to you."

"Is this true?"

"Yes. I brought half a hairpin and box as a proof." He took them out of his sleeve and gave them to Gao Lishi, who handed them to the emperor.

Li Longji carefully examined the tokens that he had given her. They made him think about Lady Yang and he wept again and said, "The separation of the hairpin and box signifies our parting. Now we are alone and apart, unable to meet again." He held the tokens in his hands, then spoke to Gao Lishi, "These are earthly things. How could they have been taken to heaven? When we rebuilt the grave, they were not in it. How can we be sure they came from Lady Yang? How did the necromancer come by them?"

Gao Lishi had already spoken with Yang Tongyou and told him what had been said. "Lady Yang told the necromancer about a secret vow Your Majesty and Her Ladyship had made on the seventh night of the seventh moon in the Palace of Eternal Youth."

"Yes, that happened." Li Longji now believed him.

Yang Tongyou said, "Take comfort, sire. Lady Yang has another message for you."

"What is it?"

"She said that during the Mid-Autumn Festival the Dance of the Rainbow and Feathery Garments will be performed on the moon and she will be present. She asked me to lead Your Majesty to the moon to meet her."

"Why didn't you tell me that earlier?" Now he was completely convinced and said to Gao Lishi, "What is the date today?"

"It is the end of the seventh moon; there is only half a month till the Mid-Autumn Festival. Please rest now, sire."

"As she has consented to see me again, I no longer feel ill." Happy, he waved the necromancer away.

Time flew. Half a month passed in the wink of eye. There was a clear sky on the fifteenth night of the eighth lunar month and the Milky Way could be seen clearly. Necromancer, Yang Tongyou, waited a long time outside the palace gate to fly to the moon with the old emperor.

织女娘娘，她告之贵妃娘娘在海外蓬莱仙山……"

"见着没有？"李隆基急不可待地问道。

"见到了。贵妃娘娘闻知太上皇不适，两眼泪流，一再要贫道代为转达她对太上皇的厚恩深情。""此事可真？"

"并非虚言。贫道携来娘娘的金钗一股、钿盒一扇为凭。"

李隆基接过钗、盒，仔细察看，果然是当年旧物，睹物思人，不禁恸哭："这金钗拆对，钿盒劈开，就好似朕与妃子，如今各自别居，形单影只，见了此物，怎不伤怀！怕也难同心再合，旧盟重续！"他沉吟半响，对高力士说道："呀，这钗盒乃人间之物，怎能到了天上？前日修造新坟，墓中已不见此物，朕正疑心，今日如何在道士手中。"

杨通幽乃禀道："娘娘还说了天宝十年七夕之夜，与太上皇密誓于长生殿中。"

"此事果然。"李隆基知杨通幽所言不虚。

"万岁爷，不要烦愁。娘娘还有话说。""还说什么？"

"娘娘说，今年中秋之夕，月宫奏演《霓裳羽衣曲》，娘娘也在那里，要贫道引着太上皇，到月宫相会。"

"既有此言，何不早说！"此刻李隆基倒深信不疑了，又问高力士："如今是几时了？"

"如今七月将尽，离中秋之期只有半月，请万岁爷保重龙体。"

"妃子既然答允与朕重见，寡人还有什么病，一点儿也没有了。"李隆基喜孜孜地挥手，杨通幽适时退下。

岁月如流，半月之期，转瞬之间已届，八月十五之夜，碧天如水，银汉无尘，杨通幽早已在南内伺候，只待太上皇一出宫，当即领他飞天而去。

After a while the moonlight was joined by lights shining from the palace. When the old emperor left the palace, Yang Tongyou advanced a few steps. "Your Majesty, the necromancer greets you."

"Master, don't stand on ceremony. Please take me to the moon palace tonight. I have waited from noon to dusk to see the moon. Now I am depending on you to lead me up to the sky." Li Longji was full of hope.

"Your Majesty, the moon is high; let us go up into the sky."

"It is a long way to heaven, master. Are we going to fly there?"

"Set your heart at ease, sire, I'll manage." As he said this, he threw out the magic duster in his hand and it changed into a bridge. Li Longji saw the necromancer walked on the bridge which went on and on and almost disappeared. He followed him closely. On either side there was nothing but mist. After a while, he heard fairy music and was happy.

Lady Chang'e, the mistress of the moon, had already made arrangements for Lady Yang to meet Li Longji.

When Yang Yuhuan arrived, she asked to see Lady Chang'e and the fairy attendant replied, "Her Ladyship left word for you to wait here, madam. After you have met the emperor, she will join you both."

Presently the emperor arrived. He hesitated and the fairy attendant asked, "Are you the emperor from the earth?"

"I am."

"Lady Yang is waiting for you. Please come in and meet her."

"Where are you, my darling?" His legs carried him on giant strides.

"Where is the emperor?" Lady Yang went out to greet him.

They met, fell into each other's arms and wept. They talked and wept and wept and talked without end. Those standing nearby were all deeply moved.

"The mistress of the moon is here!" announced a fairy attendant. Li Longji ceased crying to meet Lady Chang'e and thank her.

Lady Chang'e asked them to sit down and said, "I congratulate you both on attaining godhead which means that you can love for ever. Say no more of the past. The Weaving Maid has asked the Heavenly Emperor to make you lovers in heaven. As the night is excellent and the moon is round, I shall give you a congratulatory feast." The fairy attendants then brought in wine.

They heard the music of the Dance of the Rainbow and Feathery

稍顷，只见瑶殿灯火通明，与碧天月光相映，太上皇已步出殿外，杨通幽上前迎接："太上皇，贫道这厢有礼。"

"仙师少礼。今夜将请你导引去月宫，晌午以后一直盼望黄昏，真是望眼欲穿啊！直到此刻，方见碧天银华，就全靠你导引前往了。"李隆基满怀热望地说道。

"太上皇，夜色已深，就此同行吧。"

"仙师，天路遥远，怎生飞渡？"

"太上皇，不必担忧，待贫道施法。"说罢，将手中拂子随手抛出，顿时化做一座仙桥。李隆基见道士上桥而去，渐行渐远，几乎看不见身影。他不敢迟延，赶紧跟上桥去。只见两旁香雾蒙蒙，不见任何物事。行不多时，听见阵阵仙乐自远而近，令人心旌神摇。

此乃月宫主人嫦娥登场，她前日应织女娘娘之请，相助蓬莱仙子于此会见李隆基。

不一会儿，杨玉环果然按时前来。一进月宫她连忙请见月主嫦娥娘娘，仙女回答说："嫦娥娘娘已有吩咐，请你在此先见过太上皇。"

话音刚落，太上皇身轻如叶，已飘至月宫，正犹疑不决之时，仙女已迎上前："来的莫非是人间太上皇么？"

"正是。"

"杨玉环已到，请进来相见。"

"妃子在哪里？"李隆基大踏步飞奔而入。

"太上皇在哪里？"杨玉环趋步迎出。

两人终于相见，抱头痛哭，互诉思念之情，说了又哭，哭了又说，无了无休，仙女们无不动容。

Garments and Lady Chang'e said, "This is the music of heaven and Lady Yang improved it. Now I have borrowed it to accompany you two to the heavenly palace."

The lovers were able to meet each other in the palace of the moon because they remained true to each other after passing through cities of woe and seas of grief. The story of the vow in the Palace of Eternal Youth has been handed down from generation to generation.

“嫦娥娘娘来了！”仙女招呼道。李隆基此时只好收泪，与嫦娥娘娘相见，感谢她提供的方便。

嫦娥娘娘却吩咐仙女招呼二人坐下，说：“太上皇，玉环，恭喜你们了，从今以后，情缘永续，往事休提了。织女娘娘已为你们奏请天帝，鉴于你们二人情缘不断，心意坚定，命你们于天上成就夫妇。值此良宵佳会，人圆月圆，正应置酒庆贺。”话音刚落，自有仙女捧酒过来。

旋即又有天女奏起《霓裳羽衣曲》，嫦娥娘娘解说道：“此曲原为天上所有，蓬莱仙子听闻后翻为新曲，更胜旧曲多多——今日就借此曲导引，送太上皇、玉环同去天宫。”

真是情根历劫，到底相共，真情生死不变，方能月宫相聚，长生殿中盟誓，流传万古无穷。

图书在版编目(CIP)数据

长生殿:英汉对照/(清)洪昇著;陈美林改编 .
—北京:新世界出版社,2000
ISBN 7-80005-553-1

I.长 ... II.①洪 ...②陈 ... III.英语-对照读物,
文学-英、汉 IV.H319.4:I

中国版本图书馆 CIP 数据核字(1999)第 65246 号

长 生 殿

原　　著:洪　昇(清)
改　　编:陈美林
翻　　译:黄　裳、刘　彤
责任编辑:张民捷
版式设计:李　辉
出版发行:新世界出版社
社　　址:北京阜城门外百万庄路 24 号　　**邮政编码**:100037
电　　话:0086-10-68994118(出版发行部)
传　　真:0086-10-68326679
经　　销:新华书店、外文书店
印　　刷:北京外文印刷厂
开　　本:850×1168　1/32　　**字　数**:160 千　　**印　张**:7.375
版　　次:2000 年 1 月(英、汉)第 1 版第 1 次印刷
书　　号:ISBN 7-80005-553-1/I·027
定　　价:20.00 元
